DATE			

By Shelley Shepard Gray

Sisters of the Heart series
Hidden • *Wanted*
Forgiven • *Grace*

Seasons of Sugarcreek series
Winter's Awakening • *Spring's Renewal*
Autumn's Promise • *Christmas in Sugarcreek*

Families of Honor series
The Caregiver • *The Protector*
The Survivor • *A Christmas for Katie* (novella)

The Secrets of Crittenden County series
Missing • *The Search*
Found • *Peace*

The Days of Redemption series
Daybreak • *Ray of Light*
Eventide • *Snowfall*

Return to Sugarcreek series
Hopeful • *Thankful* • *Joyful*

Other books
Redemption

The Promise of Palm Grove

AMISH BRIDES OF PINECRAFT, BOOK ONE

Shelley Shepard Gray

AVON

INSPIRE

An Imprint of HarperCollinsPublishers

FIRST EDITION

Designed by Rhea Braunstein

Illustrated map copyright © by Laura Hartman Maestro
Photographs courtesy of Katie Troyer, Sarasota, Florida

Library of Congress Cataloging-in-Publication Data has been applied for.

ISBN 978-0-06-233770-2

15 16 17 18 19   OV/RRD   10 9 8 7 6 5 4 3 2 1

This book would not have been possible without two very special ladies with incredibly generous hearts.

Thank you to Clara for spending one afternoon showing me all around Pinecraft. Thank you for chatting with me in gift shops, introducing me to ladies, and letting me ask you far too many questions. I loved every second of our time together.

~and~

Thank you to my lovely editor, Chelsey Emmelhainz, for your expertise, encouraging words, and enthusiasm for all things Pinecraft! Thank you, too, for making this, my twenty-fourth novel with Avon Inspire, feel fresh and exciting and new. I'm so blessed to be working with you!

We can make our plans,
but the Lord determines our steps.

PROVERBS 16:9

We are not put on this earth to see through one another,
but to see one another through.

AMISH PROVERB

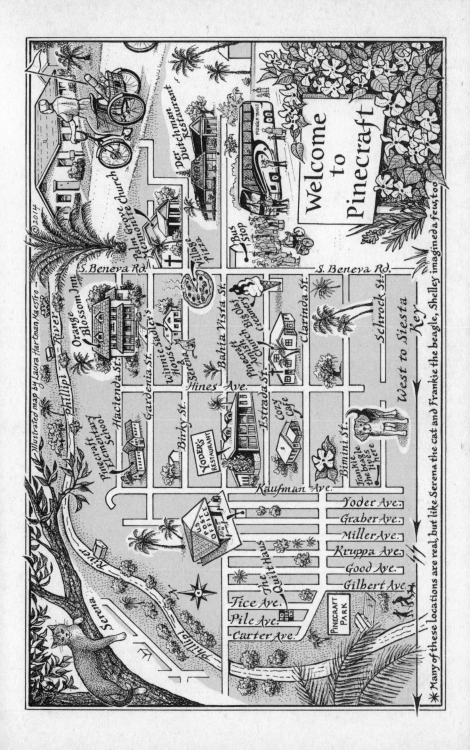

Chapter 1

Beverly Overholt dreamed in color now.

Pinks and yellows, blues and reds. Green, purple, indigo, orange. So many vibrant colors, so much promise.

So very different than her dreams had been when she was in Sugarcreek, Ohio.

As Beverly swept the front porch of the Orange Blossom Inn, her home for the last three years, she took care to carefully clear away each stray piece of Spanish moss that had fallen from the oak trees dotting the yard. And as she did so, she reflected again that God was so good. He was so good because He reminded her in dozens of ways each day that change was possible.

Every morning, He gave her the beautiful sunrises over the Gulf of Mexico, warm weather, and gentle rains. Flowers and blue skies, palm trees and always, always the hint of happiness.

In more ways than she could ever name, the Lord promised new beginnings. Renewal. Paradise.

Even for someone like her, who for so long had been struggling to make something beautiful out of the ashes of her life.

Back in Sugarcreek, for a time, Beverly had thought the Lord's decisions would revolve around her dreams. She'd grown up a little sheltered, a little spoiled. When she'd decided the time had come for her to marry, she'd carefully chosen Marvin Ramer out of all the eligible men in her church district. He'd seemed delighted to have claimed her interest. Then, just a few months later, Marvin asked her to be his bride.

And because it had been what she'd anticipated, she'd accepted. She hadn't been head over heels in love, but she hadn't expected to be. Instead, she'd yearned to fall in love with Marvin over time. She'd known he would make a good husband, and she knew she could be a good wife to him. That was important.

Her family had been happy. His family was thrilled. Their friends were pleased. She'd been gratified. She'd also gone to sleep every night imagining that she'd spend the rest of her days as his wife.

But then he'd found someone better: Regina Miller, her best friend.

It had been devastating.

Little by little, her world had unraveled. Her parents wondered what she'd done wrong. Her friends snickered behind their hands. And everyone else, after a few disruptive days of shock, had resumed their lives.

She, on the other hand, had suddenly been all alone.

And that was how her dreams had faded from beauty and brightness to something far different. Lingering in her consciousness as looming, shadowy, haunting shades of gray.

Lost in thought, lost in the memories that she usually kept firmly locked away in a corner of her heart, Beverly rested her hands on the top of the broom. She gazed at the front yard, with its green lawn and dotting of citrus trees, and recalled Marvin's expression when he'd told her that he didn't love her anymore . . . and that maybe he never had.

"Beverly? Beverly, what in the world are ya doing?"

Blinking, she righted herself. Remembered she was in Pinecraft now. At her inn.

She forced herself to smile brightly at the group of ladies coming her way. Two were on shiny red bicycles, the other three were simply standing. All were wearing brightly colored short-sleeved dresses, the colors of rainbow sherbet, along with white *kapps,* just like her.

And all of them were gazing at her with more than a little bit of amusement.

Hastily, she leaned the broom against her building's white siding and trotted down the worn wooden steps. "Sorry, I guess my head was in the clouds. Did you all say something?"

"We've only been calling your name for the last two minutes," Wilma Schwartz, one of her closest neighbors, said. "What were you thinking about? You looked like you lost your best friend."

Thinking that was far too close to the truth, Beverly forced a smile. "I wasna thinking about anything worth remembering." Noticing that all five of them were looking especially bright-eyed, she asked a question of her own. "What are you all doing today? Having *kaffi* break?" The six of them got together at the Cozy Café at least once a week.

"Goodness, Beverly, you really did get up on the wrong side of the bed," Sadie Fisher teased. "It's Wednesday. What do you think we're about to do? The bus is due to arrive any minute now."

"Already?" Panic set in. "Boy, I really lost track of time this morning."

"Do you want to join us or would you rather walk over on your own in a little while?"

Meeting the Pioneer Trails bus was a major social event in Pinecraft. Several times a week, especially during the busy tourist season, the buses pulled in with great fanfare. Everyone greeted them, anxious to see who was coming to beautiful Florida. Though she used to worry that she would one day spy Marvin and Regina arriving, or Ida and Jean—Marvin's sweet sisters, who she'd been so close to—that had never happened in the three years she'd been living in Pinecraft.

Instead, she typically greeted guests who had made reservations to stay at her inn.

And in the rare times when no guests were arriving, she enjoyed standing in the background and watching everyone else embrace their friends and family. She also loved watching the absolute glow of happiness that transformed most of the newcomers' faces when they stepped off the bus and felt the wonderful warmth of Florida. Being in sunny Sarasota was always a welcome change from the long winters of the Midwest.

"I've got guests coming. Of course I'll join ya. Let me go put away this broom and close up the *haus*."

"Hurry, now, we're going to get ice cream at the creamery, too."

"You're going for ice cream? What's the occasion?"

"It's *Mittvoch*," Wilma said with a complacent smile.

Yes, indeed, it was Wednesday. And Wilma's statement was one of the many reasons Beverly so loved living in Pinecraft. The sun shone, flowers surrounded her, new people arrived all the time . . . and ice cream wasn't something to have only a few times a year.

Here, ice cream, like life, was something to be enjoyed as often as possible and without a smidgeon of guilt. It was things like this, she believed, that now kept her dreams bright and soothing, beautiful and full of hope.

It was what kept her thoughts firmly on the future instead of the dark memories of her past.

"Let me go get my purse," she said. "A strawberry ice cream cone sounds *wonderful-gut.*"

"WE'RE ALMOST THERE!" Mattie practically crowed into Leona's ear. "The bus just turned on Bahia Vista. Oh, look! There's a sign for Yoder's Restaurant. We've got to go get a slice of pie there as soon as possible."

Leona Weaver shared a smile with Sara, who'd been her seat partner for the last sixteen hours during the long journey on the Pioneer Trails bus from Walnut Creek, Ohio, to Sarasota, Florida.

While most of the thirty-five people on the bus had fallen asleep around midnight and slept a good five or six hours, Leona and her cousin Sara had been too excited to do much except whisper to each other, attempt to read their novels, and stare out the windows.

Or, in her future sister-in-law Mattie's case, give a constant commentary about what she saw and when she saw it.

Though she had a feeling some of the other people on the bus were wishing that Mattie would have kept some of her observations to herself—starting about eight hours ago—Leona couldn't fault her sweet friend's enthusiasm.

The fact was, they were on the trip of a lifetime and for the first time in just about forever, it was only the three of them for two whole weeks. Two weeks of no chores around their homes, no part-time jobs. And two whole weeks without Edmund.

Edmund!

Her fiancé. Her private reason for the vacation. The reason that her stomach was in constant knots.

"There's the sign for Pinecraft Park!" Mattie exclaimed, startling her out of her thoughts. "Leona, you'd better start getting your things together."

"They are together, Mattie. Settle down."

Mattie smiled back at her sheepishly. "I'm sorry. I'm just so happy that we're all here together."

"You don't need to apologize. I'm just as thrilled to be here," Leona replied. And she was. Though, she wished she was a little *less* thrilled about getting a break from Edmund. Somehow, some way, she was going to have to learn to adjust to his overbearing ways.

"We are just about there, girls," a grandmother said from three rows up. "Now, tell me again where you are staying?"

"The Orange Blossom Inn," Leona said. "I can hardly wait to get there."

"I've never heard of it."

"It's on Gardenia Street," Sara said. "My older sister stayed there for a week last year. She said it was cozy and pretty."

"I bet it will never be the same after the three of you stay there," another woman teased. "You girls look like you're ready to enjoy yourselves, for sure and for certain."

Leona grinned at Mattie and Sara. "We are ready. I'm hoping it's going to be the best two weeks of my life."

"You mean, until you marry Edmund," Sara corrected.

"Oh. *Jah.* Of course I meant that," Leona replied quickly,

just as the bus pulled to a stop and a resounding cheer erupted around them.

As she followed her girlfriends down the aisle, each step bringing her closer to the sun and the beach and the many expectant people standing outside, Leona wondered what she was going to do.

How in the world she was going to learn to always put Edmund's wishes first but still retain some happiness in her heart?

Chapter 2

Girls, we've been abed long enough," Mattie announced with the enthusiasm of a blow horn. As if to emphasize her point, she clapped her hands. "Come on, now, wake up!" she barked, just as if Leona and Sara were some of her students at the Amish school.

Leona responded by throwing her covers over her head.

Sara's response was far more direct. "If you clap at me again, I'm going to ask Miss Beverly if she has a spare room for you. As soon as possible."

Looking offended, Mattie turned to Leona. "You don't want me in another room, do you?"

Leona pulled back her covers just enough to glare at her with bleary eyes. "I do if you're going to wake us up like this every morning."

"Fine." Mattie folded her hands behind her back. "Now that I'm promising not to clap, you two need to get up. It's a quarter after seven."

"In the morning?" Her mind was in such a fog, she really wasn't sure.

"Of course not, silly. It's the evening. Come on, now. If we don't get up we're going to have wasted the whole day."

Leona feared she was right. "I cannot even believe we just spent the first five hours in Sarasota sound asleep."

"*Some* of us slept for five hours," Mattie corrected. "I, on the other hand, have already been awake for a whole hour."

With a yawn and a stretch, Leona got to her feet. As she blinked owlishly, she noticed that Sara was looking decidedly worse for wear.

"Next time we get on a bus for hours and hours, we are sleeping for the majority of it," Sara announced as she fumbled on the top of her bedside table for her eyeglasses. "I feel terrible."

Mattie walked to Sara's side, picked up the glasses, and placed them in Sara's hand. "I know you do. I felt pretty groggy myself until I took a shower and put on a fresh dress."

For the first time since she'd woken up, Leona looked at Mattie closely. Instead of putting back on her long-sleeved gray dress, she'd changed into a chambray blue short-sleeved cotton one. She looked fresh and cool. Like she'd already pushed the cold Ohio winter to the back of her mind. "You look pretty, Mattie."

"*Danke.*" Smiling at her, she said, "I was so excited to wear one of my new dresses, I couldn't resist changing."

"I'm going to do the same thing. I've been anxious to put on my raspberry-colored dress." Leona grinned. "And flip-flops!" For some reason, the idea of being able to wear flip-flops instead of black tennis shoes or boots felt especially decadent in January. "Let's get cleaned up and get out of here."

"And eat. I'm starving," Sara said as she started digging around in her suitcase.

Mattie, ever their travel guide, said, "Sounds like we've got a plan. Pizza first, then ice cream. Then exploring."

Sara gave Mattie a smile before heading into the bathroom for a quick shower and to change.

Since she had a couple of minutes, Leona took a better look around their large room while she unpacked her own summer dresses. They were on the third floor of the Orange Blossom Inn, and from the moment Miss Beverly had led them inside the sprawling, beautifully decorated cottage, Leona had been completely charmed.

Each room in the inn was painted a cheery color. The entryway was the exact color of orange sherbet, the library a fresh violet. The kitchen was decorated in shades of green, bringing to mind mint chocolate chip ice cream. Even their bathroom was as bright as a summer day. It had glossy yellow walls and sported yellow gingham curtains. Blinding white towels were neatly arranged on shelves.

But their spacious attic room was her favorite. Though at first glance it looked deceptively plain, with its frosty white walls and dark red cherry planks underfoot, it was actually a warm and adorable space. All three of them had gasped in pleasure when Miss Beverly had opened their door and shown them the shelves lined with Christian romances, the trunk filled with extra blankets, quilts, and down pillows, and the charming claw-footed tub in their adjoining bathroom.

Each of their twin beds was covered with bright quilts. Coordinating rag rugs dotted the floor, and two large dressers painted bright red lined the walls. Their room also sported white wicker furniture decorated with bright pink-and-green-paisley-printed cushions.

Within moments, they'd each claimed a bed, pulled out their nightgowns, and changed clothes, ready to nap.

Then they'd promptly fallen asleep.

Now, while she looked around the room and tried to regain

some of her enthusiasm, Leona was having a hard time locating it.

Maybe she was simply groggy and desperately in need of a hot shower, or maybe it was that the second day of their vacation was almost over already. But Leona knew her spirits were dwindling. She needed to regain control of herself, remember how much she loved and trusted Edmund.

The sooner the better, too, because time was running out.

With a sigh, she pulled out her new dress. If anything could chase away her doldrums, it would be this dress with its cheery color.

"You okay?" Sara asked as she returned to the room, her wet hair streaming down her back.

"I'm fine. Just a little sleepy still, I guess."

Sara's eyes narrowed. "Are you sure that's all that's worrying you?"

"Of course," Leona lied. Because, really, how could she ever admit how she was feeling? Sara and Mattie were so excited about Leona's upcoming wedding, as was practically everyone else she knew. It seemed as if no one could talk about anything but the menu and the colors and the cake and how so very happy she was going to be.

Sara, once again her sweet self, murmured, "I bet you're missing Edmund. Don't worry, when we get back, you'll never be without him again."

Leona smiled wanly. Though they were supposed to help her feel better, her cousin's words only served to remind her that she was having more doubts than ever about pledging her heart to Edmund.

They would be so hurt and mad if she even hinted that she feared he really wasn't the right man for her.

But she couldn't share that. Mattie and Sara had already

spent hours helping Leona design the wedding invitations and sewing napkins for the reception. And Sara's brother Paul was one of Edmund's best friends.

And she couldn't even bear to think about what Mattie would do. All Mattie could seem to say was how they were going to be sisters forever now.

Luckily, Sara entered the room, which meant it was Leona's turn to shower and change. "I'll be fast," she promised. And she was. Having taken a quick shower, she got dressed with little fuss, and after drying her hair as best she could with one of those fluffy white towels, she ruthlessly pulled it back and pinned it into a neat bun.

Then she made a promise to herself. She was going to make this the happiest two weeks of her life. And that happiness would have no choice but to spill over into the rest of her life. That positive attitude was therefore going to seep into her prayers and her thoughts concerning Edmund.

Surely then, the Lord would see fit to bless her with a fresh heart and new attitude. All of her doubts would fall away, leaving only the determination to be everything Edmund needed her to be.

She tested out that positive attitude when they walked to the pizza parlor and devoured a large pepperoni pizza. It continued next door, when she ordered a mint chocolate chip ice cream cone.

It felt like God was rewarding her for her efforts. The smiles became easier and she began to relax and simply be with her two best friends.

And then they started walking. Block after block they went, smiling shyly at other Amish folks they passed, some wearing *kapps* much like theirs, signaling that they were from Holmes

County, too. Eyeing other girls' dresses with pleated skirts from Indiana and some of the more colorful ones from a church district in Lancaster County, her spirits lifted further.

"I think I'm going to like it here," she said.

"Me too," Mattie said, her smile, as usual, making Leona smile, too.

Leona was just about to suggest that they go read the message board in front of the post office, where visitors left messages about upcoming parties or events, when they heard the unmistakable sound of masculine laughter.

Sara was on that like a dog after a bone. "Come on, girls."

Mattie froze. "Why?"

"To see the boys, of course."

Leona shook her head. "Sara, we can't simply go search for boys."

"You can't because you're engaged. But I'm not. Nothing is stopping me," she called over her shoulder. "Come on." And with that, she darted down Birky Street and turned left on Beneva.

After exchanging a pained look with Mattie, Leona hustled down the sidewalk after Sara. There was no way she was going to let Sara get into trouble on her own.

After practically running down the block, Sara came to a sudden stop at the front yard of the Palm Grove Mennonite Church.

"Now what's wrong?" Mattie griped before she, too, seemed transfixed by the sight before her.

Feeling like the lazy part of the three musketeers, Leona hurried over to catch up, then found herself just as captivated.

And then she had to remind herself not to stare quite so blatantly.

But what a sight it was!

"What are they doing?"

"It looks like there's something in the tree."

Two men about their ages had surrounded a tree, chins lifted, and were staring up at something nestled in the branches. Leona followed their gazes. Then stifled a gasp.

A third man was more or less reclining on one of the branches like he was seven years old again. One leg was swinging, his blue shirt was untucked, and his straw hat had floated down to the base of the tree. And he was grinning like he was having the best time in the world.

Leona swallowed.

Yes, it was obvious that they were having a good time. Every minute or two, they laughed, egged each other on, and made jokes about bees.

Bees!

Especially the man in the tree—who she'd just happened to notice had sandy brown hair, very tan arms, and a dimple.

She knew he had a dimple because from the moment she'd spied him, he'd either been laughing, teasing his buddies, or grinning.

He lit up the scene. And, she had a feeling, he most likely lit up wherever he was all the time. Unable to take her eyes off of him, she realized he was the type of man she used to dream about when she went to sleep at night.

He looked confident and happy. Comfortable with himself and with everyone else, too.

Just then, that man glanced in her direction. Within seconds his gaze had turned intent. Far more serious.

And though it was truly a fanciful thought, Leona imagined that she could actually feel his gaze. And that he was thinking the same thing that she was—that for the first time in forever, something significant was about to happen.

That look was compelling and scary and intense. Enough to take her breath away. Instinctively, she took a step back. "We should go."

"No way," Sara said. And then did the exact opposite. She walked a little bit closer. "I want to see what they're doing."

"But it's none of our business."

"We won't get in the way, Leona," Mattie said. "Don't be so timid. I mean, weren't you saying on the bus that you wanted to meet new people?"

She had said that. But she hadn't been talking about handsome men. She'd been thinking more along the lines of girls their own age. "Yes, but—"

"But nothing," Sara whispered. "They're cute and they look nice. And they're Amish, so even my *mamm* wouldn't get mad."

At that, Leona felt her lips twitch. Sara's mother constantly warned Sara about talking to *Englischers,* especially young, handsome *Englischers.* "Fine."

"Hey!" one of the guys called out.

"Hey, yourself," Sara said, flirting right back.

"Did you need something?"

"*Nee.* We were just wondering what caught your attention. What's in the tree?"

"A cat. A mighty determined, mighty skittish *katz.*"

Mattie laughed. "I guess it takes three Amish men to rescue a cat in Pinecraft?"

The man's smile grew wider. "Obviously, and we're still having a time of it. Perhaps you three ought to come over here and give us a hand."

Before any of the girls could comment on that, there was a

rustle of leaves followed by a lazy, loud meow. Then, next thing they knew, a sleek gray cat with white paws gracefully leapt from the tree like it was the headline attraction in a carnival show.

"She's out! Catch her!" the man in the tree called as he started his descent.

The blond who had been flirting with Sara reached for the cat, missed, and stumbled as he attempted to regain his balance and run after the wayward cat at the same time.

In response, the cat meowed, lifted her chin, then darted toward the girls.

"Oh!" Sara said. "She's pretty."

"She is mighty pretty," Leona agreed as the cat pranced over to her legs and circled around her ankles. Then she looked up at Leona with gray-blue eyes and meowed.

Before she thought about it, Leona bent down and picked it up.

"Meow," the cat uttered again before snuggling close, purring her contentment. Hugging it close to her, Leona glanced helplessly at her girlfriends and at the three men who were now all turned to her and gazing at her with looks of wonder.

And then, the man from the tree branches stepped forward and grinned. "Perhaps it doesn't take three Amish men at all. Just one pretty blond girl."

Leona knew he was teasing.

She knew he was being a mite too forward.

She knew she was engaged and shouldn't encourage any familiarity.

But for some reason, all she could do was stare at him, cuddle the cat.

And smile right back.

Chapter 3

Almost a minute had passed and the blond still hadn't said a word.

Which meant that Zachary Kaufmann was beginning to feel more than a little awkward.

Studying her face, he inhaled, and started wondering what he should say next—which was something that didn't happen often. It was also something that his friends and neighbors would have said had likely never happened to him.

He'd lived in Sarasota, Florida, for most of his life. His family had made the decision to move to Pinecraft from Lancaster County when his mother's parents had opted to retire there. Though he'd been only six, he vividly remembered his first winter spent in Florida. Instead of it being snowy and cold, the sun had been shining. Instead of breaking the ice on their horses' troughs, his chores had consisted of keeping his mother's flower bed watered and weeded.

He'd taken to life in Florida without hardly a skip in beat. As had his parents. His father found work with a local contractor, and his mother got right on as a teacher's aide at a local school, Pinecraft Elementary. His older brother and sister had settled into their new school easily, too. His *grandmommi* and *granddawdi* had loved having their grandchildren close by and spoiled them often. Over time, he'd made some good friends, Jeremy and Danny.

He'd led a charmed life and felt more than a little blessed. The only problem he had wasn't a problem at all, but something that, in the back of his mind, he was always focused on:

His little sister, Effie, and her disease.

When she turned ten, she'd been diagnosed with Perthes disease. When the doctor had first told them about this childhood disorder that usually affected children's hips and legs, they'd all stared at him in shock. The diagnosis had come completely out of the blue.

Though it was a rather mild condition and she functioned better than many other children in her situation, she'd still been in a lot of pain and had spent most of the first year in a wheelchair.

She was a strong girl at heart, however, and was determined to do anything the other kids her age could do. She worked hard with her special teachers and therapists and now spent many of her days on her own two feet.

Though the rest of them were mighty impressed, Effie took it all in stride. She would be the first person to tell anyone that she was just as capable as anyone.

Zack knew she was, too, but she did have special needs. And he wasn't really sure why or how, but over time, he'd become her primary caregiver. They were close and their temperaments meshed well. Besides, she was important to him. So important that he couldn't imagine ever not being a part of her life.

And though he wouldn't exactly tell this to anyone, he had a strange feeling that the reason he was suddenly thinking about Effie as the blond girl held his neighbor's cat was because he knew that she was a tourist.

Which meant she probably lived far away.

Since he was always going to want to live near his sister, it was likely he was always going to live in Sarasota.

And that meant, of course, there could be no future between him and this girl. And that, he decided when she returned his smile, was a real shame.

When she still said nothing, merely petted the cat, he knew he had to say something.

"It seems Serena likes you," he said as he walked to her, concentrating on keeping his voice casual and ignoring the punch he'd felt in his stomach when he noticed that she was pretty. Approachable, too. Like she could be anybody's friend if they gave her just a couple minutes of their time.

She raised her brows. "Serena?"

"It's the cat's name."

"Ah. She's pretty. Is she yours?"

"No way. She's my neighbor's. Mrs. Sadler loves her."

Danny came up to his side and smiled at the girls. "Zack is Winnie Sadler's go-to guy. She calls him to rescue cats, get her mail from the post office, grocery shop—"

"It's not that bad. I'm simply available."

"Or an easy mark," Danny teased, his eyes turning warmer. Immediately, Zack felt a surge of jealousy and glanced at Danny. Then, when he noticed that Danny wasn't looking at the blond but at the green-eyed girl with the freckles dotting her nose, he calmed down.

The girls looked at each other and giggled in the way only

girls in groups could. Then the blond smiled at him. "So you're name is Zack?"

"*Jah*. I'm Zachary Kaufmann. And this is Danny, and the guy over there by the church entrance is Jeremy."

"Nice to meet you. I'm Leona. Leona Weaver. And this is Mattie and Sara."

Jeremy joined them, and they all began their round of introductions again.

"You tourists?"

Leona nodded. "We just arrived from Ohio today. What about you?"

"We're some of those rare people in Pinecraft who live here year-round."

One of the girls sighed. "You are so lucky."

"We think so," Zack said. "It's a nice place to live." Then, before he thought better of it, he reached close, intending to grab the cat and lift it out of Leona's arms.

Serena, contrary as ever, squirmed and fussed. So he had to stand a little closer. Of course, that meant he got way too personal with Leona. She blushed as he attempted to get hold of Serena without brushing his hands across places he shouldn't.

And her blush made him feel even more awkward. Something he couldn't remember feeling in ages.

The cat made her displeasure known by releasing an especially irritated meow.

"She's mad now, Zack," Jeremy pointed out.

"Yeah. I had better go return her to Mrs. Sadler." Bracing himself to be clawed, he grabbed Serena out of Leona's arms as quickly as possible.

Luckily, it was less awkward than it could have been. Serena gave in gracefully. After swiping at him in a halfhearted way, she relaxed in his arms.

When he sighed in relief, Leona giggled. "It was nice to meet you, Zack."

"Same here." He nodded. "Bye, now."

Then he turned away and started walking. Behind him, Danny and Jeremy were saying their goodbyes to the girls. Knowing that they were only seconds away from giving him all sorts of grief, Zack picked up his pace.

He didn't slow down or look back toward the church until they'd walked almost a full block. Only then did he dare to glance at the church's front yard. The girls were long gone and the yard was completely empty now.

The only thing that caught his eye was the church's cross.

Which was fitting. Once again, the Lord was directing things His way. Here, He'd given Zack an absurd situation, a wayward cat, and the prettiest girl he'd ever seen.

And Zack had lost his heart that quick.

He had no idea how it was going to work out. All he knew was that the Lord had seen fit to show him a hint of everything that could be. The promise of a future.

The promise of what a life with the right woman could be like.

WITH A SENSE of accomplishment, Beverly sealed the top of the second envelope, then flipped it over, carefully wrote her sister's name and address on the front, and finally placed a stamp on the upper right-hand corner. She'd done it. She'd written another letter home.

Around two years ago, after she'd been in Pinecraft for seven or eight months, she'd stopped ignoring all the phone calls and letters she'd received and started writing people back. At first, she had been overwhelmed with the number of people who'd contacted her. It seemed as if her parents had practically given out flyers containing the address and phone number of her new home, which was her Aunt Patty's bed-and-breakfast.

When everything fell apart, Beverly had asked her Aunt Patty if she could stay with her for a while, and since they got along so well, Patty invited her to stay on. A few years after that, Aunt Patty passed on into heaven, leaving the inn in Beverly's capable hands.

Though Beverly hadn't been in a hurry to answer any of their phone calls, she had kept a log of everyone who had left her a message. She'd also kept everyone's letters in a pretty white wicker basket. When she felt ready to start returning their notes, she'd begun picking out two a week and writing to them.

It had been a slow yet cathartic experience, but, to her surprise, it had also begun to be rather enjoyable. It turned out that she liked telling people about life in Pinecraft. She liked describing the things she'd been learning about running an inn. She enjoyed relaying stories about guests who'd stayed with her.

Most of all, she liked telling everyone that she was okay. Because she was okay. Little by little, she'd stopped thinking about Regina and Marvin and how disappointed her family had to be, and started thinking about her plans for the upcoming week. She'd stopped reliving painful conversations, trying to figure out what she'd done wrong with Marvin, and started trying out new recipes for afternoon teas.

Most of all, she began to actually look forward to the mail coming each day, because the notes she received had little to do with the wedding that never was and were more often filled with daily news and questions about life in Florida.

So even though she still wasn't quite ready to return to Sugarcreek, not even for a visit, and she'd so far successfully pushed aside her sisters' and parents' wishes to come to Pine-craft, Beverly knew that life had gotten much better.

Now all she had to do was hope it would continue.

Chapter 4

The hard plastic braces that supported her legs were starting to dig into her skin, but Effie Kaufmann pretended everything was fine. And it actually kind of was, because she wasn't in a wheelchair today.

That meant, at least for a while, that people would notice her first and not the chair. Maybe they'd see that she was wearing one of her new dresses that her mother had sewn for her on a break from work over Christmas.

Maybe if they noticed her new dress, someone would also notice that it was almost the exact shade of her blue eyes. And if they did that, it would be pretty amazing, because hardly anyone ever noticed that she had pretty eyes. They were her best feature, and she didn't even think she was being prideful for admitting that she had a best feature.

As far as Effie was concerned, she'd been dealing with people overlooking everything about her—except for her bad legs—for two years now. She'd learned pretty quickly that life for a girl her age wasn't real easy when folks looked at the wheelchair first and her second.

But even though she was wearing a new dress that covered her braces and matched her eyes, and she was standing instead of resting in her wheelchair, she still wasn't feeling great. That was too bad, because she was standing in line at Yoder's, which was the very best place in Pinecraft for pie. She didn't get to go there all that often, either. Which was another reason she should have been smiling.

But she wasn't. Standing in the long line for almost thirty minutes was putting a strain on her legs. This was longer than she'd ever stood without taking at least a five-minute break. If the wait was much longer, she was going to have to swallow her pride and tell her brother, Zack, that she had to sit down.

As if he could read her mind, he leaned down next to her. "Not too much longer now, Eff. The hostess just seated that group of four, so there are only three more couples ahead of us."

"That's *gut*. The line was longer than I thought it would be."

"I was thinking the same thing." Looking apologetic, he added, "I promise, if I would have known the wait was going to be this long, I would have suggested we go someplace else."

He would have, too, Effie realized. He always put her needs first. "I'm glad we didn't."

"Sure?"

Zack really was the best brother in the world. He was handsome and easygoing. He took time with her and never acted like he wished he was doing anything else. "I'm fine."

But she mustn't have sounded all that fine because his eyes scanned her face for about the twentieth time since they'd gotten in line. She knew what he was doing; he was looking for signs of strain. Signs that he needed to escort her to a bench or a chair immediately.

And he would do that in a heartbeat. He absolutely would.

And though her legs would be really grateful for the break, the rest of her would feel completely embarrassed.

"Sure?" he asked again.

"Positive." She started to smile, but it faltered when she saw two girls from her class sitting at a table with their moms. They were the popular girls, the girls who everyone wanted to be around. The girls who were invited everywhere.

The opposite of her.

Zack noticed her glance and her subsequent frown. "Do you know those girls?"

"*Jah*. They're Melanie and Jennifer C."

His lips twitched. "Jennifer C.?"

"We've got three Jennifers in our class." But only one Effie, she thought with a grimace. She loved her parents, she truly did. But sometimes she surely wished they'd given her a less weird name.

Okay, she wished that a lot.

"Do you want to go over and say hi? You can if you want."

"That's okay." Her muscles were so sore, she knew that her gait was going to be even more uneven than it usually was.

"Are they not nice?"

"They're fine, Zack. Don't worry about it." And that was part of the problem, Effie thought. It would almost be easier if they were the type of girls who were mean all the time. But they weren't. Sometimes, Melanie would seem almost friendly—but then, when she was surrounded by her friends, she would whisper mean comments about someone just loudly enough to be heard.

Luckily, Effie had never been one of Melanie's targets. Usually, she ignored Effie or smiled in a distracted way before passing her by.

Effie didn't care for girls who did that sort of thing, which was why she'd never been too disappointed that they weren't better friends.

But she knew if she walked over there, both Melanie and Jennifer would act like she was their long-lost friend. They'd talk to her as if they actually all talked together when they were at school, which they did not. They were really good at being nice in front of a lot of people.

Then things would be even more awkward, because Zack would remember their comments. He'd remember their names, too, and then he would start asking if she had plans with them.

Which she wouldn't, of course.

The hostess sat another table and they moved up again in the line. Then at last, five minutes later, they were seated, too. Of course, they had to walk right by Jennifer C. and Melanie. A walk, unfortunately, that was really slow, because she'd been standing in one place for so long.

When the girls looked up and smiled, she smiled back. "Hi."

"Hi, Effie," Jennifer C. chirped. "Did you come for pie or supper?"

"Both," she replied, because it wasn't like she could ignore them. Then she noticed both of their eyes kept darting her brother's way. "This is my brother, Zack."

"Hey," Zack said.

And both girls blushed and giggled. "Hi."

After their *mamms* said hi, too, Effie followed her brother and the hostess to the table. But just as she was walking, a man in front of her abruptly scooted back his chair and got to his feet.

His motion meant she had to sidestep in the crowded, narrow space between two tables, putting even more pressure on her already tired legs. The muscles in her legs twitched. She shifted her hips in an attempt to support the weight.

But it was too much. Her left leg buckled. Right there, in front of Jennifer C. and Melanie.

Instinctively, she reached out for the side of a table. A chair. Anything to help prevent her from falling completely on the ground.

And in that split second, her embarrassment reached a new level.

Next thing she knew, a woman about Zack's age leapt out of her seat and wrapped a reassuring arm around Effie. Immediately, her muscles righted themselves and she regained her balance.

Just in the nick of time.

"Easy now," the woman said with a reassuring smile. "Don't rush yourself."

Effie was breathing hard, both from the effort of holding herself stiff and from the awful knowledge that half the people in the place were now watching her fight to stay on two feet. "*Danke.*"

"You okay?" the woman whispered. "You didn't fall, but I fear you might have pulled a muscle or strained yourself."

The lady really was very kind. "I'm *gut. Danke,*" Effie said again. "I'm sorry for the trouble." With effort, she pulled herself away from the woman's grip and righted herself—just as Zack reached her other side.

"Effie, you good?" Zack asked, his voice sounding unnaturally loud in the lull of conversation.

"*Jah.*" But she wasn't. She wished she could run to the bathroom or right out of the restaurant. Or rewind the last five minutes.

"*Gut*." He smiled.

Effie returned his grin. And then, just like that, everyone in the restaurant went back to their private conversations.

Happy the drama was over, she breathed a sigh of relief that he wasn't making a big deal out of what had just happened. "I think your legs are getting much stronger," he murmured. "Used to be, you could never have righted yourself so quickly. All that swimming the doctor recommended really has been helping."

As nice as it would be to take that credit, Effie knew she couldn't. "Zack, actually, it was this lady's quick reflexes which saved the day. I would have fallen if not for her." Effie looked to her right, intent on showing Zack who had been so kind.

But it turned out that she didn't need to say anything at all . . . because Zack was staring at the woman with an almost starstruck expression.

"Leona?"

"*Jah*. And you are Zack, right?"

"I am." His chest puffed up a bit.

Leona smiled brightly. "I can't believe that we ran into each other again. What a small world."

"Well, this is Pinecraft," Zack replied. "It is a rather small world. I'm sure we'll run into each other all the time. That said, I can't believe you're lending a helping hand again. First you helped me with Serena, and now here you were, just in time to help my sister."

"I'm glad I could give you that hand."

"This is my sister Effie. Effie, this is Leona. She's the girl who caught Serena last night."

"Hi."

Leona inclined her head in a friendly way. "Nice to meet you."

Feeling awkward, all of a sudden, Effie stumbled over her next words. "Thanks again for helping me out."

"Again, it was nothing. I'm glad I happened to be sitting close by." Her gaze darted toward Zack, hesitated, then she smiled at Effie again. "Well, I should go sit back down. It's pretty crowded in here. Enjoy your meal."

"You too." Zack looked like he wanted to say something more but he turned to Effie instead. Firmly wrapping an arm around her, he guided Effie to their table and held her chair out as she sat.

"I'm sorry, Zack," Effie said, feeling her cheeks heat.

"For what?"

"Causing a scene."

"You didn't cause a scene."

Looking at him more closely, Effie realized that her brother was being completely honest. He hadn't seen anything wrong with his awkward sister stumbling in between the tables. He probably didn't have a clue that Jennifer C. was no doubt going to tell everyone how Effie couldn't even walk through a restaurant. And with her luck, their story would reach Josiah Grimm, the cutest boy in their class.

"Zack, I almost fell down in the middle of Yoder's. Your friend had to leap out of her chair to catch me. It wasn't one of my best moments." She smiled at him before dipping her head to read the printed paper menu. Maybe she shouldn't have even said that much, but while she felt that it was best to show him she wasn't going to let it ruin her whole day, she also felt obligated to point out the extent of her flaws.

"Hey."

She popped her head up. "What?"

"Don't worry about it, okay?" For once, even his eyes

weren't smiling. Instead, his whole expression was serious and solemn. "Things like this happen to everyone. I promise. It feels big because it happened to you, but everyone else has probably already forgotten it. It's only a big deal if you make it out to be."

She knew he was probably right. But she also knew that he would never be able to understand what it felt like to be a twelve-year-old girl with a wheelchair and plastic braces attached to her legs. "I just wish I was normal."

Something new entered his eyes and he leaned forward. "Don't ever say that again. You *are* normal. You are fine."

"Zack, you're right. I am fine . . . but I'm not like everyone else."

"Everybody's got something, Effie," he said, his voice thick with emotion. "You just happen to have some problems with your hips and legs. That doesn't mean you can't do things, because you can. It doesn't mean you're not as good as anyone else, you surely are."

"Okay," she whispered, hoping he would stop.

But her brother was on a roll. "You know, Effie, *Gott* doesn't give us anything He doesn't think we can't handle. He's given you this problem, but He's also given you a lot of gifts. Remember that."

His voice was so intense, his expression so fierce, that Effie nodded. There was no way she was going to even think of arguing with him about this. Especially not in the middle of Yoder's. "I'll remember."

"*Gut.* Now, let's have lunch, okay?"

She nodded, and when the server came, she ordered the special, which was barbecue chicken. Zack did the same. Just as she geared up for what was probably going to be round two of the 'Effie is normal' discussion, she noticed that he was looking beyond her. At Leona.

"Leona is really pretty," she said. "She seems mighty nice, too."

"Yeah."

"How did you meet her?"

"Last night, Mrs. Sadler asked if I could try and get Serena out of the tree in the front of Palm Grove."

Effie refrained from rolling her eyes, but just barely. "Serena doesn't need help getting out of trees. Especially not the ones in the front of the Mennonite church. She's up there all the time."

"Well, I know that, and you know that. Serena probably knows that, too."

"But?"

Slowly, his lips curved. "But Mrs. Sadler loves that cat. And she was fretting. When she knocked on our door, she was near tears. What could I do?"

Privately, Effie thought he could have told Mrs. Sadler that Serena had come down from the tree just fine the day before. But she wasn't Zack. And Zack always put other people first.

"Okay, now I get why you were trying to rescue Serena. How did Leona come into play?"

"She was walking by the church with her girlfriends and they saw Danny, Jeremy, and me trying to get Serena out. Actually, I was in the tree."

She paused. "Wait a minute. You were climbing the tree?"

"Oh, *jah*. I was half stuck in there, too. We were laughing something fierce." He leaned back and braced his hands on the edge of their table. "It was obvious that Serena didn't want anything to do with us. However, it was also becoming obvious that some bees, ah, didn't appreciate us being in their space."

"Oh, Zack. It's a wonder you three didn't get stung."

He shrugged off her worry. "Next thing I knew, Serena jumped down from the tree limb like it was six inches off the ground instead of six feet, and pranced over to Leona. Right then and there, she rubbed herself against Leona's legs and meowed. Leona bent down and picked her up, just like that cat was her long-lost friend."

Serena wasn't known for being an especially cuddly cat. That, Effie thought, was one of the reasons she escaped so much. If Mrs. Sadler had her way, Serena would be in her arms or on her lap all day long. "Did Leona get scratched up?"

"*Nee.* Fact is, Serena didn't fight her at all." He shook his head in wonder. "It was something to see." He looked beyond Effie again, his gaze settling on Leona.

"I bet. So that's how you met Leona?"

"Yeah. I introduced myself. Well, all three of us boys did. Leona and her friends are down from Ohio on vacation."

Effie felt her spirits sink, though she wasn't quite sure why. The actual population of Pinecraft was pretty small. She didn't know all the Amish, of course, but she recognized most of the folks who lived in her area. Still, if Leona were a local, Effie would have remembered her. With her blond hair, brown eyes, and high cheek bones, Leona was so very pretty.

And, judging by the way Zack kept looking in her direction, it was fairly obvious that he thought Leona was attractive, too.

After their server brought them their drinks, Effie made a decision. "Zack, why don't you go over and see if they want a tour of the area or something?"

"What?"

"All right. Maybe not a tour. But maybe you could show them how to get on the bus to go to Siesta Key. It's a little tricky, at least the first time. I mean, everyone says that. And then, since you'll be on the bus with her, you could go to the beach, too."

Something flickered in his eyes before he firmly tamped it down. "I bet she'd think that was a bit much, me going up to her table and offering to take her to the beach."

"I bet she'd think that was nice. How else is she going to figure things out? I'm pretty sure she wouldn't ask you to take her."

"Why wouldn't she?"

Effie rolled her eyes. "Because she's the girl, Zack. Even I know that answer."

"I don't know. I don't want to say the wrong thing. Or scare her off."

"You don't have to say another word to her if you don't want. But I kind of think she would be relieved if you offered. Ain't so?"

"You think?"

"*Jah.* Those girls have probably been wondering how much it costs, how to get tickets, where it stops . . . all that stuff. I've read the guides. If you don't know the streets, it don't make much sense. It's much better to be with someone who knows what to do and where to go." She smiled then, really pleased that she was able to help him out for once.

Her brother cracked a few of his knuckles, something he always did when he was thinking hard. "You may be right."

"I know I'm right." Eager to help him, since he was always looking out for her, Effie added another thought. "I think there might be another reason she's gonna be glad you asked."

"Why is that?"

"Because I saw her looking at you the same way you've been darting glances at her."

"Really?"

"Really."

Zack frowned. "A girl like that is probably taken, though, don'tcha think?"

"You won't know unless you start talking to her, silly. It's not like she's going to be wearing a ring on her finger like the *Englischers* do."

"You're probably right," he muttered under his breath.

Effie almost laughed. Her brother was one of the most confident people she'd ever met. Nothing ever seemed to fluster him. Not his life at home—which basically amounted to taking care of everything—not his friends, not even her handicap. He took everything in stride.

Except this girl. Yep, there was something about this Leona that had his stomach in knots and set him on edge. And though she was only twelve, she thought it was cute. "Go on and ask before she leaves."

He braced his hands on the table, obviously ready to push away, then paused. Indecision shone brightly on his face, so vividly that Effie could have sworn a ticker tape of thoughts flickered in his eyes.

At last he stood up. "I'll be right back," he murmured, then walked over to Leona's table.

Taking a sip of iced tea, Effie smiled to herself.

Thank you, Lord.

When she'd arrived at Yoder's, she'd only been thinking about herself. About her legs, about her handicap, about the girls in her class and how she wished she'd never heard of Perthes disease.

But now He had given her the opportunity to concentrate on someone else. To be the encourager, the strong and confident one. It was a nice change. It was a *really* nice change.

So much so, she hardly noticed when Jennifer C. and Melanie walked by, waving at her slightly before they followed their mothers to the cashier.

For the first time in a long time, what she wanted and how she was feeling didn't matter to her at all. Not one bit.

Chapter 5

Beverly loved having three young guests in the house. The girls in the top attic room were polite, had sunny dispositions, and chatted a mile a minute. When the house seemed especially quiet, Beverly had discovered that if she stood in the middle of the stairwell, she could hear the girls' voices.

Snippets of conversation would float downstairs, shared laughter punctuated by teasing, and then accompanied by strains of thoughtful silence. It was all music to her ears.

It wasn't that she tried to listen to private conversations, of course. Instead, she simply enjoyed the reminder of another time when she'd felt nothing but hope. A time when her future was so bright that she'd viewed all of her goals and dreams as completely possible.

The girls had been here four days now, and seemed to have settled into a routine of sorts. They were the last guests to arrive for breakfast but lingered at the table the longest. Then, after a round of discussion—and there was always a lot of discussion—they'd set off to explore Pinecraft and the surrounding city of Sarasota.

Later, they would return, their hands laden with shopping bags and lots of stories about the things they'd seen. Then, with more chatter and smiles, they would meet Beverly in the living room for informal tea.

Beverly had a pretty good idea that their devotion to the hour in her living room had much to do with cups of hot tea, and freshly baked lemon bread and sugar cookies. Free food was the best food, especially to girls on a budget.

But they also seemed to enjoy hearing Beverly's perspective about Pinecraft, the tourist season, the beach, and their various concerns. In no time, they became fast friends with Wilma and Sadie, too, as well as all of Beverly's friends who stopped by for tea on occasion.

There really was something about the bright-eyed girls that brought out the best in everyone at the Orange Blossom Inn.

As she set out a platter of carefully sliced grapefruit Bundt cake next to the tray of thinly sliced turkey and watercress sandwiches, Beverly wondered what their conversation would be centered upon today.

Or, perhaps, they had elected to do something else with their afternoon.

"You sure put out a great spread," Wilma said as she fixed a plate, piling it high with the desserts. "You've got the luckiest guests in the area."

"And maybe the luckiest friends as well?" Beverly countered with a meaningful look at Wilma's plate.

Wilma had the grace to look embarrassed. "You don't mind, do you? I mean, I know I'm not one of your guests, but it always looks like you have more than enough."

"Of course I don't mind. I love playing hostess every afternoon. I'm glad that you can stop by so often."

"And we like taking you up on your hospitality," Wilma said just as Sadie entered through the front door. "Sadie, just in time," she called out, just as if she was the hostess! "Beverly made her cream cheese grapefruit Bundt cake today."

Sadie, the oldest one of their group, smiled. "Oh, I know all about the grapefruit Bundt. It's better than *gut,* why, it's *wonderful-gut.* Why do you think I'm here early?"

"Help yourself to a plate," Beverly offered just as she heard a burst of giggles and a trio of footsteps scamper down the stairs.

Sadie looked toward the wooden stairs and smiled. "Looks like the girls will be joining us again."

Beverly winked. "I think so, too."

Wilma filled her mug with hot water just as the girls appeared, their faces wreathed in smiles. One of them had a pink nose, too.

"Good afternoon," Beverly called out. "Will you be joining us for tea today?"

"Oh, yes," Mattie said. "Believe it or not, we plan our afternoons around this."

"I believe it," Wilma quipped. "I do, too."

Beverly chuckled. "I host a tea in the hopes that folks will come. I'm glad you do. So, are you having a good day?"

Sara, the quietest of the trio, nodded. "We thought about going to the beach, but we weren't up for it. I think all this traveling has gotten the best of us."

"We fell right asleep last night in the middle of a conversation," Mattie said as she heaped her plate almost as high as Wilma's. "I woke up in the middle of the night with my reading glasses on."

"I've done that a time or two," Beverly admitted. "I like to

read at night. Sometimes I can't put my book down. I keep telling myself, just one more page."

"And then one more, and one more," Sadie said with a
wink. "I've done that a time or two, myself."

Beverly lost track of the girls' conversation as her other
guests appeared. Currently, she had all seven of her guest
rooms filled, which pleased her a great deal. She liked being
busy, and she liked being able to put a little bit of money aside
to save for a rainy day.

Unfortunately, her other guests weren't quite as outgoing
or cheery. One couple was older and seemed to have regretted their decision to come to Pinecraft from the moment they
boarded their bus. All they did was grumble about the fact that
they weren't home. Two other couples never came to tea and
barely ate any of Beverly's breakfast. They seemed to have their
own plans and agenda.

The last room was occupied by a mother and daughter who
didn't seem to bring out the best in each other. The daughter,
who seemed to be about fifteen or sixteen was a complainer,
her mother only less so.

They, however, liked to linger at their meals and sit in the
living room. After struggling to make conversation with them
the first day, Beverly now did her best to avoid them.

But she still felt obligated to make sure the tureens were
filled with hot water, the trays were kept plentiful, and everyone's needs were met to the best of her ability. She circled the
living area, chatting with each group, pouring more tea and
lemonade, bringing more napkins and spoons, and generally
doing everything she could to ensure her guests became repeat
visitors.

She'd just finished her second lap when she spied one of

the girls staring intently out the window. There was such a look of worry in her eyes that Beverly took a seat next to her. "Leona, is everything all right with you?"

"Me? Oh, *jah.*"

"Are you sure? I don't want to pry, but you look a little melancholy."

Leona smiled weakly. "That's not it at all. I just was thinking about someone."

"Your fiancé?" The girls had told Beverly when they arrived that they were in Pinecraft to enjoy one last trip together before Leona said her vows.

"*Nee.*"

Beverly blinked. Leona's voice was a little sharp. She wondered if she was feeling a little homesick. It certainly wasn't her business. "Please let me know if you need anything else," she said, and stood.

"I've got a problem," Leona blurted.

Beverly sat back down. "You do?"

After darting a glance at her friends, who were chatting with the whiny fifteen-year-old, Leona said, "See, I made a friend here."

"Yes, that happens a lot."

"You don't understand. The friend I made? It's a boy." She shook her head. "I mean, a man. I mean, he's local. His name is Zack Kaufmann. Any chance you know him?"

"Yes, I do. All of us in the community know pretty much everyone, at least by sight."

"Is he . . . is he a nice man?"

"He seems to be. His father, Frank, has done some remodeling for me. I'm pretty sure Zack helped him out from time to time."

Leona heaved a sigh of relief. "That's good to know." After another quick look at her friends, she leaned closer. "Miss Beverly, he and his friends have offered to take us to Siesta Key, to show us how to get on the bus and everything."

"That was nice of him. Those buses can be tricky."

"I don't know, though."

"Okay. Well, if you don't want to take them up on their offer, I'll be happy to show you what to do . . ."

"That's not it," Leona said, moving a little closer to Beverly. "The thing is, I want to take him up on his offer. I think it would be a lot of fun to spend the day together."

"Then, what is wrong?"

"I'm engaged."

Things were starting to come together. "I remember. Are you worried your fiancé will get jealous?"

"I'm worried that I don't even want to tell him that I'm going to the beach."

"Why not?"

"Edmund, well . . . he ain't a man who likes surprises. Or for me to do things he doesn't approve of."

"I see."

"He's good man," Leona said quickly. "Just, um, a bit controlling." After darting yet another look at her girlfriends, Leona shared, "I'm not thinking about being unfaithful, of course. But I'm worried that going to the beach with a man will seem disloyal." She grimaced. "As well as the fact that I *want* to go with him."

"Ah. What do Sara and Mattie think? Do they think your fiancé will get upset if you all go to the beach with your new friend?"

"*Jah.*"

"Any reason why?"

"They know how Edmund is. They don't think I should do anything to make him cross at me." Taking a breath, she added, "They're excited about the wedding, you see. They're excited about everything." She looked like she was about to add something more but jumped to her feet instead. "*Danke* for the treats. They are mighty *gut*."

"I'm glad you liked them. If you're done, I'll take your plate."

"*Danke*," she whispered before walking over to her friends. Moments later, the three of them darted out the door.

"Is she okay?" Wilma murmured as she walked over to take the still-full plate out of Beverly's hands.

"I'm not sure."

Sadie gestured toward the slice of cake that looked hardly touched. "She either didn't like your cake or decided she wasn't hungry."

Beverly laughed. "Maybe she's watching her figure. Young girls do that, you know."

"Oh, you," Wilma said. "I wish you wouldn't say things like that. It makes you sound far older than you are."

"Sometimes I feel far older than my years," she quipped just as her front door opened and a pair of women walked in, their eyes wide. "Hello, may I help you?"

One walked forward, then stopped and stared at her. "Beverly, look at you! Aren't you a sight for sore eyes! And you look lovely, too. Just as pretty as a picture."

Beverly felt as if her whole body had just frozen. "Jean? Ida?"

"Of course," Jean said.

"What in the world are you two doing here?" She hated to sound so inhospitable, but she was beyond shocked to see Marvin's sisters.

"We figured we might as well surprise you, since it was becoming obvious that we weren't going to receive an invitation anytime soon," Jean said.

Then, to Beverly's shock and amazement, Jean scampered over, tossed down her colorful quilted duffel on the floor, and enveloped her in a fierce hug.

"Oh, Beverly," she murmured. "I missed you. Do you have room for two surprise guests?"

"I'll make room," she promised, once she found her voice.

Though at the moment, she wanted to do nothing more than run upstairs to that attic room and shut the door behind her.

What in the world were Marvin's two sisters doing in Pinecraft? And more importantly, why in the world had they sought her out after all this time?

Chapter 6

"Will you be okay with just hamburgers, French fries, and Jell-O salad for supper, Zack?" his mother asked as she walked into the backyard.

Zack was watering his mother's vegetable and flower beds—something his brother Karl was supposed to do but he hardly ever had time for, seeing how he now had a full-time job at the Pinecraft Inn. Almost a year ago Karl had received a promotion and he was now assistant manager of the motel. As far as anyone in the family could tell, this new title meant that he now got to work nights, weekends, holidays, and whenever the manager needed a day off.

Zack didn't mind taking care of the yard and house, though. Both of his parents had their hands full with their jobs.

Things were especially difficult now, seeing as how his sister Violet had recently chosen to leave the order and become active in the Mennonite church. Though she wasn't shunned or anything like that, there was definitely a new gap between her and the rest of the family. Their parents suddenly didn't expect as much from her. He also privately thought that maybe Violet didn't offer to do as much as she should.

"Hamburgers are fine," he said as his mother walked to his side. "Anything is fine. You know that."

Her turquoise blue dress fluttered in the breeze. When he glanced her way, he noticed that the color complemented her already pretty features, especially her blue eyes—the same color eyes he'd inherited from her.

"Are you sure? I've got a meeting this evening with Effie's physical therapist, so things are a little out of sorts."

"Not out of sorts," he corrected. "More like how they always are. Busy."

Crossing her arms over her chest, she sighed. "I suppose so. Are you sure you don't mind staying here with Effie? Again?"

She asked him this at least once a week, and his answer was always the same. "Nope."

"You're sure you don't have other plans?"

This question, on the other hand, was new.

Turning off the hose's spray nozzle, Zack looked at his mother more carefully. She looked apprehensive; her lips were pursed into a firm line. Come to think of it, she looked a bit more stressed than usual, and she also seemed to be hinting at something, too. But, for the life of him, he couldn't guess what it was.

"Mother, maybe you could save us both some time and talk to me about what is really on your mind."

"Well . . . Effie mentioned that she met a young woman named Leona today at Yoder's."

"She did. And?"

"Effie also said that Leona was very nice."

"Leona *is* very nice."

"So . . ."

His mother's look conveyed all sorts of things. Things he wasn't ready to discuss with her.

Things he hadn't even thought about discussing with Leona.

Therefore, he decided it was time to nip her matchmaking glow in the bud. "Mamm, if Effie told you all about Leona, I'm sure she told you that I just met her."

She nodded. "I know. But—"

"Leona seems to be a nice girl and all, but she's only here on vacation."

"That's it?" His mother didn't even try to look not crestfallen. "Effie made it sound like there was something special between you two." She looked like she was tempted to add more but hesitated.

He was glad about that. Zack could only imagine what romantic notion Effie was conjuring up between him and Leona. "There could be if she didn't live in Ohio," he allowed, "but she does."

"So you aren't going to see her again?" A line formed between her brows. "Effie told me something different."

Lord, save him from meddling little sisters! "Actually, there's a chance I might see her tomorrow. I told her I'd take her and her girlfriends to Siesta Key."

"Oh!" A dimple appeared in her cheek.

"It doesn't mean anything. I merely offered to take her because the bus can be so confusing."

"Oh, *jah*. It is confusing, for sure." Smiling softly, she added, "It also gives you lots of time to spend together. Hours."

Zack exhaled as he attempted to find his patience. "Mamm, don't push."

"I'm not pushing."

"You are. And you are pushing too much. What is meant to happen will happen. The Lord will take care of it, He always does." Zack paused. "You and Daed taught me that, remember?"

"I know. It's just that you've given up so much for us." Gesturing toward the garden and the flowers, she said, "I feel like you've put your life on hold so the rest of the family can get their needs met."

"I've never felt that way."

"Truly?"

"Not at all. Stop worrying, please. And tell Daed to stop worrying, too." His parents were of the same mind on most everything. It was rare for one of them to be worrying about something without the other doing the very same thing.

She bit her lip, her expression a picture of indecision. "All right, then. I'll go make you and Effie those hamburgers."

"*Danke.*" Making a shooing motion with his hands, he said, "Now go on in. I've got this."

When the door closed again, he turned the hose on and faced away from the windows that lined the back of the house. After giving the hose a good yank, he started watering his mother's pride and joy: her eight grapefruit, orange, and lemon trees.

And then he at last gave in and contemplated what he really thought about his life.

His mother hadn't been far off the mark when she'd said that it seemed like he'd put his life on hold for everyone else.

It was true; he had.

When he'd graduated from school at age fourteen, he'd leapt into all of his father's odd jobs with both feet.

His *daed* worked for a big company that specialized in refurbishing vacation properties. Every day, his father was out in Sarasota, Siesta Key, or Longboat Key working. It was a good job, and his father had always enjoyed it because the jobs never lasted beyond a few weeks, he got to be outside a lot, and he didn't have to worry about paperwork. All he had to do was show up and put his skills to work. He was especially good at removing and installing countertops and kitchen and bathroom hardware. So good that even other contractors asked for him to take a side job here and there because they didn't know of anyone else who could do the work so quickly and efficiently.

Zack had stayed by his father's side for a good year. In that time both he and his *daed* learned a very important lesson. Loving someone didn't mean that it was always best to work by their side eight or ten hours a day.

Instead, he'd slowly begun to pick up the slack around the house. When Violet began dating a Mennonite boy—which had meant lots of arguments with their parents—Zack had taken over some of her chores. When she got a job working in a Christian bookstore, he'd taken over even more of her responsibilities.

During this time his brother Karl began working more hours at the motel and their mother continued her job, working as an aide at Effie's school.

And so Zack began doing even more yard work. He began taking care of the grocery shopping, too. Eventually, he started doing the laundry, too, since it wasn't too hard to wash a load and then hang out the clothes on the line to dry.

When the neighbors noticed that he was around quite a bit, they'd started asking him to do odd jobs for them. Jobs like staying in their homes for a week or two while they traveled up north to see family and friends. Because he wanted to make some money and contribute financially, he did that, too.

But most of all, he helped with Effie. He was in charge of helping her with her physical therapy exercises every day. He made sure he was home to greet her school bus when their mother had to stay after school for meetings. He took her to lunch when she was on vacation, to the beach on Sunday afternoons, and basically tried to ensure that she didn't sit by herself when she wasn't at school.

Thinking about all he did—none of which was all that important but still took up a lot of time—Zack realized that he was a fairly busy man. Yet none of what he did was only for himself.

He'd never minded that. He loved his sister. He liked his family, he liked being needed, and he liked that none of it gave him reason to lose sleep at night.

He'd never regretted his choices, that is, until he met Leona Weaver.

There was something about her golden hair, brown eyes, pretty smile, and friendly nature that struck him as special and unique.

Unfortunately, he had an idea that when she found out that he didn't actually have an important job or lofty goals, the warmth in her eyes was going to fade real fast. He was fairly sure that no woman would find anything appealing about a man who spent his time cleaning, gardening, and caring for a little sister.

Why wouldn't a beautiful girl like Leona feel exactly the same?

He couldn't blame her. He didn't want to blame her.

It was just that, for the very first time, he wished he was a little bit more special. A little bit more perfect.

A little bit more.

Chapter 7

Leona knew she had to tell them. She had to. Otherwise she was going to go bald, because every time Mattie and Sara started talking about the upcoming wedding, she had the terrible urge to start pulling her hair out.

She just about had a heart attack when Mattie told her that she'd started counting down the days until they'd be sisters, and they now had less than sixty days to go.

After supper, as the three of them leaned on the fence at Pinecraft Park, watching the men and women play shuffleboard and the boys play basketball on the green cement court, Leona mentally practiced various ways to tell her girlfriends that she was having second thoughts about marrying Edmund.

And though she'd considered several scenarios, running the gamut between being bold and honest to evasive and shy, Leona knew neither Sara nor Mattie were going to take the news well. It was more likely that they'd take the news badly. Really badly.

So, instead of being open and honest, she held her thoughts to herself for a little bit longer. Worried her bottom lip. And tried not to think about how shocked and disappointed those girls were going to be. How upset and irritated and dismayed everyone in her whole family was going to be with her.

To make matters worse, she wasn't going to blame them one bit. She'd made many mistakes. She'd accepted Edmund's suit when she wasn't completely sure he was the right man for her. She'd kept her worries and doubts to herself because she hadn't wanted to risk upsetting her mother, who had so enjoyed planning her wedding. Then, when she started being sure she didn't want to have a lifetime of being expected to follow her husband's wishes without discussion, she knew something had to change.

Time and again, she tried to discuss her worries with Edmund. But true to form, he ignored her wishes.

Now all of this timid behavior was going to cause a lot of heartache.

"Leona, oh my gosh. There's that guy again," Sara said with a careful head tilt toward her right.

"Who?"

"Zack."

"Zack?" With all her might, she attempted to look only mildly interested. But inside, her heart was pounding.

"*Jah,*" Sara continued. "You know, he's that man who was chasing after the cat. And then we saw him at Yoder's yesterday with his sister Effie, and he offered to take us to the beach."

Leona turned and looked in the direction Sara was pointing. Then she forced herself to contain the smile that was threatening to form when she located Zack. He was standing with his sister and a couple of men and women his age. His arms were crossed over his chest; his hat was tilted slightly forward in an effort to shield his eyes from the setting sun.

"Pinecraft is so small, I guess we're bound to be seeing some of the same people over and over. Ain't so?"

Mattie leaned closer, peering across the crowded park that was made up of shuffleboard and basketball courts, grassy areas and a covered pavilion. "Do you see any of his friends? All I see is his sister."

While Sara gave Mattie an exasperated look, Leona couldn't keep from glancing at Zack. And his sister, too, of course.

When Effie caught her eye, she gave a little wave.

Leona waved back. "That Effie is so cute. And sweet, too, didn't you think?"

Mattie waved at Effie, too. "You said it. I was never that sweet when I was her age." With a wink, she added, "And I know you weren't, either, Sara."

"Oh, stop," Sara ordered, though her lips were curving upward. "But you're right. I wasn't. But you were, Le."

"I wasn't," Leona protested. For some strange reason, she did not want to have been the sole goody-two-shoes at twelve.

"Oh, yes, you were," Mattie retorted. "You were perpetually happy. Perpetually thoughtful and considerate, too." Scowling, she added, "It was *so* fun to be friends with you back then."

Leona did not appreciate her sarcasm. "What is that supposed to mean?"

"It means, we always got compared to you, Leona," Sara said. "And, according to my mother—"

"And mine," Mattie added.

"We always came up short," Sara finished.

Leona winced. She *had* been a bit of that type of girl. Actually, she'd kind of prided herself on her good attitude and the ability to always get along with others. Looking back on it, she realized she'd probably been a bit too full of herself and more than a bit insufferable. "Sorry."

Sara waved off the apology. "Oh, stop. You can't help who God made you to be."

"I think your sweet, sunny disposition is what Edmund has always liked about you," Mattie said. "We're all secretly hoping you'll rub off on him." Pulling her lip in between her teeth, she murmured, "Maybe one day you will."

She wasn't so sure about that. "Well, um, I don't know."

"Don't worry, we all think that once you are married, Edmund will be far more easygoing," Mattie said. "Mamm and Daed and I were just talking about that the other day."

Ugh. Every conversation came back to her upcoming marriage. And Edmund!

Needing to put some space between what her girlfriends were saying and what was churning inside her, she pushed back from the metal fence. "I'm going to go say hello to Zack and Effie."

"Do you think that's wise?" Sara asked.

No, she did not think it was. But Sara surely didn't need to know that. "Why wouldn't it be?"

Sara leaned in closer. "Because I think he likes you."

"Really?" With effort, she attempted to look only mildly interested.

Sara gave her the type of look that came from knowing each other for most of their lives. It pretty much told Leona to stop acting so clueless. Then she nodded slowly. "I really do think he likes you. At Yoder's, he couldn't seem to take his eyes off of you. Your back was to him, but I faced him. Every two or three minutes he would look our way and stare at you."

"There's nothing wrong with making a new friend or two while we're in Florida."

"I don't disagree, but I think we should concentrate on making girlfriends, not boyfriends."

"We're not fifteen, Sara. We can be friends with men."

"That may be true, but I don't think that is what Zack is thinking about. Plus, he doesn't know you're engaged."

"I know." She bit her bottom lip. Did she sound as muddled as she felt?

Mattie folded her arms over her chest and lifted her chin. "I'm just gonna say it, Leona. You were looking intrigued by him when we first met him at that church. You were not acting like an engaged woman. You also didn't immediately refuse his invitation to the beach."

Leona flinched, not because Mattie's words were cruel but because she feared Mattie was exactly right. She had been delighted to speak with Zack again at Yoder's, and she hadn't bothered to hide her pleasure even a little bit.

However, no matter how much she wanted to retreat and ignore all things Zack, there was something about him that had caught her interest and her imagination and she knew it had little to do with his blue eyes and everything to do with the qualities that made him Zack. She'd noticed it when she'd heard him laughing in that tree.

It had deepened when he'd pulled that silly cat from her arms and teased her about being the only person able to capture a cat.

And then there was the way she'd noticed him with his little sister. He'd been gentle with her but not condescending. It made her wonder how he would act toward other important people in his life.

It made her wonder how he'd act with her, if she were important to him.

"I hear what you're saying, but I think it would be rude not to say hello. Do you two want to join me or stay here?"

Sara looked incredulous. "You're still going to go over there?"

"*Jah.*" She didn't bother with excuses or explanations. She had none that would make any sense and she realized that. All she did know was that she felt like something was propelling her forward. Something greater than her common sense.

She also felt a little nervous, almost like she knew she would regret it for the rest of her life if she didn't make that short walk to see him. It made no sense, but at the moment, it didn't need to make sense. All she knew was that she wasn't going to ignore the feeling.

"Again, would you like to join me?"

"I'm going to stay right here," Mattie said.

Treating Leona to yet another scorching, extremely meaningful look, Sara nodded. "Me too."

Right then and there, Leona knew they were going to start talking about her. She didn't appreciate it, but at the moment she was willing to be the subject of their irritation in order to visit with Zack again. She truly felt as if there was a reason they kept running into each other and she intended to figure out what that reason was.

"You two are being silly, but if that's how you want to be, I won't try and change your mind." And with that—which was a pretty good parting shot, if she did say so herself—she walked over to Zack and Effie.

They both were facing her as she got closer. Effie was smiling broadly. Zack was looking pretty pleased, too, though only a warmth in his eyes conveyed his feelings.

When she got within speaking distance, he stepped forward. "I was just about to walk over to say hello."

"I'm glad I saved you the trip, then. It's so nice to see you again." She took special care to smile at Effie, just to make sure that the little girl understood that Leona was including her in the greeting. Tonight, Effie was holding some kind of crutches. When she saw Leona's eyes dart to them, her expression stilled.

Zack smiled. "Are things okay? It looked like you and your girlfriends were having a pretty intense conversation."

"I wouldn't call it intense. We just were talking."

Effie raised her brows. "They're looking at us now and they look kind of mad."

Leona refrained from turning and glaring at Mattie and Sara, but only barely. Honestly, couldn't they try to be a little more easygoing?

"Are they mad at you?" Effie asked.

"Ef, that ain't none of our business," Zack chided. "Sorry, Leona."

When Effie's cheeks started coloring, Leona made sure that she shrugged off her worries as much as she could. "Don't worry about us. Three girls, together twenty-four-seven. You know how that goes."

Zack's lips twitched. "Actually, I don't."

She laughed, liking his sense of humor. "I guess you wouldn't. Suffice it to say that every once in a while we don't agree on something. It's no big deal, though. It will pass." Eager to stop thinking about how it was very likely that Sara and Mattie's irritation with her wasn't going to pass any time soon, she brightened her smile. "So, how are you two?"

"I'm only okay," Effie said.

"Just okay?"

Looking at her brother, Effie frowned. "Zack made me do all my exercises tonight. And that is why I'm in my braces tonight and have to use my crutches."

He pressed his hand on her shoulder as he explained. "Effie works with a physical therapist, so every day she has to do exercises to help her limbs grow stronger."

"That's great. I mean, you were walking at Yoder's when we saw each other yesterday. So that means your therapy must be working, right?"

Effie nodded. "I'm getting better but the exercises still make me sore and tired."

"And grumpy," Zack added.

"I wouldn't be so grumpy if you weren't being so pushy, Zachary."

Leona chuckled. "Effie, I think you're really blessed to have a *bruder* who will give you his time to help you do exercises. I don't have a brother, but I'm imagining most wouldn't be so nice or so patient."

"Zack's always helped me. He helps me do everything."

"That's admirable, to be sure." Leona liked how Effie jumped to her brother's defense. Looking his way, Leona smiled, and was surprised to notice that he was blushing.

"It's nothing. I just help out when I can."

"Zack does everything for everyone. He even does laundry sometimes."

"Wow." This time she was the one who was trying her best to keep her expression even and not judgmental. But the truth was that she was a little taken aback. She'd never heard of a man doing a household's laundry.

If anything, he looked even more uncomfortable. "Effie,

there's Amy. She's been waving at you for a good five minutes. You should go over and say hi."

After gazing at her brother and Leona, her eyes lit up. "All right. See ya, Leona." She started walking toward a girl about her age who was standing with her parents.

"'Bye, Effie."

"Sorry about that," Zack said. "I'm pretty sure the last thing you wanted to hear tonight was my life story."

"I like learning more about you." Plus, as far as she was concerned, he was going to have to share a whole lot more information for her to have any real idea about his life story.

"Yeah?"

"Yeah. Especially since what I'm learning is that you are a really nice guy. I meant what I said, Zack. I really do think Effie is blessed to have a *bruder* like you."

He still wasn't meeting her eyes. "Both my parents work, and my brother and sister are busy with their own lives. Someone needed to be around for Effie."

"That's really kind of you. I mean, I bet a lot of people, men or women, wouldn't want to make that sacrifice."

"It's not a sacrifice," he protested, his eyes flashing, almost like she'd just offended him. "I enjoy being with Effie. She's a great kid. I'm glad I can help her out."

"I'm glad you can, too."

His smile warmed. "Leona, have you given any more thought to going to Siesta Key tomorrow?"

She definitely had. She really did want to go with him. She wanted to get to know him better. But she was also worried that she was about to make a terrible decision and ruin everything she had with Edmund . . . and maybe even life-long friendships with Sara and Mattie. "I don't know if my girlfriends want to go."

"Even if they don't, will you still come?" he interrupted, almost like he was ready to put any excuse to rest. "We wouldn't even have to stay all day. We could leave around nine and be back by two. I, uh, need to be back in time to get Effie off the bus, anyway."

She liked the way he said that. Not like he resented it, more like he wasn't sure how she would react but he still wanted to be honest.

And because of that, she listened to what her heart was saying. Maybe it was her heart, maybe it was her guardian angel . . . maybe it was the Lord himself, but somehow everything inside of her was clamoring for her to accept his invitation.

To spend just a little more time with him.

Even if it meant that she was going to have to face the consequences and risk making Sara and Mattie even madder at her.

Even if it meant risking her relationship with Edmund.

"I'd love to go."

"*Gut*. I mean great. That's just great. We can all meet here at nine in the morning."

"No matter what, I'll be here."

"Me too." He smiled at her then, and it was warm and sincere and tempting.

And it scared her and excited her and made her happy.

And, she was starting to realize, she hadn't been really, really happy in a very long time. Not since she'd realized that a lifetime by Edmund's side would likely drain all the happiness out of her.

After discussing what she should bring to wear and how much money she might need to have with her, they parted ways. Then, reluctantly, she joined her girlfriends who were looking at her with twin mutinous expressions.

The moment she reached their side, Mattie spoke. "Well, do you feel better now that you've gotten that out of your system?"

She did, but she wasn't so eager to share that. She was also getting a little tired of her two best friends in the world treating her like she was a disobedient child. "You don't need to be so judgmental, Mattie."

"You're chatting with men while being engaged to my *bruder*, Leona."

This was true.

But it was also true that she wasn't so sure being engaged to Edmund was the right thing for her. Not if she was so eager to go to the beach with Zack.

Not if she was willing to risk everything to go to the beach with Zack.

Therefore, she steeled herself, then did what she needed to do. "I'm going to Siesta Key with Zack tomorrow. Would you both like to join us?"

As their expressions turned livid, Leona did the only thing she could. She resigned herself to the drama that was about to ensue.

Chapter 8

Four hours had passed since Marvin's sisters had entered the Orange Blossom Inn and rattled Beverly's carefully controlled life.

Now, as stars slowly dotted the evening sky, the three of them were once again sitting together, chatting on the front porch, just as they had when back in Sugarcreek.

They weren't talking, however. Instead, each seemed lost in their thoughts, something that Beverly was grateful for since she couldn't seem to do anything but relive Ida and Jean's arrival.

She'd been too shocked to do much but settle into autopilot at the time.

Earlier, Beverly had gone from friendly and cordial to defensive and stiff the moment she'd spied Ida and Jean. And if her body language hadn't given everyone in the room the warning that something was very wrong, Beverly was pretty sure her cool greeting had conveyed to one and all that some sort of trouble was about to ensue. And she wouldn't have wanted to be a part of the conversation, either.

In fact, the only people who hadn't looked all that ill at ease were the two women who had caused her transformation. Instead, they'd merely smiled as if Beverly had greeted them like long-lost relatives, then carefully stowed their rolling suitcases against the wall.

When they'd started walking around the gathering room, inspecting the many knickknacks and books that lined the shelves, Beverly had become flustered. She'd turned away and gone to the kitchen, supposedly to refill a pitcher of water, which made no sense, given the fact that everyone but Ida and Jean had left. But at least it gave her some much needed time to prepare herself to talk to the two women she'd once imagined would be her sisters-in-law.

The sisters looked exactly the same as she remembered. Both were almost ten years older than Marvin. To Beverly's best knowledge, neither of them had ever married, though she remembered Jean was being courted by a sheep farmer. Marvin had said that Ida was once courted, as a teenager, but the romance had never quite bloomed.

Jean had always been a soft-spoken woman. She had a sweet, malleable personality, which matched the extra thirty or so pounds she carried on her delicate frame. Beverly wondered if she and that sheep farmer had ever married and if she was still as submissive to her sister's wishes as she used to be. In all of her letter writing to her friends and family in Sugarcreek, Beverly had never felt brave enough to reclaim her friendship with the two women.

And while some people made mention of Marvin's family every now and then, most didn't, no doubt out of consideration for Beverly.

When Beverly had returned from the kitchen with the

water pitcher, she'd watched from outside the doorway as Ida helped herself to a generous slice of lemon cake, and, having set it on a small side table, as she poured herself a steaming mug of tea and got some ready for Jean.

Beverly had been unsure how to handle things. The cowardly part of her had wanted to act like the perfect hostess, invite them to sit down and begin chatting about nonsensical things. If she'd tried hard, Beverly was sure she could have pretended that they were merely long-lost acquaintances who wanted to do nothing more than catch up on trivial matters.

Like talk about the weather, perhaps.

But she'd realized, as she lurked outside the room, that something had happened in the three years since she'd last seen Marvin's family. She'd become stronger. No longer was she going to be content to retreat inside herself.

Now, hours later as the three of them were sitting on the front porch and quietly watching the stars, Beverly knew it was time to say something.

No longer could she hold her pain and insecurities tight to her chest, burying them while she pretended nothing bothered her. Since she'd been in Pinecraft, she'd begun to stand up for herself.

They needed to see that she had become stronger.

She also wanted to understand what had brought them all the way to her inn. Were they merely curious about how she was doing, or did they have news for her? She needed to know.

After the three of them smiled at a father walking by with a very sleepy little girl in his arms, she broke their silence. "Ida, Jean, I'm sorry I've been so distant," she began. "Seeing you both was quite a shock."

Ida, always the bolder sister, simply nodded. "*Jah,* I imagine it was."

Feeling their expectations, she struggled with the best way to begin. "So . . . I mean, so, you see . . ."

"I just have to say that your baking is as *gut* as it ever was, Beverly," Ida said. "I always told Marvin that I'd never met a better baker. Why, you could have opened your own shop in Sugarcreek. I'm sure of it."

"Maybe you could even open one here in Sarasota," Jean said brightly. "I mean, if you don't think it's too late."

It was. It was too late for a lot of things, including this reunion. "Thank you for the compliments. I'm, uh, glad you liked the food"—she paused but at last blurted—"Listen, I'm sorry. I simply don't understand why you two are here."

"I can see why you'd be thinking that. It has been a long time," Jean replied.

"Yes."

"We meant to come down soon after you moved here, Beverly. Years ago."

"Years ago?" Beverly was dumbfounded.

"Oh, *jah*." Ida nodded. "But then I slipped on some black ice and tore a ligament or some such in my knee." Raising her foot, she looked at it. "I had to have surgery, you see."

"It was awful," Jean added with a meaningful wave of her hand. Just as if they'd had coffee together last week.

"I'm sorry . . ."

"Then, last year, we were going to come down but my Jason got the stomach flu, and you know how that goes."

"Jason?"

"Oh! You might not have heard. Me and Amos got married soon after you left," Jean said with a smile in her voice. "Ten months after that we had Jason."

"Oh! Congratulations to you and Amos. And, uh, I'm sorry Jason got sick."

Jean shrugged. "He was soon fine, but his illness did ruin our plans. But that's the Lord's will, I suppose. Everything is out of our hands."

"That's one of the reasons we didn't warn you that we were coming," Ida explained. "We didn't want to have to explain if we had to cancel again."

Since Beverly hadn't known they'd ever planned to visit her, she thought it was a moot point. But that said, she decided to get to the heart of the matter. If Marvin had taught her anything, it was that no good came from pushing things off or pretending they weren't happening.

And since her last question had set off a great many comments about the state of their lives—but nothing that provided any answers—she decided more bluntness was necessary.

"I'm sorry, but I still don't understand why you decided to pay me a visit."

Ida's gray-blue eyes were guileless. "Why wouldn't we want to see you?"

"Because Marvin and I . . ." She couldn't believe it, but her eyes filled with tears. Even after all this time, his rejection hurt.

"There was no Marvin and you anything, dear," Jean said with a surprising bit of tenderness lacing her voice. "Marvin fell in love with Regina right under your nose, that's what he did."

Well, she wouldn't have put it quite that way, though she supposed her statement summed up what had happened.

"Yes. Yes, that's what he did."

Ida pursed her lips. "I hope you didn't think we condoned such actions."

Beverly hadn't thought that. But then, well, she hadn't really thought about much beyond the pain she was feeling.

"I didn't know what to think," Beverly at last admitted. "I guess I imagined that we wouldn't have anything to say to each other."

Ida gave a little cluck of disapproval. "Really? I thought we always got along. I thought we were friends. Did you not feel that way?"

"Oh, *jah*. I mean, yes, I thought we were friends." She bit her lip, tried to get herself to not say another word, but then went ahead and said it. "But you all seemed to get along just fine with Regina. I mean, I heard you did."

"We had no choice, dear," Jean said. "Marvin married her."

"And Marvin is our baby brother," Ida added.

Looking pained, Jean continued. "However, we did tell Marvin that we were disappointed with his actions at the time. We told him quite forcefully, too."

"Not that it mattered," Ida finished. "He always was a willful boy."

"He liked to be first in line— always," Jean continued, then glanced at Beverly meaningfully, like Marvin's selfish habits somehow correlated with why he'd practically left her at the altar.

"I am sorry you're still nursing old hurts, Beverly, but it has been three years," Ida said as she leaned back a bit. "It's time to move on."

"I have moved on. Obviously." To prove her point, Beverly waved a hand around the porch. It was freshly painted, and surrounded by beautiful flowers. She'd made her Aunt Patty's tired inn into a showplace.

"Yes, you moved to Sarasota and took over this inn of your aunt's," Ida said, not sounding all that impressed. "Your mother told us all about that."

"It's a great inn."

"It is beautiful, that is true. I love the orange trees dotting the front lawn," Jean said. "I bet it smells heavenly come spring."

"It does. The orange blossoms are very pretty and do smell nice."

Ida crossed her legs. "It was kind of you to give us your bed."

"I want you both to be comfortable. Tomorrow, when I have a room available, I'll help you get resituated."

"That's mighty kind of you," Ida said. "Where will you sleep tonight?"

"There's a small room near the kitchen with a pullout couch. I don't rent it out much, but I'll be fine in there."

If they could go to so much trouble to make sure she knew they hadn't forgotten her, she could offer them her hospitality. Their slightly garrulous, very matter-of-fact ways stripped away a lot of the barriers she'd built around her heart . . . and those painful memories.

They sat quietly for another few minutes, Ida gasping when she spied a shooting star.

Smiling at Ida's reaction, Beverly let herself relax. Perhaps this visit was going to go just fine.

Then Jean coughed. "Beverly, dear, we should probably tell you something, in order to get everything out in the open, you know."

"Oh?"

For the first time, Jean seemed uncomfortable. "Well, you might not have heard this, but Marvin and Regina are happy together. They have a little girl now, too."

They had a baby? A new flash of pain lit her heart, surprising her with its force. It seemed that every time she thought she was over Marvin and Regina's love affair, she'd discover some new detail about their life and that pain would resurface just as if her heart had never healed.

"I . . . I'm glad. Really glad," she bit out. Then, before she said she was glad for a third time, she got to her feet. "Hey, how about you two relax here for a little bit? I should go inside and make sure none of the other guests need anything."

"All right, dear, take your time," Ida said.

Beverly was pretty sure Ida added something after that, but she'd already walked through the screen door. Thankfully.

All she could think about at the moment was that Marvin and Regina were happy. And that they had a baby. They'd thrived in her absence.

Until that moment, she'd begun to believe that she'd been thriving, too. But maybe she'd only been focusing on the inn. Maybe she'd forgotten that there was more to life than putting all her efforts into making a comfortable space for people to spend a few days of their time.

And though she definitely did have some good friends here, she spent many more hours of the day simply chatting with strangers, never letting them get too close. Never letting herself get too involved.

She'd especially never taken the time to return men's smiles when she passed them on the sidewalk. She'd definitely never accepted any invitations to go to breakfast or lunch. Or for walks on the beach. Or to grab a cup of coffee.

She'd been carefully, deliberately, keeping herself alone.

Just so she wouldn't get hurt again.

It had taken a visit from Marvin's sisters to shake her out of her self-imposed isolation. To make her realize that she didn't have to be alone, and once more, she hadn't ever had to be that way.

It was definitely time to stop living in what could have been and start making plans for herself. Maybe, just maybe, it was time to remind herself that she wasn't old.

That she certainly wasn't too old to one day fall in love again.

Chapter 9

Leona was having trouble keeping up with her two best friends. She had a very good idea that it was because they were currently acting nothing like her two best friends.

"Come on," she called out from behind them as they practically race-walked down the sidewalk like they were about to enter the next Pinecraft 5K. "You shouldn't be so mad at me."

"You made a date with a man who is not my brother, Leona," Mattie said over her shoulder. "Of course I'm going to be mad at you." *Of course,* she said this loud enough for several people around them to overhear.

Which made Leona mad enough to finally catch up and grab Mattie's arm. "Slow down, wouldja? Please? I'll be happy to talk with you both about why I said yes to Zack."

Sara looked pointedly at her over her shoulder. "Do you really think that you could have a *gut* reason, Leona?"

She did. Well, she thought she did. But that didn't mean Sara and Mattie were going to see things that way. "I think I have a real *gut* reason. I do. But I'm not gonna try to explain myself while running down the sidewalk."

Mattie glared. "Does it really matter where we talk?" She yanked at her arm, and looked ready to charge ahead.

"I think so. This is important to me."

Sara looked her way again. However, this time her expression was more sympathetic. "You're right, Leona," she said slowly. "There is a time and place for everything, and it certainly isn't out here in front of the rest of the world." She tempered her speed a bit.

"*Danke*," Leona said under her breath. "So can we please go sit down somewhere and talk?"

Sara looked around, and then pointed to a pair of benches right outside the front of the Palm Grove Mennonite Church. "Let's go sit down over there."

"In front of the church where she met *him*?" Mattie asked, drawing out the last like it was an awful curse word.

"Oh, stop, Mattie," Sara said. "We need to talk, and this is as good a place as any. It's not like it's the church's fault."

Leona hid her smile, but, secretly, she felt like raising her hand in triumph. There weren't too many people who could stand up to Mattie's strong personality, but Sara had no problem meeting Mattie word for word, time and again.

When they sat down—Mattie and Sara side by side, Leona on the bench right across—Leona tried to think of the right way to describe everything that had been slowly building up inside her for months, but she knew there wasn't any graceful way to admit how she'd been feeling. Worse, she knew what she was about to tell them might very well end their friendship.

"I don't know where to start," she finally said.

"Just start in the middle," Mattie said in typically Mattie fashion. "No matter what you say, we're going to talk about it for hours."

Sara's lips twitched. "At least that long. Maybe even a couple of days."

Mattie's eyes lit up in amusement. "That's what we do, *jah?* We analyze everything that happens to us so many different ways, we're all sick of the topic by the time we're done."

And then, to Leona's amazement, she smiled.

That smile was everything Leona needed. She stopped worrying about the perfect way to explain herself.

"About five months ago, I was walking with Edmund after work," she said slowly, remembering that afternoon in startling clarity. "It was the end of September and tons of tourists were on the streets. You know how that goes."

"Fall foliage." Sara nodded.

"Anyway, we were walking. I was tired from working at the fabric store, and Edmund was tired from working in the fields. There were tons of cars around us. Buggies, too. And bicycles. It was really crowded." Her voice got softer as she remembered everything she'd been feeling.

She'd been so hopeful for their future. So grateful that she wasn't going to have to worry anymore about finding the perfect man.

Looking at her intently, Maddie nodded. "And?"

Leona took a deep breath. "Anyway, we were stopped at an intersection, waiting for the traffic to clear so we could cross . . . when all of a sudden a stray dog trotted down the sidewalk and looked about to dart out onto the street. It was a little thing. Anyone could tell it was a young dog, not a little puppy, but nowhere near full grown."

Remembering her panic, she inhaled. "Without thinking much about it, I ran over and tried to hold on to it so it wouldn't get hurt."

Sara leaned forward. "What did you do then?"

"Edmund stopped me before I got ahold of it and told me to leave it alone. That it was a dirty, stray dog. That it wasn't my problem."

As Sara's eyes got wide, Mattie tilted her head to one side. "So all this is about my *bruder* not wanting you to grab a stray dog that could have had some disease or bitten you?"

"*Nee.*" Leona grabbed hold of the edge of the bench and prayed for God to give her better words. After a pause, she said, "It was the start of me realizing that he and I are different. Really different. Edmund and I ended up arguing on that street corner. I wanted to save the dog, and he didn't want to deal with it. Then I said something about how I hoped one of our dogs never got loose . . . and that's when he told me he didn't ever want to have a dog."

Mattie shrugged. "Edmund doesn't really like dogs. He never has."

"I know that. But, see, I do. I like dogs. I like them a lot. I like cats, too. I've always had pets. I had imagined that we'd get a little poodle or cocker spaniel or something after we got married. Something to keep me company when he was working such long hours. But he told me it wasn't up for discussion."

"So this is about him not wanting you to have a pet?" Mattie looked just as impatient as ever.

"No, this is about me realizing that while I thought I loved him, I wasn't looking forward to doing what he wanted all the time."

Sara tossed her head a bit. "Marriage is full of compromises, Leona. Our mothers have said this time and again."

"I realize that. And I even understand that I'll need to let my husband be in charge of our household. But after our little argument on the corner, I started listening to Edmund a whole lot more closely. Not just the sweet things I wanted to hear, but also the things I used to kind of ignore."

Leona steeled herself, then said, "When I did that, I discovered that a lot of the things he never wanted to have or do were things that I had always wanted and planned on doing."

"Like what?" Sara asked.

"Like having a pet. Like keeping my job for a little while. Like seeing my family as often as possible. Like planning trips to Indiana or out west or even trips here to Pinecraft. Edmund didn't want to do any of that. And as the days have crept closer to our wedding, he's become a little bit more adamant about how he expects his wishes to be obeyed."

Sara's eyes widened. "Oh, Leona."

Grateful that Sara, at least, was starting to realize how she'd been feeling, Leona nodded. "I've been pretty worried. I don't want to be ordered about for the rest of my life."

"Did you talk to him about this?" Sara asked.

"Some." She winced, thinking about how awkward those conversations had been.

"But he didn't want to hear it, did he?" Mattie asked quietly.

Leona shook her head. "I'm not saying Edmund isna right. I'm not saying he's not entitled to have the kind of marriage he wants. I'm not saying I want to break things off," she said in a rush, "but I have started wondering if he and I are really meant for each other." She shrugged. "How can we be right when I feel so worried about our future?"

"Oh, Leona," Sara said again. Her voice was tinged with sadness now. And, if Leona wasn't mistaken, it was also filled with a new understanding.

That understanding felt like a gift. "When I talked to Zack, there was something about him that made me feel hopeful for the first time in ages," Leona said. "He made me remember that I haven't said my vows yet. And that marriage is a long time."

"Marriage is forever," Mattie murmured.

"See, when I saw Zack sitting in this tree, it made me wonder if, one day, I could have a relationship where I wasn't always giving in. Where I wasn't the only one compromising," Leona said. "Where, if I wanted a silly dog to keep me company, I could have it . . . even if my husband didn't understand. He'd love me enough to know that I needed that dog to be happy." She waved a hand. "I hardly know Zack, but I know that I want a man who values the person I am." Almost whispering, she said, "Not just the idea of who I could be."

Hearing their silence, Leona looked down at her hands, which were now clasped tightly in her lap. "I'm sorry, you two. I wasn't trying to deceive you and I'm not trying to hurt Edmund. But I feel like I need to at least spend some more time with Zack. I think I owe it to myself."

Mattie closed her eyes. "Edmund is going to be hurt."

Leona nodded. "I know. I promise, I don't want to hurt him. But here's the thing: I talked with him about all of my feelings months ago. And then weeks ago. And then a couple of days before we got on the bus. Every single time, he's acted like what I want and what I think isn't important." Her words hung in the space between them, reminding Leona of how many times she had held her tongue but silently fumed.

As her cousin and Mattie stared at her, making the seconds that passed seem like minutes, Leona started to feel even more awkward. "Maybe, um, what I feel and think really isn't all that important," she said, though she didn't necessarily feel that way. "Maybe you both think that my feelings don't matter."

"But maybe they *do* matter," Sara whispered. "Maybe they matter a lot."

Leona looked at Sara more carefully and noticed that there was a new emotion in her eyes. Less judgment, more empathy. Leona felt the muscles in her back relax. "I hope so. I want to count. I want what I think to be of some importance, especially to the man I intend to spend the rest of my life with."

Turning to Mattie, she braced herself. "I'm sorry you are upset with me. I don't blame you. Edmund is your brother, after all. I don't know what else to say, though."

"You said everything you needed to," Mattie said. "What is between you and Edmund is your business, not mine. But I think you need to call him."

"I'll call him tomorrow and tell him that I went." Mattie was right; being honest and open was always best—even though Leona knew she'd told him how she felt before, and it was Edmund who was determined to only hear what he wanted to hear.

"Oh, *nee*," Mattie insisted. "If you are going to Siesta Key tomorrow morning, you need to call him tonight."

Looking apologetic, Sara nodded. "I have to agree. You can't go to the beach with a man without letting Edmund know."

Leona felt a new knot form in her stomach as she realized she was going to have to do just that.

Just a few minutes from now, she was going to have to call Edmund and tell him she was about to spend the day with another man.

For sure and for certain, he was not going to take the news well. Not well at all.

Chapter 10

Using only the stars and the glow of a full moon as his guide, Zack walked around the house, made his way through his mother's garden, and crossed the back porch, taking care to avoid the two squeaky wooden slats lining the patio as he did so.

Only then did he unlock the back door and step inside the house. He was returning home a full hour later than he usually did, and though he was far beyond the age of being held to a curfew, he didn't want his return to be remarked upon.

The last thing in the world he wanted was to have a discussion with his parents at one in the morning about where he'd been or what he'd been doing.

Or, in his case, who had been on his mind for the last couple of hours.

Now, as he took off his straw hat and light jacket and tossed them both on the back of the couch in the dark living room, he couldn't help but think about Leona Weaver some more. She was cute—there really was no other word for it. She acted cute and she looked that way, too.

She just also happened to affect him like no other girl ever had.

Which was why he wasn't in the mood to do anything but keep his thoughts and their conversation to himself. The morning was going to come soon enough. Besides, chances were good that his parents already had a pretty good idea how he'd spent most of his night, thanks to one little sister.

Effie, being Effie, would have probably come home and given their parents a minute-by-minute report of every word he and Leona had exchanged. It had been obvious that she liked Leona and had been excited to see that Zack liked her, too.

And he did like her. He liked her a lot. What he wanted to do was spend the rest of his night thinking about her and anticipating seeing her in the morning.

However, though he'd been fairly stealthy, he obviously hadn't been quiet enough. Before he could bend down and take off his boots, he heard the telltale shuffling of his father's leather-and-sheepskin slippers on the tile floor. Right behind him was his mother's familiar, noisy stride. Zack had always thought his mother stomped instead of walked. The contradiction never failed to take people by surprise, considering she was such a small and slender lady.

"Oh, *gut*," his father said when he entered the room. "You're back at last."

"Yeah," Zack said. "Sorry it's a little later than usual. I hope you weren't worried."

"We weren't worried," Daed said, "but we did want to talk to you."

"Really? Is, uh, something wrong?" Though he didn't actually want anything to have happened, Zack couldn't quite keep the optimism out of his voice. If they were worried about something besides him, that would mean he wasn't about to be peppered with a bunch of questions he didn't want to answer.

"Not at all, Zack," his mother said as she rushed forward with a happy smile. "Come sit down. Do you want a glass of water? Or a snack? I could make you a turkey sandwich."

It had to be close to one thirty. No, he did not want to sit in the kitchen with his parents and drink a glass of water and eat a turkey sandwich. "Can we talk tomorrow night?"

His father's brow wrinkled. "Tomorrow night?"

"I'm free in the morning," his mother said. "Well, until it's time to take Effie to school."

"That's less than six hours from now." Zack knew the last thing he wanted to do was have a serious conversation with his parents when he was still groggy. " I won't have any time to chat in the morning. I have plans tomorrow."

"Oh, we know." Pointing at one of the chairs with one heavily calloused finger, his father glared. "Sit down, son. This won't take long. We just wanted to get some information about Leona."

"I'd really rather not do this now." Actually, he really didn't want to discuss Leona anytime soon.

"I don't see why not," his mother murmured. "Nothing like the present."

"I don't agree." He did not appreciate being questioned the moment he walked in the door. He especially didn't appreciate being asked questions about a girl he hardly knew.

"Have a seat, Zachary," his father said, his voice a bit firmer.

Zack sat because it didn't matter how old he was, he was still his father's son.

As did his mother, though she didn't look half as serious

as his father did. Instead, she looked like she was holding back a grin.

Because he didn't dare roll his eyes, he folded his arms over his chest and looked steadily from one parent to the other. "Let's get this over with, then. What do you want to know?"

"Zachary, stop being coy," his mother chided. "Tell us about this girl you are taken with."

"I'm not being coy. There's nothing to tell. Her name is Leona. She's about my age, though I haven't asked her specifically yet. She's from Ohio and she's here on vacation with her girlfriends. She's blond and she's very pretty. And that's about all I know about her. Effie shouldn't have been telling tales about me."

"She wasn't telling tales. But she did say that she likes Leona," his mother said. "Very much so."

"I'm not surprised about that. Leona is a likable person."

His mother's tentative smile transformed into a delighted grin. "Zachary! This is so *wonderful-gut*! I've never seen you so smitten."

"I am not smitten." Actually, he wasn't really quite sure what smitten even meant.

"Zachariah." His father's firm use of his given name told Zack everything he needed to know. It was time to start sharing information whether he wanted to or not.

"Fine. I think I like her. I know she likes cats and is friendly to strangers, whether they are men her age or little girls wearing leg braces. Finally, I know I want to get to know her better."

"Sounds like you know plenty." His father raised a brow.

It took everything Zack had not to comment on that.

"And you're taking her to the beach tomorrow?"

"*Jah.* I offered to help her and her friends, since the SCAT buses are kind of hard to navigate the first time."

His mother's expression softened. "That is true."

"*Danke* for sharing about Leona, Zack. We're only asking because we're happy for you."

"We're only friends."

"Maybe she's the one," his mother said with a smile.

This was why Karl had chosen to be so independent so early. It was nearly impossible to be a grown man in his parents' house. In their eyes, he would always be fourteen or fifteen, a boy on the verge of manhood.

"I don't know about that. Ohio is pretty far from Florida. And again, I hardly know her." Perhaps, if he kept repeating this to himself, his words would eventually sink in for both himself and his parents. He really needed to stop thinking about Leona.

"You two can figure out that problem eventually," his mother said in an offhand way. Just like they were discussing whether or not to eat a third slice of pizza. "It's time that you had something for yourself."

"Past time, I think," his father added.

There was something in the way his father sounded that sent warning bells through Zack. His parents didn't sound judgmental. Instead, they sounded a little despondent about the way he'd been handling himself. About the choices he'd been making with his life.

"I haven't been putting myself last."

"It might not seem that way to you, but I think you have," his mother said.

"I would know, don'tcha think?"

His father talked over him. "Zachariah, it's not that we

don't all appreciate everything you do for the family. Why, day after day you organize your schedule so that everyone else can do what they want to do."

"It's not like that." They were making him sound like some kind of saint. That definitely wasn't the case. "I like being here for Effie. I also do several jobs for people in the neighborhood. I bring in money every week."

"We know you do a lot. But that doesn't mean that you don't need to put yourself first from time to time." He lifted a finger and shook it. "Don't forget that even the Lord expects us to care for ourselves."

"I won't forget." He hadn't thought he had forgotten.

But what was funny, he realized as he headed upstairs, was that he hadn't been thinking about himself . . . he'd been thinking about Leona.

Chapter 11

Growing up in a new-order Amish church community, Leona had always been rather pleased to have a phone in her home, but it wasn't like her parents had encouraged her to call her friends or have long conversations or anything like that.

Still, simply walking to the kitchen to call work was a whole lot easier than hiking out to a phone shanty when it was raining or snowing outside. She also liked the ability to get information quickly or talk to someone without having to wait to receive a letter.

Now, though, she would have gladly changed places with a girl brought up in a more conservative order. Then she would have had no option but to write Edmund a note. If that was the case, she would have been able to convey all her feelings and thoughts on paper. If she made a mistake or worded something wrong, all she would have to do is scratch out her words or throw away the paper and begin again.

Once her carefully written note was completed, she could have walked down to the Pinecraft Post Office, posted that letter, and then settled in to wait at least a week for a response. And what a week that would be! She would be in her own world of oblivious bliss. She would have no earthly idea how mad Edmund might be at her. Instead, she could have even imagined that he wasn't mad at her at all, that he completely understood her point of view.

That would be a stretch of the imagination, to be sure. After all, he'd never really embraced her point of view. But if she tried real hard—and consoled her frayed nerves by eating lots of coconut cream pie—she could do it.

She knew she could summon her courage and competently explain herself to him. And maybe he'd even listen to what she had to say.

But as perfect as those things sounded, it was never going to happen. It didn't matter if they were face-to-face, trading letters, or talking on telephones across the country, Edmund was not going to be of a mind to listen to what she had to say.

But she could try.

That was what the Lord promised, she supposed. As she sat and mused, she remembered a line from Psalm 37, one of her mother's favorite Psalms. *Commit everything you do to the Lord. Trust him, and He will help you.* That verse had always given her mother comfort.

Now, as Leona reflected on the beautiful, meaningful words, she realized that the verse comforted her, too. She might be sitting alone in the kitchen, but she wasn't actually alone. God had promised that He would help them through times of trouble. So He was there in spirit.

But it wasn't like He was going to pick up the phone and converse with Edmund for her.

That was her job.

Taking a deep breath, she picked up the receiver, and carefully dialed his number, punching in each number of the calling card her parents had bought her in case of emergencies.

Guilt hit her again as she realized that calling Edmund to tell him that she was going to the beach with another man probably wasn't what they'd had in mind when they'd spent their hard-earned money on the card.

But since this conversation affected the rest of her life, she thought that it maybe *was* an emergency. At least it felt that way to her, especially since her best friends in the world had determined that Leona make this call.

After three rings, a somewhat distracted voice answered. "Hello?"

It was Edmund. Leona gulped. Well, she surely hadn't imagined that he would be the one to actually pick up the phone.

And now that he'd answered, what in the world was she actually going to say? How did one start this conversation?

"Hello?" he asked again, his voice sounding irritated.

"Hi, Edmund," she said in a rush. "It's me."

"Yes?" His voice wasn't exactly warm or welcoming.

Maybe he wasn't sure who it was? "You know, Leona."

"I know it's you, Leona."

"Oh." Again, she had hoped he would sound a little happier to talk to her.

"What did you need?"

What did she need? *That* was all he had to say after not speaking to her for four or five days? For some reason, that response gave her a bit of a backbone.

Danke, Gott.

"I don't need anything, Edmund," she said a bit tartly, matching his tone. "I simply called to check in with you."

"Oh."

"*Jah*." Her mouth went dry. This was obviously going to be even more difficult than she'd imagined it would be. "So. How are you?"

"I am fine."

As silence filled the empty space between them, Leona curled her finger around the telephone cord and realized that he hadn't asked about her. As a matter of fact, so far, he sounded as if her phone call was nothing more than an interruption to his day. Feeling more uneasy—and a whole lot less guilty than she had just a few minutes before—she got down to business. "Edmund, I wanted to let you know that a man asked me to go to the beach tomorrow."

"What did you tell him?"

"I, um, told him I would go."

"You did?" He sounded incredulous. Finally, there was some emotion.

"*Jah*. It sounded like fun. I didn't want to pass up the chance to see Siesta Key with a local. They know all the best places to go."

The minute she said those words, she realized that she hadn't quite done her motivations justice. Yes, she did want to see the beach, but what she really wanted was to get to know Zack Kaufmann better. Even if she never saw him again after the day at the beach, Leona knew she needed to spend time with a man who was so different than Edmund.

"I'm not pleased to hear this news, Leona."

"I didn't think you would."

"Then why did you say you would go?" He paused. "Are you going to let him court you?"

His words sounded so judgmental. And a bit scary. So she added, "He isn't courting me. It's nothing like that."

"It sounds like it."

Did it? Had she quickly said yes to something that was far more significant than she'd given it credit for being?

"I don't think Zack and I are going to go alone. Mattie and Sara will most likely go. As well some of his friends."

"Zack?"

"*Jah*. It's short for Zachary. I mean, Zachariah." The minute she uttered those words, she wished she could have swallowed them. Too much information!

"It sounds to me like you're going on a date, Leona."

"Well, I suppose it is." She closed her eyes. Mattie had been right. There was no way she should have even considered not telling Edmund about her trip to Siesta Key.

She must have been in a fog when she'd told herself that Edmund would only treat her news with indifference. Had she really imagined he would accept her news as if it didn't concern him one bit?

"Why on earth would you make these plans?" he nearly shouted in her ear.

"Um . . ."

"Why would you even be talking to men?" he continued. "You are an engaged woman, Leona."

"I know."

"Well, then?"

Oh, but Edmund sounded mad. And not mad in an irritated-for-interrupting-his-evening kind of mad. No, this was him being very much put out with her.

Rather surprised at his response, and feeling lower than a snake in the grass, she struggled with a response. "Like I told you, a day at the beach sounds like fun." Yet even to her ears, it was a terrible excuse.

"Leona, you and I both know you didn't say yes because you wanted to go to the beach."

He was exactly right. And she owed him the truth. Gathering her courage, she tried to explain herself. "Edmund, I have to admit that I also told Zack I would go because of everything that has been happening between you and me."

"Nothing has happened."

That was kind of the point, she realized. They weren't growing. Instead, he kept making decisions and she kept trying to appease him. "Edmund, you know I've been unhappy. You know I have been wondering about our future." She didn't bother to start listing all the times she'd attempted to start a conversation with him about her concerns. Surely, he remembered them just as clearly?

A disparaging noise slid through the phone line. "Honestly? You want to talk about the future now? While we're sitting hundreds of miles from each other?"

"Well, *jah.* Actually, I'm a bit surprised that you even remembered I've been worried about our future. Why, every time I bring up my concerns about our compatibility, you push them aside."

"Because your concerns aren't relevant."

"Well, um, they're an issue to me. How could you say my feelings aren't important to you?"

He sighed. "Obviously you are suffering from a case of nerves. Don't forget, our relationship is no fly-by-night type of thing. I courted you properly."

"*Jah,* I know that."

"When it was time, I asked you to be my wife. You said yes right away. Do you remember that?"

No longer able to continue to sit, she jumped to her feet. "Of course I do."

"Then how could you throw that away?"

She closed her eyes. "Edmund, you are exactly right about

my part. I did say yes. I should not be thinking about anything else." A new surge of guilt and anxiety rolled through her. What was she doing? She'd given a man a promise! Everyone was making wedding plans! Mattie had been planning for them to be sisters.

She really needed to get her act together and tell Zack that she couldn't go to the beach with him. And then she was going to need to stay away from him. Stay away from that church, too.

"Edmund, listen. I—"

He interrupted her. "I'm not sure what is going on with you, but I had hoped being around Mattie and Sara might have had a calming influence."

Abruptly, she tossed her new decision to the floor. "Calming?" she bit out. Had he even met his sister Mattie? She was the opposite of calm! And for that matter, why did he actually think that she needed someone to calm her down? She was one of the most unflappable people she'd ever met.

Well, until lately.

He continued on. "Since you're still struggling, you need to listen to me, Leona. My mother said all engaged couples experience second thoughts. It's natural. The excitement of courting and the engagement announcement wears off, and it's replaced by wedding preparations and stress."

"You've been speaking to your mother about me?"

"Of course. She said you're going to get back to yourself as soon as the wedding is over. She said sometimes brides have a difficult time dealing with all the pressure and plans."

"Boy, thank goodness you talked to your *mamm* about my moods. Did she mention anything else?" she said sarcastically.

He ignored her jab. "I truly feel you're going to regret your impetuousness, and probably sooner than later. This means you need to cancel your plans, Leona. I'm sorry you let your emotions get the best of you, but I guess it couldn't be helped. You do tend to jump into things without much forethought."

Since agreeing to marry him was a good example of this, she wasn't all that pleased that he brought it up. "Hey, now—"

"My *mamm* said you'll probably be having second thoughts when you are carrying a baby, too. Hormones, you know."

Leona almost laughed. Edmund, the man who would hardly talk to her about the possibility of owning a dog or cat, was now chatting about them having a baby. And her hormones! It would have been horribly embarrassing if she wasn't so peeved.

"You talked to your mother about me being pregnant?"

Edmund skillfully ignored her irritation again.

"She's been a great help, Leona. I'm sure she will be helpful to you in the future, too. She said I'll be used to your mood swings by the time we are expecting."

"Mood swings?"

"*Jah*. It's what we've been talking about, Leona. Your hormones."

Reaching out, she pressed her hand on the wall, practically bracing herself for what had to be one of the most uncomfortable conversations she'd ever had in her life. "I do not want to discuss hormones with you, Edmund. Ever."

"Then I suggest you stop making such impulsive decisions."

That would be the smart thing, if she was solely concerned about making sure he was happy with her for the evening.

But she was thinking about a lifetime. And she just wasn't sure. "I am not."

"If you make this choice, we are finished."

Finished. He'd just threatened to end their relationship as calmly and quietly as if he was changing his mind about what he wanted to eat for dinner.

And though she'd often thought he was heavy-handed and had too many concerns about how happy she was going to be married to him . . . she was shocked. "Edmund, you would break up with me over the phone? You don't want to wait until I come back from Pinecraft?"

"I'm not the one who has doubts and regrets. You are, Leona. Remember, this is your doing. You called me. However, now that you have decided to see other men, I realize I have doubts, too. Serious ones."

This *was* her doing. He was going to put the blame for the breakup on her shoulders. "Then I guess we're breaking up."

"You're not going to change your mind? You're still going to go to the beach with this man?"

"*Jah.*" Even to her ears, her voice sounded hoarse and harsh. Like the wind had gotten knocked out of her.

She waited a second, half hoping that he was suddenly going to start apologizing, start telling her that he wanted things to change, that he wanted her to be happy. That everything she was asking for wasn't too much to ask.

But he didn't.

"I guess this is goodbye, then," she murmured, feeling like a stranger. "I'll call my mother to tell her that the wedding is off. I trust you will do the same with your parents."

"You needn't worry about me informing my parents."

He sounded as bitter as she felt. Without a doubt, he would tell his parents that she'd strayed.

He would no doubt tell everyone in their church district that he was the innocent party.

"Goodbye," she said before hanging up.

Then, still feeling the sting of that conversation, and before she chickened out, Leona picked up the phone. Intending to call her parents and her sisters, Rosanna and Naomi, too.

It was better to disappoint her fiancé, her fiancé's sister, her cousin, her parents, and her sisters all at one time. Then, hopefully, she would be able to find a quiet place to go cry. And then cry some more.

Chapter 12

Who do you think is going to show today?" Danny asked Zack as they walked to the SCAT—Sarasota County Area Transit—bus stop.

Zack shrugged. "I don't have any idea. I thought that for sure both of her girlfriends would want to come, but from the way they were glaring at us last night, I started to get the feeling that they were unhappy about Leona talking to me."

Danny grunted. "Those girls must have been taking lessons from my sisters. They're always unhappy about something."

"True," he said, enjoying the opportunity to give Danny grief about his sisters, who everyone far and wide knew were his constant source of pain. "They're unhappy with you pretty much all the time."

"Like I said, they're mighty trying on a man's patience."

"Not at all. They seem to get along great with everyone else," Zack said around a grin.

Danny grimaced. "I irritate them as much as they irritate me. We can't seem to help ourselves."

Zack grinned but didn't say anything more on the subject. Danny had the misfortune of having four sisters. Somehow, the Lord had seen fit for him to be born smack in the middle, too. That meant that he had two who bossed him around and another two who tried their best to boss him around.

To make matters worse, his mother—although a mighty nice lady, to be sure—adored her girls and never would hear of anything critical about them. Their household was always abuzz with talk about cooking, diets, boys, and all sorts of other things girls liked to talk about. "It's no wonder that you're such a good fisherman. If I were you, I'd be fishing all the time."

"Daed says we are truly blessed to live in Florida. The plentiful fish in the Gulf are his saving grace." His smile broadened. "Not that he'd ever tell Mamm or my sisters that!"

They were almost at the bus stop. The bus came every hour, and it was pretty obvious that they weren't the only people planning to spend the day at Siesta Key. All around them were men and women about their age holding canvas tote bags likely filled with sandwiches, towels, drinks, and sunscreen.

As they approached, he scanned the crowd for Leona.

"See her yet?"

"Nope."

Danny pulled out his cell phone to check the time. His parents and the bishop had allowed him to have it since he needed one for his job, but he'd told Zack more than once that he used it as his watch as much as he did to make phone calls. "We've got less than ten minutes."

"Ten minutes is a pretty long time. I bet she doesn't want to get here too early."

"Maybe not." Danny slipped his phone back in a pocket,

then smiled at a couple of their friends. "I'm gonna go say hi to Adam."

Zack nodded, then retreated to lean against the fence that divided the stop from some private property. It was getting so crowded that he wanted to stay out of the way but still be able to see Leona when she approached.

Unfortunately, as the minutes passed, he didn't see the slightest glimpse of her. He was beginning to get worried.

Maybe she was standing him up. Part of him wouldn't be surprised if she did. After all, she was only in town for a vacation. Maybe she started having second thoughts about spending the day with a man she didn't know all that well and would likely never see again after she left.

He'd be disappointed about that, but, he supposed, he could understand. Just thinking about his little sister contemplating spending the whole day with a man no one in her family knew made him grind his teeth.

Besides, if Leona's girlfriends didn't think it was a *gut* idea for her to be with him, Zack felt pretty certain it would be another mark against him. Girls seemed to only want to do things in groups. She might think that keeping them happy was far more important than keeping a date with him.

Looking right and left, Zack scanned the crowd yet again, searching for the wholesome-looking girl with the striking brown eyes and golden hair.

He still didn't see her.

He swallowed back a lump of regret. He wasn't going to be devastated if she didn't show up, but, boy, was he going to be disappointed.

"Any luck?" Danny asked when he returned to his side.

"Nope."

"If she don't show, do you still want to go to the beach?"

Part of him didn't. He had plenty to do, and he usually never went to the beach with just one friend. It was a lot better to go in a group.

But he'd already roped Danny into it. "If you want to go, we can. We can hang out with Adam and his friends." Trying to warm up to the idea, he added, "We can go for a few hours, then head back early, no worse for wear."

"Just with better tans," Danny quipped.

"Exactly," he said with a smile, then resumed his scan of the crowd.

Still no luck. And to make matters worse, their bus was looming in the distance, no less than four stoplights away. He needed to resign himself to the idea that she had changed her mind. Well, he shouldn't have gotten his hopes up.

Danny stuffed his hands into his pockets. "Should I tell those guys that we're still going?"

Zack scanned a group of girls who were walking up the sidewalk. They were all about Leona's age, and one even had golden hair like she did. But as they got closer, he noticed that they wore pleats in their skirts. They were from Indiana, not Holmes County.

She wasn't here.

Turning to Danny, he nodded. "Yeah, tell them that we'll hang out with them. Maybe we can play volleyball or something." They weren't his close friends, but they were nice guys.

But just as Danny was about to turn back, he elbowed Zack in the ribs. "Ha! Looks like we won't be hanging out with Adam and his buddies after all." With a smirk, Danny pointed to their left. "Look who is walking up the sidewalk."

Zack turned, then stared. There was Leona, wearing a

pretty turquoise-colored short-sleeved dress. Her eyes were glowing, and a smile played on her lips. Next to her was one of her friends, the girl with the auburn hair and freckles.

"What do you know?" Danny murmured. "Mattie came, too."

"Were you hoping she'd come?"

Danny didn't meet his gaze. "I didn't say that."

Instead of questioning his buddy, Zack pushed off from the fence and wound his way through the maze of people. "Hey, Leona," he said when he got close. "You made it."

She turned to him instantly with a bright, eager smile, which made him really happy. "*Jah*. Are we late?"

"Nope. You're just on time." And as she smiled again, looking even more pleased, he finally relaxed. She'd shown up and she was obviously happy to see him.

Already things were off to a really good start.

LEONA SMILED AT Zack. For the first time in almost twenty-four hours, she felt like she was able to breathe freely.

And now she knew that all the pain and tears she'd been going through had been worth it. Something special was brewing between the two of them. It was obvious in the way he looked at her.

And more obvious was the way she felt drawn to him. Why, even in Mattie's company, she could hardly bring herself to look away from him.

She didn't know if it was merely infatuation or the beginnings of a real relationship, but at the moment, she was so disheartened with how everything had ended with Edmund, she didn't care. All she did know was that she'd done the right thing.

If she'd really been in love with Edmund, no other boy

could have struck her interest. She had a feeling that if she'd been as in love with him as she'd hoped to be, she never would have even wanted to leave him to go to Pinecraft.

And since she was feeling only relief that she'd told him everything, she knew she'd made the right decision.

After she'd called Edmund, she'd called her parents. From the very first second that her mother had heard the worry in Leona's voice, she asked what was wrong.

That concern had been like a dam bursting in Leona's soul. After taking a deep, shaky breath, Leona had told her mom everything. Told her about Zack and his sister Effie, about the cat. And how disappointed Sara and Mattie were with her. Finally, she had relayed how her conversation with Edmund had gone.

"He was ready to end it right there and then?" Her mother sounded surprised. Mighty surprised.

"*Jah.* I couldn't believe it. I mean, I knew Edmund might be upset with me, but I thought he'd want to try to work things out."

"Leona, you did tell him that you were going to go to the beach with Zack," she pointed out in her matter-of-fact way.

"I told him I was going to take Zack up on his offer to accompany Mattie, Sara, and me to Siesta Key. I didn't say I was prepared to run away with him. There's a difference, I think."

"Mind your tongue, daughter."

"I'm sorry." And after double-checking about Leona's state of mind, her mother asked what she wanted to do.

Leona knew the cautious thing to do would be to bide her time until she returned to Walnut Creek and spoke to Edmund in person. And maybe that was the right thing to do, too. But she simply couldn't bring herself to do that. At last, she needed to be honest with herself—and her parents. "The wedding is off."

After a barely muffled sigh, her mother replied. "All right, then. I'll start contacting everyone."

Leona closed her eyes. "I'm sorry. I'll pay you and Daed back. I know you had to put lots of deposits down on everything."

"We'll talk about money when you get home."

"Is Daed gonna be mad at me?"

"You're our youngest daughter, dear. We want you to be happy."

That wasn't an answer. Which, of course, was an answer in itself. "Are you mad, Mamm?"

"*Nee,*" she said after a pause. "I wish you would have made this decision a few months ago, but I'm not mad. If you don't feel in your heart that marrying Edmund is the right thing to do, then you shouldn't marry him. Marriage is forever, you know."

Her *mamm* was so wise. Leona knew she was so blessed to have a mother who cared more about love and happiness than plans and money. "I am really sorry. I know I'm causing you a lot of trouble."

Her mother chuckled. "*Jah,* you are. But we still love you. This is a hard moment, but things will work out. They always do, *jah?*"

That had been music to her ears, and exactly what she'd needed to hear in order to feel some of the pressure in her chest start to lift. "*Danke, Mamm,*" she'd murmured. "I love you, too."

After she hung up, Leona had forced herself to go upstairs and tell Mattie and Sara what had happened.

When she opened the door, she'd half expected to have found all of her things already packed. Instead, both Sara and Mattie were sitting on their beds, their eyes red with tears.

"What happened?" Sara asked.

"Edmund said we were finished if I went to the beach."

Sara's eyes turned to saucers. "What do you mean by 'finished'?"

"Our whole relationship would be done. That he would end our engagement."

Mattie leaned forward. "How did you respond?"

"I said I was still going to go the beach." Looking at her two best friends' sad expressions, Leona felt lower than a starfish clinging to the ocean floor. "I'm sorry. I know you both are disappointed in me, and I don't blame you."

She chewed on her bottom lip, attempting to make some sense of what she was doing. "All I can say is that marriage is forever, and that forever is a long time. And when I thought about being married to someone who always had to be right and expected me to always blindly obey, I just couldn't do it. I couldn't."

Standing in front of them, she braced herself for the worst. Would they kick her out of the room? Start yelling at her?

But instead of making her feel even more guilty, both girls burst into tears and ran to her side. Next thing she knew, they were in their own small huddle, all three of them with arms around each other. All three of them sobbing.

"We've been feeling so bad for being mean to you, Leona," Mattie said.

"What?"

"I've never been in love. I don't know what I would do in your shoes," Mattie continued. "All I do know is that while I love my brother, he would drive me to drink."

Leona had been so shocked, her tears had momentarily stopped. "I can't believe you said that!"

Mattie shook her head. "I love him dearly, but he's more than a bit controlling. He always has been." Lowering her voice, she added, "I was secretly hoping you would be a good influence on him."

Sara grinned. "I feel bad, too. You've been my best friend forever. Friends don't treat friends the way I treated you this evening. Who you want to marry is your business, not mine. And it sure isn't my place to tell you what to do. No matter what you decide, I'll support you."

And that, of course, made Leona burst into tears.

This morning, Sara had bowed out of the beach, saying she was eager to visit the library and have a quiet day to herself. Since Sara was kind of a loner by nature, Leona understood that.

Mattie, on the other hand, was eager to go to the beach. They'd mutually decided not to speak about Edmund or marriage, to simply concentrate on having a good day.

And now they were almost to Siesta Key. Zack and his friend Danny kept glancing their way.

And they were going to spend the day at the beach.

God had given her a new day, and she was so very grateful for that.

Chapter 13

Out of all the places I've thought of taking you, the last place I considered was the Selby County Library," Beverly told Jean and Ida as they walked along the tree-lined sidewalks of downtown Sarasota toward the large library. "Do you two really need new books?"

"Of course I do," Ida said. "It's a long bus ride down here to Pinecraft, you know."

Actually, Beverly didn't know. When she'd made the decision to move to Pinecraft, she'd asked some of her Mennonite friends if they'd let her ride in the car with them. Then, after she'd gotten settled, the moving company had moved her things down.

"It is a long drive," she said. "And I suppose it is a good walk to Selby."

"Do you come here often?"

Beverly shook her head. "Not really. I never have much time to read anymore." Because she was now Mennonite, she was able to have an e-reader, which she was finding so handy.

Now she could get a good deal on brand-new books. "I should come here more often. This is a wonderful library."

"Best in the whole state," Jean said. "It won an award, you know."

This was news to her. "Really?"

"Oh, for sure and for certain! You should learn more about your new home, Beverly," Jean chided.

"You're right, I should." Actually, Jean was very right. When Beverly had first moved to Sarasota, she'd been so hurt and dismayed, she'd hardly done much but try to get through each day. Then, slowly, she'd gotten acclimated to the slower pace and easy atmosphere of Pinecraft.

After Aunt Patty had passed away and Beverly had taken over the inn, work had consumed her. Each day revolved around her inn's guests and their whims and needs. Only late at night, when her to-do list was done and she was so tired she could hardly stand up, did she think about herself.

But unfortunately, by that time of night, she stuck to the basics: trying to remember if she'd showered, eaten; if she needed to press a dress or buy a new pair of sandals. Only now did she feel like she was ready to stop sticking her head in the sand.

"Now that I feel like I have everything in control at the inn, I'm sure I'll get out and about more," she promised.

Ida and Jean exchanged glances.

"What are you two smiling about?" Beverly asked.

"Nothing, dear. It's simply that you're never going to be completely in control. The Lord is."

"I know that." And she kind of did. But privately, sometimes she kind of didn't. After all, why would the Almighty encourage Marvin and Regina to see each other when Beverly had been ready to commit herself to him for life? That hardly seemed fair.

"I hope so," Ida said. "Now that we're here, we'll make sure you get out and about every day."

"That will be nice, but please, don't forget that the inn is my job. I have to cook and clean and keep everything running smoothly, you know. If I don't do these things, they won't get done."

Ida brushed off Beverly's comment with a careless wave of her hand. "Don't you worry about that none. We can help you cook and clean."

It seemed they had an answer for everything. "I couldn't let you do that."

"*Gut,* because we weren't going to ask, we were just going to tell you what we'd done after the fact," Jean said.

"You two never change."

"I surely hope not," Jean teased. "I kind of always liked the way I was."

Beverly chuckled as they entered the large library through the wide glass double doors. She smiled as Jean and Ida stood in the large area and gaped. The main entrance boasted a beautiful archway aquarium that led into a large, expansive rotunda.

Immediately, the two ladies looked like children in a candy store.

"Oh, heavens," Jean said. "This is a wonderful place."

"And so big," Ida murmured. "How about we meet you back here in an hour?"

"An hour?" She'd been hoping she could be back at the inn within the hour.

Jean frowned. "Oh, I bet you want to look around as well. Is an hour enough time?"

"One hour is plenty of time for me," Beverly answered quickly. Looking at the circulating desk, she remembered she'd wanted to sign up for a library card anyway. "Meet me at the desk and we'll check out your books."

"Right." Ida nodded, then walked over to a sign indicating new fiction.

Feeling at a bit of a loss at the unexpected free time, Beverly waited in line, showed her identification card and proof of address, and got a library card.

Then she wandered over to the mysteries and, giving into temptation, decided to find a book or two to read. As she started walking along the stacks, glancing at the titles, she felt her body immediately relax.

This was probably what she needed to be doing as often as possible. Taking time for herself. Taking time to relax. Her favorite verse from Psalm 46 rang in her mind: *Be still and know that I am God.* Perhaps it was time to be still for a bit and let the Lord take care of the rest.

And as she pulled out two Anne Perry books, realizing with a bit of dismay that she hadn't been keeping up with Anne's latest releases, she skimmed the back of one of the books as she walked to a chair . . .

And promptly ran into a very tall man holding a very large stack of books. "Whoa," he muttered, just as he reached out to clasp her arms.

Which, of course, was the wrong thing for him to do, because the books fell like a waterfall onto the floor, toppling onto her toes and scattering like a spray of water.

"Oh!" Beverly cried. "Oh my gosh, I'm so sorry." Kneeling down, she attempted to pick up the books as quickly as possible.

The man knelt down, too. Then, there they were, picking up too many books, too close together. She lifted her chin and met his gaze, then blinked because he had really dark brown eyes that somehow managed to look warm and assessing at the same time.

"I really am sorry," she said. "I wasn't watching where I was going."

"Nothing to be too concerned about. It's just books that fell, not hot coffee." His black golf shirt strained along the muscles in his chest and shoulders as he reached for the last of his books.

As he got up, she got to her feet, too, thinking that he really was tall. Why he had to be over six feet!

Then, she of course had to bend back down to grab her purse and those two mysteries that had caused all the trouble in the first place. Feeling that he'd been exactly right, that she was on the verge of making a big deal about nothing, she smiled at him sheepishly. "Sorry," she said. Again. Obviously, it was time to go sit in a corner and hide out until Ida and Jean were ready.

Luckily, there weren't any other people in the immediate vicinity.

"Well, um, enjoy your day."

The corners of his lips curved up, revealing perfect teeth, which just happened to go with his perfect jawline, perfectly trimmed dark hair, and unusually expressive eyes. "I will. Thanks. You, too."

She'd just taken a step away—thinking few men could pull off a pair of khakis and a golf shirt and flip-flops like he could—when he said, "Hey, do you live here in Sarasota?"

"I do. Are you visiting from out of town?"

"Yeah, but I'm actually thinking about moving to Sarasota. Do you like it here?"

With relief, she donned her cool and professional inn demeanor. She could talk about the beauty of her adopted city all day long. "Very much so."

"Are you a native?"

"Not at all. I'm from Ohio. I moved here three years ago."

"And you haven't ever been tempted to leave?"

"Never. What about you? Where are you from?"

"Pennsylvania. Near Philly."

"Ah."

"I've been exploring the area for days. But when the manager of my motel suggested I come here for more information, I became hooked on this place. It's one of the nicest libraries I've ever been in."

"Yes. Well, um, it's won an award, you know."

"I bet it's won a ton of them. Hey, any chance you have a minute to talk?"

"I do." Then afraid she sounded way too eager, she sputtered, "I mean, I have a couple of minutes. I'm here with two ladies, but they're going to be awhile longer."

"Great."

Suddenly, she couldn't help but agree. Yes, it was great that Ida and Jean were taking their own sweet time.

It wasn't so great that she seemed to be tripping over her words and acting like she was standing in the lunch line next to the cutest boy ever. "I'll be happy to answer any of your questions." She pointed to a pair of comfortable-looking leather chairs. "Want to sit down?"

"Yeah. I do."

As they walked, he looked over at her, seeming to notice

her dress and the small lace covering on her head. "Are you Mennonite?"

"Yes. Are you?" He wasn't wearing especially conservative clothes, but some branches of the Mennonite church were rather progressive.

He shook his head. "No, though I grew up in a fairly conservative church."

"I grew up Amish." With a shrug, she said, "When I moved here, I decided to not be baptized in the faith."

"We each have to follow the Lord's will in our own way," he murmured.

She liked that. Liked how he phrased his statement. And really liked that he wasn't being judgmental. Smiling, she sat down and set her things to one side, then leaned forward. "So, what are you interested in? Have you been to Pinecraft?"

"I've been to the Der Dutchman Restaurant. Does that count?"

"It counts. Have you been to Pinecraft Park yet?"

"*Nee.*" Pointing to the books on the ground, he said, "I've been getting a bit of information about the lay of the land. I'm going to be running a local bed-and-breakfast."

"I guess we were meant to meet," she said with a laugh. "I own a B and B."

He shook his head. "That's crazy. Talk about it being a small world! Hey, by the way, I'm Eric Wagler."

"I'm Beverly Overholt."

"Pretty name."

"*Danke.*" She shrugged. "Is this B and B you're gonna be working at already running?"

"It is. Maybe you know of it? It's called the Orange Blossom Inn."

She blinked. "Are you sure that's the name of it?"

"I'm positive. Why?"

"That's the name of my inn."

"Wow, that is strange." He opened up a plastic folder that was secured with a rubber band and fished through some papers. "Yes, my lawyer said it was called the Orange Blossom Inn. On Gardenia Street."

"That is absolutely my inn." Feeling that he was playing some awful, terrible game with her, she glared. "So, what are you talking about, saying that you're going to be running it?"

"I had a neighbor, John Eicher, for almost twenty years. When he passed away, his lawyer contacted me. It seems John had been leasing it to his ex-wife for decades." With a shrug, he said, "I guess she passed on a couple of years ago."

"My aunt, Patty Eicher, passed away to heaven two years ago. Why did no one do anything about it then?"

Eric shrugged. "From what I understand, John didn't have much communication with his ex-wife. A full year went by before he'd heard she'd passed away."

"I find that hard to believe."

Eric's whole posture changed, becoming more assertive. "Maybe you should try a little harder, then, because it's the truth. From what I understand, part of the problem was that someone took over the lease right away, so nobody in Pennsylvania realized Patty was gone."

"That someone was me."

"Well, you should have taken care to tell the mortgage company you wrote the checks to that Patty Eicher had passed away. By the time John discovered Patty had passed away, he was in poor health. Four months ago he died. And because he never had children, he left the inn to me in his will."

Beverly shook her head. She felt sorry for John and for Eric's wishes, too, but his loss wasn't her problem. This was her livelihood they were talking about. "I made no attempt to be sneaky, Eric. When my Aunt Patty got sick, she told me that she wanted me to continue running the inn."

He folded his hands over his chest. "She should have also told you that the Orange Blossom Inn was part of her divorce settlement. John kept the rent low so she'd always be able to afford to run it. Supposedly, she really loved it here in Sarasota."

"She did. And she really loved the inn, too." Beverly didn't even try to hide her frustration and the pain in her voice. She'd just received a huge shock, and if what this Eric said was true, then she was about to lose everything that was important.

All over again.

"I thought the Orange Blossom Inn was mine," she murmured.

"Then I guess we've got a problem, Beverly." His voice didn't sound so harsh, but there was no doubt that he meant every word.

"I guess we do." She knew there were a hundred things she should be asking Eric, a hundred things she should clarify, starting with why he hadn't stopped by the inn yet. But at the moment, all she knew was that she needed to put some space between them. Her throat was tight and she was starting to fear that she might start crying.

Standing up, she grabbed her books and hugged them to her chest. "Excuse me, I must be going."

"Right this minute? Beverly, wait. We need to talk about how to handle this."

"I know we do. But not right now."

"If not now, when?"

"I have no idea. I need to look at Patty's paperwork." That was, if she could still find it. "I need to call my lawyer, too."

He nodded. "How about I stop by tomorrow, then?"

So he could look at his new home. "*Nee.* That's too soon."

He looked at her steadily before replying. "I'll give you another day, but that's it. The whole reason I'm here is to see my inheritance."

She was getting the feeling that an inheritance was all the Orange Blossom Inn was to him. A piece of property in Florida. "You've made your intentions incredibly clear, Mr. Wagler."

He rolled his eyes. "It's Eric."

"Seeing as you are about to take over my life, it would be best if we kept things on a more professional level."

"Fine. I'll see you at nine in two days' time. Look for me then."

She gave him only the briefest of nods before turning away.

She now felt sick and completely empty inside. Each step felt overwhelming. Everything did. Realizing that she was never going to actually take time to read them, she set her books on a random metal cart and looked for Ida and Jean.

As promised, they were waiting for her at the circulation desk. Their arms were laden with books and they were chatting with two library employees.

When they saw her, Jean waved. "Beverly, we've had such a *gut* time here."

It took everything Beverly had to smile in return. "I'm so glad, Jean. That makes me really happy."

Chapter 14

Zack had no idea what was going on with Leona. Every time he glanced her way, wanting to share a smile about how good the sand felt on their bare feet, or how fresh the salty air smelled, she barely acknowledged him.

At first, he was worried about her comfort. Was she too hot? The noonday sun was particularly strong, especially for someone not used to it.

Or maybe she was thirsty? Hungry? Bored?

All he knew for certain was that something was wrong.

Was she mad at him? Was she regretting her decision to meet him? Did she not feel well?

Instead of smiling and chatting the way she'd done during their previous meetings, she was hardly saying a word.

She didn't seem as happy to be with him, either. Her smiles weren't as bright, she kept glancing beyond him, and more than once he'd felt her tense up.

If they'd known each other better, he would have wrapped an arm around her shoulders and offered her a comforting hug.

But that seemed like the absolute last thing she wanted at the moment.

He was glancing at her again, debating whether or not to say something, when she pointed to Mattie and Danny. "Look at them. They really seem to be getting along."

"You're right about that," he agreed, feeling more than a little relieved. Maybe she wasn't upset after all. Maybe she simply wasn't too interested in him.

"I didn't know they'd developed such a rapport, did you?"

"*Nee*. But I guess I should have," he said with a grin. From the moment they'd gotten off the bus and started walking through the parking lot and down the cement steps leading to the beach, Danny and Mattie had been talking to each other nonstop. "Danny likes to talk."

"Mattie does, too."

That was, he supposed, his opening. "Yesterday evening, when we saw each other at the park, I thought you liked to talk, too. But you seem kind of quiet today."

Her pretty brown eyes clouded. Then, to his dismay, they filled with tears.

Had he been that rude? Or was she that sensitive?

"I'm so sorry. Just ignore me, this has nothing to do with you," she said around a sniff.

"I'm not going to ignore you crying, Leona. What's wrong?"

She dug around in her canvas tote bag, pulled out a tissue, and dabbed at her eyes. "To tell you the truth, I debated whether to meet you or not today. I was worried that this would happen."

"That what would happen?" he pressed.

"I had a difficult conversation last night."

"About what? You've got to help me out, Leona," he added

when she looked like she didn't want to answer. "All I know is that you don't seem very happy. I was worried I'd done something wrong, but I have no idea what it could be."

She swiped at her eyes again. "Oh, no. I promise, my tears have nothing to do with you. I mean, well, not really."

"Not really?" Now he was really confused.

Looking torn, she leaned back on her hands in the sand. "Zack, I was engaged until last night."

"Engaged to be married?" He didn't know whether to laugh or give her more space. He'd never met anyone who'd *stopped* being engaged. They'd all gone from engaged to married. Furthermore, no one simply broke things off in one night. Did they?

"*Jah.*" She held up a hand when he was about to scoot a little farther away. "This is bad, I know."

He wasn't gonna lie. "It sure sounds like it."

"I don't know if you'd understand, but what happened last night was a longtime coming. I've been having regrets for saying yes almost from the very beginning. But I had convinced myself that I was being foolish. That I should've been happy about Edmund. But I couldn't have been more wrong."

He had no idea what to say. He couldn't believe he'd been thinking nonstop about a girl who'd been engaged. "I wish you would have told me you were promised to someone else."

"I know. But how would I have explained everything?"

Glancing at her, he couldn't help but notice how the faint ocean breeze had pulled a few tendrils of hair loose from her *kapp*. Now, as those few blond strands blew across her cheeks, he unfortunately realized she'd never been more beautiful to him.

"It wouldn't have been that hard to explain things to me,"

he said, forcing himself to focus on their conversation. "I mean, you're doing right it now."

"Zack, I promise, I wasn't meaning to lead you astray." After she took a breath, she said, "My rocky relationship with Edmund was why I came here in the first place. I felt the need to get some space in between us. To clear my thoughts. I really thought that some distance would make me realize that I'd been foolish. Instead, I knew from the minute our bus left Holmes County that I wasn't happy with Edmund, that it was going to be difficult to *ever* be happy with Edmund. Then I met you and that silly cat."

"What did I do?"

"Nothing." She shrugged. "I mean, everything."

Was she pinning part of the blame of her breakup on him? "Leona, when we first met, I was attempting to rescue a cat. That was it."

She gazed at him, her brown eyes filling with a new warmth. "I know what you were doing. But, see, you were laughing. You were simply happy. And I realized neither Edmund nor my life with him was ever going to be that way. So I shared all this with Sara and Mattie. They got mad at me. Mattie is Edmund's sister, you see."

This story was getting crazier and crazier. "Mattie is your fiancé's sister?"

"*Jah.*" She bit her bottom lip. "I mean, *nee*. Well, she is my friend, but now her brother isn't my fiancé. See, Mattie and Sara had me call Edmund yesterday to tell him that I was going to the beach with you and your friends today."

"I would have never asked you to come here if I'd known you were promised to another man," he said again. Actually, he was starting to think that he couldn't tell her this often enough.

"I know, Zack." She sat up again, grabbed a handful of warm sand, and then slowly let it trickle through her fingers. "I'm sorry if you felt I was lying to you, but I truly assumed we would just be going as friends. I mean, we don't know each other."

"You're right." He had to give her that.

After giving him a relieved look, Leona shifted again, pulling her legs up beneath her. "So, last night, I called up Edmund and told him that a local man had offered to take us to Siesta Key and that I wanted to go. He forbade me. And then he said if I did go against his wishes he was going to break off our engagement right then and there."

"Wow." Zack had never been in love, but he couldn't imagine throwing away a whole relationship over the phone. "Since you're here, I'm guessing it happened?"

She nodded. "*Jah.*"

"Is that why you are crying? Do you have second thoughts?" He felt so ill at ease, he fired off another set of questions. "Do you miss him? Did he hurt your feelings?" Though it killed him to say it, he added, "I bet if you call him back tonight and say he was right, he would take you back."

After glancing at the surf, she turned back to him. "I'm not going to do that, Zack," she said quietly. "I am sad, but not because I regret coming here. I'm sad that I put him through all of it. I'm sad that I didn't trust my instincts and the Lord's voice in my ear. I'm sad about a lot of things." Tilting up her chin, she continued. "I don't mean to make you uncomfortable, Zack. I know we hardly know each other. And I realize that we might never be more than friends this week. But the reason I said yes was because I wanted the chance to get to know you. I wanted to feel like I mattered."

He thought about her words, about what it must have been like for Leona to feel that she didn't matter. From the time he'd met her, he'd known she was pretty special. Girls like her, girls who could be so honest, who were willing to take chances like she was . . . they were fairly few and far between.

And that's when he knew what he had to do. Even if nothing ever happened between them, even if they never saw each other again after they got off the bus, he knew she needed to at least hear one thing from him. "You matter, Leona."

She smiled. "Obviously you matter to me, too."

That smile touched him. Made him feel like he was something special and that he could slay dragons.

Made him feel too much.

"How about we go see what Mattie and Danny are doing?" he suggested as he got to his feet. "I don't know what you think, but I'm pretty surprised Danny is talking to her so easily. He's usually pretty reserved around girls."

"Mattie is the same way around boys. But, you know, she did seem really eager to come here with me. I had thought maybe she was worried I was going to be moping around. Now I think I am beginning to understand why."

"Maybe this trip was meant to happen for all of you," he said as he reached down, took her hand, and pulled her up. "I've often wondered why the Lord does the things He does."

She nodded. "Today, that gives me a lot of comfort. I hope you are right. I hope His plan was for all of us to meet . . . for whatever reason. I would hate to think that I disappointed Him by breaking things off with Edmund."

Zack was tempted to point out that she actually hadn't been the one to break things off. It sounded like her idiot fiancé had simply been looking for a reason.

But it sure wasn't his place to say such a thing.

All he did know was that if a girl like Leona was his fiancé, he would have done a whole lot more to try to keep her. He wouldn't have let her go to Pinecraft without him. He wouldn't have made her feel like she couldn't talk to him or that he didn't want to listen to everything she had to say.

But more than anything, he wouldn't have broken up with her on the phone after she told him she simply wanted to go to the beach with a bunch of people.

As they walked toward their friends, the super-soft sand feeling like spun sugar under his toes, Zack knew that no matter what, he needed to keep his thoughts to himself. No good would come from him pushing his feelings on her too quickly or too forcibly.

He was simply going to do his best to make sure she had a good time with him today. If he did that, chances were good she'd want to see him again.

And then maybe even a whole lot more after that.

IT HAPPENED RIGHT in the middle of math. Effie had just turned in her assignment and was making her way back to her seat when Jennifer C. spoke to her.

For the majority of the class, this would not be a big deal. Jennifer C. wasn't a shy girl and she did talk to most everybody. Their teacher, Mrs. Bishop, really liked her, too. So did the boys. And the principal. Even the ladies in the lunchroom.

Jennifer wasn't mean. She never made fun of Effie. Actually, Jennifer C. was the type of person to hold the door open for her or ask if she needed help getting something off a counter.

Plus, she had pretty straight-blond hair, blue eyes, and two older sisters who doted on her. Whether it was just her personality, her confidence, her looks, or a combination of all of it, she was really outgoing, and she talked to everyone.

So, everyone was pretty used to her stopping them and asking about their new jeans, or what show they'd watched the night before, or what their plans were for the weekend.

But Effie was not. She was only one of five Amish girls in the class. She was shy. And, well, until recently, she'd been confined to a wheelchair. It wasn't that she didn't have a lot in common with Jennifer, it was more like she had *nothing* in common with her.

Those things meant that she was pretty much invisible to girls like Jennifer C.

"Effie, hi," Jennifer C. said from her desk. Loud enough for Josiah, who sat one row up and two rows over, to hear. "How are you?"

"I'm *gut*. I . . . I mean, I'm fine, Jennifer," she said, hoping she sounded more mature and together. "How are you?"

She smiled. "Great. I think I got a hundred on the test."

"I think I did good on it, too. Not a hundred, but at least an A or a B." Effie paused, unsure of what else to say.

"Melanie and me and a couple of other girls are going out for ice cream after school. Do you want to come?"

She was getting invited out to ice cream? More than anything, she wanted to say yes, but she was afraid that her legs weren't going to be strong enough to support her for a long distance.

And the only thing worse than not getting invited to go out with the girls was making a fool of herself in front of them.

"Thanks, I'd love to, but, um, I told my *mamm* that I'd ride the bus home."

"Couldn't you call her?"

"*Nee*. I mean, no. She's working. But thanks." She started walking back to her desk, realizing that their brief exchange had been witnessed by all of the other kids around them.

"Maybe another time?"

Effie felt her cheeks heat. "Yes. Sure. That would be great," she said right before she took her seat. As casually as possible, she darted a look Josiah's way. He was looking at her. When their eyes met, he smiled.

Smiled!

Now she was completely flustered. Luckily for her, Mrs. Bishop started telling everyone to get their things ready so they could switch classes. With a sigh of relief, Effie concentrated on doing just that.

Only when the bell rang and she was waiting until the rush of kids eased before she ventured out of the room, did her best friend in the class, Rosemary, walk to her side.

"What was that about?" she asked.

Effie didn't need to ask what Rosemary was talking about. She knew. Gosh, most likely, everyone was thinking the same thing. "I don't know."

"You sure?"

Effie shook her head. "Really, I have no idea at all. But I have a feeling I'm going to find out pretty soon."

When Rosemary walked away, Effie forced herself to get her things together and start walking, too. And as she made her way down the hall, for once she wasn't worried about keeping her limping to a minimum. Instead, she was wondering what had just happened with Jennifer C.

No one suddenly decided to want to be someone's friend without a reason. Was it because of Zack? Though he was much older, that didn't stop most girls from wanting to be around him.

Or was it because her mom had seen them talking at Yoder's? Maybe she'd felt sorry for Effie, thinking she needed more friends. Sometimes moms loved to mess everything up with their good intentions.

Whatever the reason, Effie wasn't sure what to think about Jennifer's new friendliness. All she did know was that she didn't trust her. And that there was no one in her family who would understand why Effie felt that way.

Chapter 15

People flock to those boys like flies to sugar water," Mattie whispered as she picked up her bottle of water from the little hole she'd dug for it in the sand, and took a fortifying sip. "I don't know whether to be impressed that they're so well liked or a little concerned that we've elected to spend so much time with them."

Though Leona didn't much care for the fly image, she couldn't deny that her friend's comment was true. All day long, Zack and Danny had been introducing them to their friends— and they had a lot of friends.

Some were boys, like Adam and his three buddies on the bus. Others were girls about their age. All of them had been nice and had seemed genuinely happy to meet two girls who were visiting from Ohio. When they'd gotten off the bus, Zack had guided them to the most beautiful beach she'd ever seen. It seemed to go on for a solid mile, and the sand under her feet was soft and white and felt like silk along her skin. After Leona had taken a moment to stop and admire it all, Zack pointed to a group of men and women.

"There's Adam and a couple more of my friends. Do you mind if we join them?"

"Of course not."

He'd smiled. "Good. You're going to like everyone, I promise."

"What would you have done if I had said that I didn't want to sit with everyone else?" Leona teased.

"I would have stayed by your side."

"You really would have?"

He'd shrugged, suddenly looking embarrassed. "I didn't ask you to come to the beach in order for you to have a bad time, Leona. I want you to be happy."

Everyone had joined them again after that, and Leona had been glad about it, mainly because Zack's words had affected her too much. It had been a long time since she'd felt that she was the focal point of any other person's attention.

Certainly Edmund had never been so accommodating.

But there was no way she would admit how touched she was. So she'd pushed off her serious mood and shrugged. "That's good to know."

His eyes had lit in amusement, but he'd said nothing more before he turned away when Adam claimed his attention.

A couple of the girls had called her and Mattie over. Soon they were helping them spread out quilts and beach towels on the smooth white sand, open up Tupperware containers full of sandwiches, chips, cookies, and fried chicken, and twist open Mason jars full of sweet tea.

Some of the boys had taken off their shirts and started playing volleyball. Some of the girls—to Leona's amazement—took off their dresses to reveal bathing suits underneath. They'd gone swimming, lain in the sun, and talked with their friends.

Leona still felt a little self-conscious in her short-sleeved dress, though at least she didn't feel embarrassment anymore about pulling it up to reveal her calves and knees as she sat on the beach. When Mattie did the same, they shared a smile. They were fitting in just fine.

Leona soon learned that it was definitely an anything-went atmosphere. The freedoms displayed confirmed some of the whispers she'd heard from girlfriends who had been to Pinecraft, that even the biggest Amish sticklers in Sugarcreek or Berlin looked the other way when they came to Siesta Key. She wondered if all the other people were in the midst of their *rumspringa* or they simply were enjoying a few days of freedom from the rules of their local church district.

In no time she and Mattie had settled in and relaxed, which brought them to their present activity, watching everyone dart back and forth in front of them.

"This day is flying by," Mattie declared suddenly. "Not only has everyone been so nice, but they've made us feel like we're part of their group."

"I completely agree. This is the first time in two hours that the two of us are sitting by ourselves. I was kind of afraid that we were going to spend most of the day feeling out of place."

"Zack wouldn't do that to you. He's been superattentive."

Leona thought that, too. From the moment he'd introduced her to his friends, he'd taken care to make sure that she hadn't been left out.

Actually, he'd been really wonderful. "It is nice of them to volunteer to go over to the snack shack and bring us back ice teas."

"They wouldn't let me pay."

"I know." Mattie shrugged. "But it is just iced tea. Best not to make a big deal out of that."

"I thought the same thing." Noticing that Mattie was once again following Danny's every move, Leona eyed her girlfriend curiously. "So, what do you think about Danny?"

"Danny? Oh, well, I think he's really nice."

Obviously there was more to that story! "And?"

"And, I don't know," Mattie said. But a new secret smile played on her lips. "Sara is going to be so sorry she stayed behind."

"She seemed pretty happy to have some time to herself." An awful thought suddenly occurred to her. "Was that the truth, or is she upset with me?"

"She's not mad at you, Leona."

"Really?" Leona wished she'd been more honest about all the doubts she'd been having about a future with Edmund. Keeping her worries to herself had only brought on a lot of hurt feelings and misunderstandings.

"Really." Mattie's voice was firm. "I meant what I said last night, and I think Sara did too. It's not our place to judge." Looking just beyond Leona, she said, "I mean, I've never had a serious boyfriend."

Seeing that Zack and Danny were approaching them, Leona scrambled to her feet.

"Girls, we brought you some iced tea and ice cream bars," Zack called out.

"That sounds so good," Leona declared before she realized she probably sounded a little too enthusiastic. Obviously, she wasn't doing much better than Mattie at hiding her interest in a certain man.

He handed her a chocolate-covered vanilla ice cream bar. "Do you like ice cream?"

"Of course. *Danke.*"

"You're welcome." Looking adorably embarrassed, he said, "It's actually a bribe."

Mattie tilted her head. "For what?"

"Well, I hate to tell you this, but I'm going to have to catch the one-fifty bus. I promised my mother I'd be home for Effie."

"Oh, that's fine."

Looking a little uncomfortable, he said, "If you don't want to leave yet, I bet some of my friends could help you get on a later bus."

Leona stared at him. "That would be okay with you?"

"Well, sure. I mean, I want you to be happy. It's not your fault I need to look after my sister."

He was right. It wasn't a big deal. But it was a big deal to her. It showed just how selfless he was. He was always putting other people in front of himself. Proving over and over again that he was worth taking a chance on. Worth risking everything she knew for the idea of what could be.

But that sure didn't mean she was comfortable with the idea of staying behind after he left. She might have told people that she'd come to Siesta Key with Zack in order to see the beach, but that wasn't the truth. She'd come to Siesta Key to spend more time with him.

"I'm fine with leaving with you," she said simply. Feeling a little bit of tension—or maybe it was disappointment—from Mattie, Leona said, "But just because I don't mind leaving, it doesn't mean you need to, Mattie. I promise, if you want to stay longer, I won't mind one bit." Actually, Leona would kind of like it if Mattie did stay longer. Then she could spend some time alone with Zack and wouldn't have to worry about being observed by Mattie.

Mattie's eyes held a good bit of longing, but she said, "I'm not going to stay by myself, Le."

"I'd be happy stay with you," Danny said in a rush. "I don't have to be anywhere until five or six."

"Really? You wouldn't mind staying with me?"

"Not at all." With a broad grin, Danny added, "I haven't stuck my toes in the water yet. We have to do that, right?"

"Oh, definitely," Mattie said, her voice a little breathless. "I'd hate to have to tell my family that I went all the way to Siesta Key and didn't even stick my feet in the Gulf."

It took everything Leona had not to tease Mattie about her comment. Suddenly, Mattie was acting like she absolutely loved the beach and the water. Leona knew that wasn't the whole reason she was electing to stay.

Sharing a small secret smile with Zack, she said, "It sounds like we have everything settled. I'll leave with Zack, and Mattie will meet me back at the inn later."

"You sure you don't mind?" Mattie asked.

"Not in the slightest. Remember what Sara said at breakfast? It's nice that we three can go on vacation together but not feel like we have to be joined at the hip."

Zack grinned. "I'm glad everything is working out so well."

"Me too."

She and Zack made plans to get on their way in half an hour. When he and Danny went off so Zack could say goodbye to some of their friends, Leona sat down next to Mattie on the beach towel. "*Danke* for coming today."

"You know you don't have to thank me. I'm really glad I came."

"Do you like Danny?" There was no reason to beat around the bush, Leona figured.

"I don't know. I think I kind of might." She bit her lip. "Is that bad?"

"I don't think so. But then, I haven't been making the best choices lately."

Mattie stared at her hard, then shook her head. "Don't do that. Don't put yourself down that way."

"I'm not, but it would be wrong of me to pretend that I am not causing you and your family a lot of pain. I bet your parents hate me."

"Of course they don't hate you."

"Mattie, I'm sure Edmund is pretty upset right now."

"I bet he is. But let me tell you something. Leona, you were upset last night. And I would never have told you this before, but you've been acting upset for weeks. Maybe even months. Sara and I both noticed. As did your sisters."

"Rosanna and Naomi noticed, too?"

"Yep. One day after church they asked me how I thought you were really doing."

Rosanna and Naomi were both married now. And since they lived away from home, Leona didn't always get to have many conversations with them anymore. For them to seek Mattie out said a lot about their concern. "I didn't think it was that obvious."

"It wasn't, but it *was* obvious that you weren't comfortable sharing whatever was wrong. Sara and I just weren't sure what it was." She shrugged. "Actually, I was thinking maybe you were simply anxious about getting married. Moving in with a man, taking a new name, doing everything differently? Those are big changes."

"Funny, I never even got that far. All I could think about was that something wasn't quite right with me and Edmund and I didn't know how to change it." Thinking about the way she'd been feeling—that deep-set worry in the pit of her stomach, and never having any relief—Leona realized now that she'd been a fool to think that she could actually make things better by completely changing herself. "I really was afraid you were going to be mad at me for the rest of my life."

Mattie glanced at her, her expression soft. Then she wrinkled her nose. "I guess *Gott* gave me Danny."

"What?"

Mattie waved a hand, "Oh, I don't mean it like that," she said. "At least, I don't think I do." She grinned. "I guess what I'm trying to say is that the first time he smiled at me, my insides got all flustered. Then, last night when we were going to sleep, I was thinking about today, hoping he would be here, too. Then, when we went for a walk and started talking, and I found myself talking and talking and talking, and he didn't even look like he minded . . . I felt really happy."

"That's nice."

Mattie nodded. "Even if nothing happens between us, I now understand what it's like to want to get to know someone better. And being willing to risk looking like a fool in order to do that."

"You don't look like a fool. You're not acting like one, either."

"Leona, do you really think that? I would be so embarrassed if I discovered I'd been behaving like a fool."

"You're not. You're being your sweet self—"

"I'm more than a little awkward," Mattie interrupted in a rush. "Once more—I have way too many freckles. I have dark auburn hair, which is a nice way of saying it's red."

"Everyone likes your freckles, and your hair is beautiful. Everyone says so."

"I talk too much. I get too excited about things. And until this trip, I always tried to keep a handle on myself." She grimaced. "And we both know how that's gone." Lowering her voice, she said, "Danny's probably already wishing he'd never agreed to go to the beach with Zack."

Grateful to be concentrating on someone other than herself, Leona said gently, "Everything you are pointing out as flaws are what I consider to be some of the most special things about my friend Mattie."

"Le, you are too sweet."

"I'm sweet, but what I'm trying to say is that maybe Danny sees you the way I see you. Maybe he's a pretty smart guy."

Suddenly, Mattie smiled wide. Her teeth were white and her cheeks looked like they might be hurting, she was smiling so wide.

Which made Leona laugh. If nothing else noteworthy happened on their trip, this day was worth it.

She knew that with all her heart.

"Hey, Leona?" Zack called out. "I'm sorry, but we really need to get going. I can't miss the SCAT."

"I'll be right there," she said, grabbing her towel, shaking out the sand, and hastily stuffing it into her canvas tote. "See you, Mattie." Lowering her voice, she added, "And have fun."

"I will." Mattie grinned as she raised her voice. "See ya." She waved. Then before Leona had even looked away, she turned and focused all of her attention on Danny again.

It was obvious that all thoughts of Leona were already forgotten.

Chapter 16

It was becoming clear that Jean and Ida wanted to discover everything they could about the city of Sarasota.

While they walked back to the inn, the ladies quizzed Beverly on the surrounding government buildings. They asked what she knew about the other hotels and restaurants nearby. They asked about the museums and the retirement communities, the shopping centers, and the signs for the botanical gardens. They picked up brochures to take excursions to some of the islands around, to visit Orlando, even Tampa.

Everything around them seemed to be cause for excitement and questions and, well, happiness. Their enthusiasm and energy were infectious. Those things also made Beverly realize that she'd spent an awful lot of time being afraid and worried.

She'd always over-thought things. It had been a curse when she was young, but it was a true liability now.

No matter what other people might have said, Beverly had always blamed herself for Marvin's abandonment. She'd been sure that he never would have strayed if she had been more fun. Prettier. More easygoing. Actually, she wasn't sure exactly what she had worried about; she simply knew that she'd worried about it a lot and had given herself a very hard time about her imperfections.

Now she knew better.

But what she hadn't realized was that she'd been entirely too focused on the Orange Blossom Inn and not on rediscovering herself and what made her happy.

However, maybe that was a blessing in disguise, because Ida and Jean seemed intent on unearthing these things in record time.

Now the two ladies were in the kitchen baking sugar cookies and key lime tarts. This was their idea. They were excited about it and had no desire for her to supervise them or help.

Which made her feel a little out of sorts. "Are you sure you don't need my help? This kitchen can be a bit confusing."

"We've got it," Jean said.

"I should warn you that those key lime tarts can be a little tricky. Sometimes the filling doesn't set like it should."

"*Nee,* I don't think this filling will be a problem. I'm trying a different recipe, you see."

With effort, Beverly bit back a sharp retort. She'd literally spent weeks experimenting with different recipes in order to serve the best items possible. The last thing she needed—or wanted—was to have her reputation spoiled by two adventurous cooks. "Um, where did you find the recipe?"

Ida held up one of her library books. "In here. All we needed were key limes, and they had those at the produce store at Yoder's."

"Ah."

"We've got it all covered. Therefore, you should go relax, dear," Jean said.

Relax? She felt like all she'd been doing was relaxing today. "Maybe."

"We'll be serving tea in two hours," Ida reminded her. "Besides, didn't you say you had some phone calls to make?"

Beverly knew it was time to call her lawyer and talk to him about Eric. "All right, I think I will go make those phone calls."

Jean nodded. "Off you go, then, dear. After, try to relax a bit if you can." Her eyes brightened. "Or putter around in your garden. I know you like to do that."

Beverly did as Jean suggested, mainly because the thought of going against those two seemed exhausting. After leaving a message for the lawyer, she picked up some snips out of her shed, walked over to her rose garden, slipped on her garden gloves, and started snipping off the deadheads and pruning the bushes.

Then she gave in to what she knew she had to think about. Her conversation with Eric. What if this place really was his?

What was she going to do? For the life of her, she didn't know if she could survive more turmoil. Or starting over again.

Thank goodness she'd put money aside. She actually had put quite a bit in the bank. Not enough to put down on another business, but more than enough to take some time to figure out what she wanted to do.

She supposed she could rent a room or lease a place for six months. Or maybe even put her things in storage and take a trip out west. Everyone always talked about how much fun those bus trips were. Maybe she should pick up some brochures about them one day soon.

Yes, taking a long bus trip might be fun. And what an opportunity, to have three or four weeks with nothing to do but make friends with her travel mates, play cards in the evening, and explore new places during the day.

She could read a book. She could read a lot of books. Take time for herself.

Thirty minutes later, her lawyer stopped by. Since he was semiretired and lived just a few blocks away, she wasn't too surprised to see him. After explaining her situation again, she gave him all the paperwork she could find.

Then, her stomach in knots, she did her best to be patient.

"Beverly? You're daydreaming again," Sadie said from the front sidewalk.

"Oh, hey. How are you?"

"I'm *gut*."

As Sadie approached, she examined Beverly through narrowed eyes. "Are you ready for tea already? Usually, this time of day, you're hustling and bustling around."

Beverly started, then looked down at her simple Timex watch. "Oh, gosh, I've been sitting out here over an hour. I guess the time got away from me today."

"I would say you've been working hard, but it doesn't look like it. It looked like you were lost in thought." Her lips twitched. "Yet again."

"I guess I can't stop that habit, no matter how hard I try."

"Can't think of a reason why you'd want to stop your daydreams. You always seem to look right pleased about them. Besides, I have a feeling they are just as much a part of you as your brown hair and brown eyes. That's who you are." Sadie winked. "Your tendency to drift off into thought is one of the reasons I like you so much, dear. I've always thought it was rather sweet."

Beverly felt even more at a loss. For some reason, Sadie's kind words made her feel kind of choked up. What was she going to do if she really was going to have to leave the Orange Blossom Inn? She'd lose all her friends. She'd be alone again. "You've been a *gut* friend to me, Sadie. For sure."

"Just like you've been to me, and to everyone you've come in contact with." She sat down next to the flowers, on a wooden bench that Beverly had painted a pale green. "Ah, it smells like heaven here."

"I think so, too."

"So, are Marvin's sisters driving you crazy? Are they being mean?"

"Not at all. Actually, they're making me wish they lived here full-time. They really enjoy life. We went to the library this morning."

Sadie smiled. "They got you to go out and about? Praise God."

"I know. It was a minor miracle. We were only gone a few hours, but getting out of here for a little while did me a world of good."

"So if it isn't those two ladies who have you in a tizzy, who is it?"

"You know me that well, huh?"

"I do. And you know me well enough to know that I'm not going to let you push off my questions."

Until that very minute, Beverly had been sure that she was going to keep her problems to herself. She hadn't wanted to burden anyone else. But Ida and Jean's arrival had forced her to reevaluate everything in her life.

The women's no-nonsense ways combined with their desire to retain her friendship, even when she wasn't being much of a friend, encouraged Beverly to rethink things.

Maybe it really was time to begin deeper conversations and reveal her real feelings with people who cared about her.

"Actually, I think I need your help, Sadie."

Sadie clapped her hands. "*Gut.* I've been waiting to feel useful all day. What is on your mind?"

"Well, I happened to meet a man at the library."

Sadie's pleased expression turned into something akin to bliss. "Truly? That is *wonderful-gut!*"

Beverly waved a hand in the air. "This meeting was definitely not wonderful."

"Oh?"

"See, I accidentally ran into him and his books fell. Then, because his books were about the area, I made the mistake of asking him if he had any questions about Sarasota."

"That doesn't sound like a mistake."

"It was," she said around a moan. "It turns out that he's here because he believes he inherited this very inn from his friend John." Thinking again of how shocked she'd been, she pressed her lips together. "What are the chances, you know?"

"It does seem unlikely. Really unlikely." Sadie's brow wrinkled. "Furthermore, it doesn't make sense, Beverly. This is *your* inn."

"It didn't make sense to me, either. When I first moved to Florida, I was so devastated by everything that had happened with my fiancé and best friend that I think I was kind of numb. I took everything my Aunt Patty said at face value." She paused, remembering her kind, elderly aunt who'd always had a reputation for having a heart of gold and the attention of a gnat. "She was so proud of this place, and I was so grateful that she trusted me enough to run it with her. All I remember her saying about the inn was that she had the lease for a lifetime."

She glanced at Sadie, appreciating that her friend was willing to listen to her problems but also not wanting to overwhelm her with too many details. But instead of looking puzzled or bored, Sadie merely nodded and smiled encouragingly . . . allowing Beverly to tell a story that she now realized she should have never tried to keep inside.

"When Aunt Patty passed away, I simply took over the lease. For the last three years, I've hardly given the owner a second thought. I simply wrote my check on the first of every month, posted it, and didn't think about it again."

"I wouldn't have, either, dear."

"After we got back from the library, I called my lawyer and left him a message with what Eric told me. He came right over and looked at the papers about the inn and Aunt Patty's estate that I'd stuffed into a back cabinet."

"And?"

"He took everything with him, but his first thoughts were that there's a mighty good chance that everything Eric said was true. Aunt Patty actually was leasing this inn from her exhusband. And she definitely did have that lease for life, but it was *her* lifetime, not her niece's," she added ruefully.

"What a story." Sadie's eyes were wide with disbelief.

Beverly nodded. "I should have remembered long before now that Aunt Patty was a pretty ditsy lady when it came down to details." Feeling terrible, she added, "Actually, it seems I have inherited that trait from her."

"I'm so sorry that this happened, Bev."

"Me too. Putting all the blame on her shoulders might make my pride feel a little better, but I truly cannot. I should have looked into things long before now."

"What are you going to do?"

"Bide my time."

Sadie waited a beat before giving her a chiding look. "That's it?"

"I don't have much choice. I want to continue here, but that may not be an option. Eric is coming over the day after tomorrow to see the inn and to talk about things."

"At least he's giving you a couple of days."

"Barely. He wanted to come over today, but I said I needed time."

"So you don't actually know what his plans are," Sadie said.

"That is true. Eric hasn't come right out and said that he wants me to leave. So he might want me here. If that's the case, then I'll start leasing the inn from him."

"I don't like the idea that some *Englischer* can pretty much pop out of nowhere and take over your life." Sadie frowned. "It don't seem right."

Beverly didn't like it, either. But she also knew if the situation was reversed, she'd do the same thing Eric was doing. "It's out of my hands."

"Well, it's in God's hands, that is true. But there must be something you can do."

"What I can do is start looking for another place to live."

"Definitely not." Getting to her feet, Sadie started walking toward the inn's back door. "Let's go on in. You might be thinking that now is a *gut* time to lie down and let some strange man walk all over you, but I for one do not. I'm going to take over this problem of yours and fix it."

"Sadie, you can't. It might be in God's hands, but at the moment it's in the lawyer's hands, too."

Instead of grinning at her joke, her friend was treated to a pointed look. "Last time I checked, lawyers worked for their clients. We're going to see what all we can discover about your ditsy aunt, her ex-husband who suddenly realized he had an inn to give away, and a man named Eric who has suddenly decided he wants to run the Orange Blossom Inn." She rolled her eyes. "Though, who would want to compete with everything you've done, I surely don't know. Can he even bake?"

The irreverent question startled a chuckle out of Beverly. "I have no idea. I guess if he can't, he's going to have to hire someone."

"I wish him luck with that."

Feeling a bit like a lost puppy, Beverly followed Sadie inside. Sadie was right. That whole matter was in God's hands in the end. "No matter what happens, I want you to know that I appreciate your support."

Sadie pursed her lips. "You can thank me when it's all over. And then you can make me a coconut cake," she said as they entered the gathering room, where Ida and Jean were already setting up the afternoon tea.

Ida popped her head up. "Did you say you wanted a coconut cake?"

"Not today," Beverly said in a rush. "Sadie was simply making me a bet."

Then, luckily, the room started filling up with her guests and no less than four of her girlfriends. Eventually, she knew she was going to have to come to terms with the fact that her afternoons serving tea might one day be a thing of the past. And she might have to look for a new place to live.

But all that could be dealt with later.

At the moment, she needed to concentrate on the job at hand. She needed to make sure that her guests were happy, that there was enough tea, lemonade, and coffee, and that the cookie trays were filled.

Those were things she could do right now, and do well.

Chapter 17

The bus ride home from Siesta Key was way too short. As each minute passed, feeling like mere seconds, Zack did everything he could to make Leona want to see him again, and soon.

Every hour in her presence deepened his feelings for her, so much so that it caught him off guard. Never before had he been so certain that he'd found the right woman.

Now, unfortunately, he was fighting a whole new set of worries. Ones that had everything to do with the fact that she was going to head back to Ohio very soon. That meant he only had days to convince her that he was worth taking a chance on.

In an effort to keep such dark thoughts at bay, from the time they'd taken their seats on the bus, he'd talked to Leona about the beach, and Mattie and Danny, and her suspicions that a romance was blossoming between the two of them. He'd asked her questions about their attic room in the inn. Then they'd told each other a bit more about their families.

Through it all, Leona had been responsive and just as

chatty. And the way she gazed at him from time to time made him feel like everything he had to say was important.

He hoped he'd been able to convey that he felt the same way about her.

Only when the bus was just minutes from their stop did he dare ask her more about Edmund.

And that was when she'd visibly retreated. "I'd rather not talk about him anymore right now," she'd said.

In a normal relationship, Zack would have given her space. It wasn't in his nature to push people too much, especially when it came to discussing things that obviously made them uncomfortable.

But each time he saw her, he became more aware that their time together was winding down. And though he'd never been in a serious relationship, he sensed that it was necessary for her to open up to him. Otherwise, when she left, they'd have more lying between them than miles and miles—they'd have her secrets.

"Leona, I know this makes you uncomfortable, but I really do want to know more about Edmund and what went wrong."

"Why?"

"Because I like you," he said simply. If she trusted him enough to tell him about her breakup, he figured he should trust her enough to be completely honest.

She blinked, then to his surprise, she looked amused. "You do?"

He couldn't resist asking. "Does that amuse you?"

"*Nee.* Of course not." She looked down at her hands, swallowed, then seemed to come to a conclusion. "I like you, too, Zack."

He couldn't help but smile, though he was trying his best

not to look like a love-struck fool. "What are you going to do about Edmund?"

"Nothing."

"Really?"

She shrugged. "It's over. It really is."

"I can't help but wonder why you aren't fighting for him." He would have never thought she was the type of woman to drift in and out of a relationship so easily. Especially when they'd been engaged.

Looking down at her hands again, she asked, "Zack, have you ever been in love before?"

"I think so."

Humor lit her eyes. "What does that mean?"

It meant he was actually starting to have fairly strong feelings for Leona. He wasn't sure if it was love, but if it wasn't, it was surely something close to that. Whenever he was around her, he couldn't seem to concentrate on anything else.

More disconcerting was the realization that he didn't want to do anything *but* be around her.

Was that love? He wasn't sure. But if it was, he didn't want the feeling to end anytime soon . . . even if feeling this way made him feel off-balanced.

But of course he didn't dare speak *that* openly. "I'm fairly sure I've come kind of close to being in love."

She shrugged. "Maybe that was how I felt. Maybe I've been really close to love. Maybe I simply wanted to be in love and he was right there. And when I thought I was in love? It was strong and sure. I knew I was doing the right thing. Now that it's over, I feel almost as sure."

"I can't imagine falling out of love like that."

"I still feel like I'm at sea, but I do know that what happened on the phone last night was the right thing. And I have to guess that perhaps Edmund thought the same. Otherwise, why would he have broken up with me so easily?"

"I can't answer that."

"I don't feel sad, exactly. I just feel a little bit hollow. Like it's time I was filled up with something good. Something new."

He nodded just as the bus stopped and it was time for them to get out. Once they'd stepped off the bus, he said, "Do you know your way back to the inn? I'm sorry but I've got to get back to the house so I'll be there when Effie gets off the bus."

She pointed down the street. "I go down two blocks then turn left?"

"*Nee.*" Unable to help himself, he curved his hands around her slim shoulders. "You go this way," he said into her ear as he carefully turned her around. When she shivered, he gave in to temptation and let his hands drift down her back, following the path of her shoulder blades before dropping back to his sides. "Then you turn right," he finished, barely remembering what they were talking about in the first place.

"Okay." She bit her lip. "*Danke.* I'm sure I'll be fine."

Zack noticed that while she said all the right things, she didn't look all that convinced. He wasn't all that convinced, either.

Thinking quickly, he said, "Give me your hand." When she did, he pulled out a pen and wrote the cross streets of the Orange Blossom Inn on her hand. And then, just because he couldn't resist, he wrote down his home phone number, too.

She let him write on her palm, but she was looking at it like no one had ever done something so impetuous before. "The two streets I understand. But why are you giving me your phone number?"

"So you can call me if you want to see me again."

"I couldn't call you. That would be way too forward."

"Maybe you wouldn't call men at home in Walnut Creek. Maybe you would be perfectly happy to wait for the chance for the two of us to just happen to run into each other sometime, but we're not in Ohio, and we're on a time crunch here."

Her eyes brightened with amusement. "A time crunch, is it?"

"You know I'm right. Before we know it, you're going to be getting ready to go back home, and if we want to see each other again, one of us will have to take the bus. So, if you want, give me a call and let me know when you have some free time before you go."

"And you'll make time to see me?"

"Of course I will." The pull he felt toward her was so strong, Zack was pretty sure he'd drop everything in order to see her again, and soon. Even if it meant calling in Violet or Karl to help with Effie so he could make that happen.

She looked at her palm again, closed it into a fist, then started walking.

The wrong way.

He darted forward, rested both hands on her shoulders, and turned her around. "This way, Leona," he murmured. "Go four blocks up until you see the cross street, then turn right."

"Okay."

"Sure?" He really needed to go. But he really didn't want to spend the rest of his evening worrying about her wandering up and down the streets of Pinecraft.

"I'm sure." Giving him a tremulous smile, she murmured, "*Danke,* Zack. Today was . . . well, it was wonderful."

"Yeah," he said. "Now keep walking forward and then turn right."

She giggled.

And he thought about that giggle the whole time he ran home, making it to Effie's stop just in time to see the bus turn the corner and pull forward.

That's when he decided he and Effie were going to have to take a walk in about an hour.

Just to make sure Leona had made it back safely.

SARA WAS SITTING on a wicker chair on the front porch of the Orange Blossom Inn when Leona walked up. Before Sara saw her, Leona peeked once again at her palm and gave thanks that Zack had seen fit to write the cross streets on her palm. She'd made it, no problem. But that didn't mean she hadn't checked and double-checked several times, just to be on the safe side.

What she should have been doing was reminding herself to try to get better at following directions, but the truth was she was hopelessly navigationally challenged. She was always getting lost or turned around. It had annoyed Edmund something terrible. He'd even accused her of getting lost deliberately, out of some misguided need for attention.

She'd been so embarrassed by his statement that she hadn't bothered to correct him.

Leona knew that she didn't get lost on purpose. That definitely wasn't the case at all. She'd just been that way all her life. No matter how hard she tried to remember the right way to things, nine times out of ten, she would become sidetracked and get lost.

Her mother had a whole cupboard of stories about how Leona had gotten lost in stores, restaurants, just about anywhere. But neither of her parents had ever gotten mad at her about it. They knew she lived much of her life with her head in the clouds and there wasn't much she could do about that.

Now she simply closed her palm around Zack's writing and held it tight. Even if she never saw Zack again, she knew she'd always remember that moment when he'd written the streets and his phone number on her palm. It had been a sweet gesture. Cute, even.

She wondered how long she could keep that ink on her hand without anyone else seeing it.

Actually, she was wondering if she was going to give in to temptation, write his phone number on a sheet of paper, and actually call him.

That was doubtful.

"Leona, are you going to stand there staring at your palm, or are you going to come up the steps anytime soon?" Sara called out.

Leona popped her head up. "Oh. *Jah.* Of course." Closing her palm again, she trotted up the stairs and took a chair next to Sara.

"What's wrong with your hand?"

"Hmm? Nothing. Why?"

"I thought maybe you got a blister or a splinter or something."

"*Nee.* No blisters." Taking care to keep her hand in a fist, she tried to shrug it off. "You know me, always daydreaming about something."

"Well, that is true." Looking at the front of the house, she said, "Where's Mattie? Did she grab an ice cream cone?"

"She is still at Siesta Key."

Sara set her library book on the small wicker table between their chairs. "You left her there?"

"Of course I didn't *leave* her. We simply met up with a couple of Zack's friends and she wanted to stay behind. I left because Zack had to go home to watch over his sister."

"I can't believe you left her there alone. What if those kids aren't nice?"

"I promise, they're plenty nice."

"But—"

"Sara, it's all right. She's with Danny. Remember we met him the other night? In front of the church?"

Sara scowled. "He's still a stranger."

"Not anymore. We all spent the day together. I think she kind of likes him, too." Feeling the worry and tension rolling off Sara, she reached out and squeezed her hand. "You should have come with us."

Sara shook her head. "There was no reason."

"Sara, we were at the beach. There are signs everywhere saying it's the best beach in the whole country. You should have felt the sand, it was super soft. You'll be glad you went next time."

"Next time? Does that mean you're planning to return to Siesta Key?"

"Of course. It's a beautiful beach. Don't you want to go?"

"I don't know."

"Sara, I thought you didn't want to go with us today because you were ready to spend a quiet day with yourself. I understood that; each of us needs some time to ourselves, I think." She paused, debated whether to speak her mind, then decided she had nothing to lose. "Now, however, I'm starting to think that maybe there was another reason. Are you mad at me?"

"Of course not."

"Truth?"

Sara glanced at Leona again, her light brown eyes looking troubled. "I'm not mad at you. But I have to admit that I'm pretty troubled by the fact that you could break up with Edmund one night and go to the beach with Zack the next morning."

"You know it wasn't like that. I've been really stressed out about all of this. I never intended for Edmund and I to break up."

She slumped. "I know. It's just, well, I'm sure everyone at home is in an uproar."

Sara's mother was Leona's mother's older sister. And though Leona loved her Aunt Jo a lot, she would be lying if she were to say that she thought Aunt Jo was as easygoing as her own mother.

She had a feeling that as soon as word got around Walnut Creek about what had happened between her and Edmund—no doubt taking about two hours, at the most—Sara's mother would have something to say about it.

"Sara, I already talked to my mother. My *mamm* didn't sound all that surprised. Actually, I think she might even have been a little relieved."

"And your *daed*?"

"She said she'd talked to him, but Mamm assumed he'd feel the same way. I did promise to pay them back." With a sigh, she added, "I'm sure my mother has probably gotten an earful from Naomi and Rosanna, too. I called them after I got off the phone with my mother."

"What do you think they told her?"

"There's no telling. Neither of them seemed terribly upset or surprised, but we didn't talk very long. They might be waiting to lecture me when I get home. Or they'll write me some long letters."

Sara treated Leona to a weak smile. "At least they didn't yell at you on the phone."

"At least." Well, Leona was pretty sure that Naomi and Kevin, her husband, were going to be pretty relieved, too. Kevin hadn't been afraid to let everyone know that he wasn't too thrilled about Edmund being his future brother-in-law. Kevin was definitely a man's man. He liked to chop wood. He liked to fix things himself. He was an easygoing, even-natured kind of person.

Edmund was none of those things.

Naomi, on the other hand, had been concerned when Leona had never seemed anxious to be alone with her fiancé.

As for her other sister, Rosanna? Well, Rosanna would no doubt simply shake her head in mild frustration. She'd always thought Leona was flighty and more than a bit impulsive.

But that said, even Rosanna had come over after Leona announced her engagement. She'd poured them both big mugs of hot tea and then proceeded to ask Leona all sorts of questions about her relationship with Edmund. Now that everything with Edmund was over, Leona remembered how concerned Rosanna had been about Edmund's opinions on marriage. Edmund had been fairly vocal about how Leona was expected to always follow his advice and directives.

"My *mamm* is surprised," Sara blurted. "I called her today."

"Oh? What did she say?"

"About what you would think. That maybe you've let the sunshine and palm trees get to your head a little bit."

Leona was a little hurt by that remark. "How did you respond to that?"

For the first time, Sara looked a little embarrassed. "I told her it was fairly obvious that you and Edmund weren't a *gut* match." Reaching out, she clasped Leona's hand. "I meant what I said last night, Le. I always am on your side."

"I really did try to make it work, Sara. I wanted to be happy with Edmund. At first, I thought I really could be."

"I know you did. And I'm sorry I sounded so judgmental. It's just that I don't understand what you are doing here in Sarasota with Zack. Are you sowing wild oats or something?"

"I'm simply having fun."

"But why reach out to a man like Zack?"

"Why wouldn't I want to reach out to a man like him? He's pretty wonderful."

"He also lives in Pinecraft. Nothing can come of you two becoming close."

"You don't know what the Lord has in store for us," Leona reminded her cousin. "I tell you what, I'm glad we're talking, and you're feeling free to be so honest. I really am glad about that. But I hope you aren't planning to be mad at me for the rest of our trip."

Immediately, Sara looked ashamed. "I'm not." Then she whispered, "I think I'm jealous."

Leona was stunned. "Jealous of what?"

"Of you."

"Me? Oh, come on, Sara. My life is obviously a mess."

"*Nee,* I'm serious. People like you, Le. They always have."

"They like you, too."

"I know. But they don't gravitate toward me like they do to you. Listen, girls always want to be your friend. And boys, well, they always think you're cute. Your parents only want your happiness. The first night here, why even a cat ran to you! You had a perfectly good fiancé and you were willing to risk that relationship . . . and here you're already thinking about a new boy. It's never been that way for me."

Leona knew it hadn't. Sara was reserved and smart. Really smart. Because of that, she didn't always have patience for schoolgirl silliness or grown-woman silliness, either.

But she was pretty, too. While Leona's blond hair, brown eyes, and average figure made her look like everyone's next-door neighbor, Sara was pretty in a way that made people look at her twice. Her hair was dark, almost black, and she had light blue eyes, creamy skin, and a delicate frame. Leona and Mattie used to tease Sara, saying she looked like one of the girls on the covers of the Amish romances.

They'd thought it was a great compliment.

Sara had not.

"Sara, you are really pretty and really smart. I've seen many a man look like he was preparing himself to talk to you, then chickening out."

"Why would they chicken out?"

"Because if they said something dumb, there was a mighty *gut* chance that you would look at them like they were foolish."

"I don't do that." Her voice was full of protest, but there was a high note at the end of it, which led Leona to believe that Sara knew exactly what she was talking about.

Deciding that they should definitely be done with this conversation, Leona chuckled. "Can we go inside now and eat a scone or something? I'm starving."

Sara grabbed her arm. "They have lemon meringue tarts."

Leona groaned. "I love it here. I could move in here," she said as they walked through the front door.

"If there was a chance that I'd eat food like this at every meal, I could, too," Sara said with a laugh. "Of course, I'd probably be as big as a whale."

After Leona ran to her room to get cleaned up, she felt light on her feet again.

At least it looked like things with Sara had been smoothed over. Now all she had to do was figure out what to do with the ink on her hand. She was pretty sure Sara wasn't going to think it was adorable.

Actually, she was very sure about that.

Chapter 18

Danny knocked on Zack's front door at a quarter to seven. The moment Zack opened it, Danny strode in, his expression serious.

"Zack, we have to talk about something."

"You look so serious, I guess we do," he replied as he led the way into the kitchen. "We're going to have to talk in here, though. I was helping Effie with her homework and we're not finished yet."

"Hey, Ef," Danny said, plopping down in a chair next to her. "What are you working on?"

She frowned. "Long division."

"Ugh."

"I'm not real fond of it, either, but I'm getting better at it. Plus, I'm almost done." Looking Zack's way, she said, "You know, I can finish my problems on my own. You don't need to sit with me."

"Nope. I promised Daed that I'd double-check your answers."

She sighed and started scribbling on her paper again.

After sharing a commiserating look with Danny, Zack motioned toward the back porch. "Let's sit out here."

"Perfect," Danny said.

Before he joined his friend, Zack said to Effie, "Bring me your paper when you're done."

"But—"

"Don't argue. I told you I wanted to do something tonight, which means we've got to get your homework done first."

"What do you want to do?" Danny asked from his seat outside on the patio.

"He wants to go see Leona," Effie called out before Zack could answer. "Even though they saw each other at the beach today."

Zack said nothing, wishing he'd acted just a little bit more reserved the first few minutes after Effie had gotten off the bus. Instead of keeping his thoughts to himself, he'd been practically grinning like a fool when he'd said hello to Effie.

Now he was going to hear about how foolish he was acting from his best friend.

But instead of bursting out in laughter, Danny looked relieved.

"Effie, do your homework," Zack said, before leading the way outside.

After the door closed, Danny said, "I don't know how you do it, looking after your sister all the time."

"She's a good kid. It's not hard."

"She's great. And she's tough, too. I read up on Perthes disease once and the books said it can be really painful. But she never complains."

"She never complains about her legs and hips. About long division and her spelling words? She complains a lot."

Danny grinned.

"So what brought you over here? We saw each other at the beach today, too."

"I wanted to talk to you about Leona's friend Mattie."

"What about her?"

"I think I really like her. When I walked her back to the Orange Blossom Inn, it felt like we'd only been together an hour instead of all day. I actually told her I wanted to see her again soon."

"Oh. That's all?"

"'That's all?' Ah, Zack, Mattie lives in Ohio."

"Believe me, I know exactly how you're feeling. I feel the same way about Leona."

"Are you two serious?"

"Of course not. I mean, we just met." However, it was becoming pretty obvious to him that he already was serious about her. His heart didn't especially seem to care that falling in love with a recently engaged girl who lived almost a thousand miles away was a really bad idea.

Danny kept staring, looking skeptical. "So are you going to tell me the truth, now? I've never seen you act this way about any woman. Are you two serious?"

Zack squirmed under his scrutiny and realized that he was going to have to be completely honest. "We could be."

Danny nodded. "*Gut.*"

"*Gut?* This isn't *gut*. I have responsibilities here."

"Maybe she'll want to live here. Or maybe you'll want to leave some of those responsibilities and think about moving to Ohio."

"I couldn't do that."

"Zack, I'm not trying to kick you out of my life, but what, really, is keeping you here?"

"My sister, this family. I have obligations."

"Everyone *is* leaning on you, but I can promise that your parents didn't decide to have four children so one of you could take care of everything." Lowering his voice, he said, "It's time, Zack. It's time to realize that you can't live your life by putting everything you want on hold. Not even Effie would want you to do that."

"What would I not want you to do?" Effie asked from the doorway, startling them both.

Danny kept his back to Effie but closed his eyes in silent mortification as Zack got to his feet. "Nothing. Danny and I were just talking."

She stepped forward. "Are you talking about you having to live here?"

"We were just talking," Zack replied. "You shouldn't have been eavesdropping. Everything that happens in this house isn't your business."

Hurt shone in her eyes. "I wasn't eavesdropping. I was coming out here to tell you that I finished my math problems."

"Okay." He held out a hand. "Give your paper to me and I'll look over it in a minute."

"You know, it's okay if you don't look it over, Zack," she replied. "I never asked you to give up your life for me. I can't believe you're using me as an excuse to keep from doing what you want."

Zack could feel the muscles in his jaw jump. "We'll talk about this later, Effie."

But instead of answering, she turned and walked to her room. And though her steps were stiff and ungainly, Zack couldn't help but notice that she was pretty steady on her feet.

When she was out of sight, he sighed. "Great."

Danny looked behind him. "How about I go talk to her?"

"No. I've got this."

Danny shook his head slowly. "You know what? I don't think you do. Let me go talk to her. I have four sisters, remember? I won't mess this up."

Because he was suddenly tired—really tired—Zack nodded. "Fine. Go ahead." Then he sat down as Danny strode inside, walked down the hall, and knocked on Effie's door.

When he heard his sister let him in, Zack thrust out his legs and tilted his head back.

It looked like he was going to need to stay home instead of visit Leona. Once again, he needed to put his family first and his wants second.

He loved his family. Helping out when he could was the right thing to do. But at the moment, he wished doing the right thing wasn't so hard.

"HEY," DANNY SAID as he walked into Effie's room. After scanning the room and pausing for a moment on her, he leaned back against the wall next to the open door. "You mad at me?"

"*Nee.*"

"A little bit?"

"*Nee.*"

"Then why are you crying?"

"Because I didn't ask for my legs to get some disease. And I never asked for my brother to give up everything in order to take care of me."

"I think everyone knows that."

Now Effie felt like she'd not only been a lot of trouble, but a whiny brat, too. Swiping at her eyes with the side of a fist, she sat up on the bed. "Danny, am I really the reason Zack doesn't have a girlfriend?"

"I don't think he's ever had a serious girlfriend because, until recently, no girl has ever interested him."

"He really likes Leona."

Danny nodded. "I think so. But that isn't why I came in here to talk to you." He sighed. "I'm sorry about what you overheard, but the problem isn't you. It's your brother. He's the type of guy who really likes being needed, but he's also the type of person who doesn't seem to mind being in a rut. For some reason, he likes putting himself second." He rolled his eyes. "Or third. Or fourth. I was kind of trying to encourage him to start taking chances."

"Do you think it worked?"

"I don't know. But I do know that I'd feel really bad if I hurt your feelings. You're a sweet girl, Effie."

"*Danke,* Danny. I'm fine. And I think you did the right thing. Zack doesn't do much for himself."

Her brother's best friend stared hard at her for another long moment, then at last nodded. "*Gut.*"

When he walked out, Effie examined her legs and thought about everything that had been happening lately.

It seemed that Zack wasn't the only person in the family in a rut. She'd been in one, too. It was time to reach out a little more, to not assume that she couldn't change her life, or change the way people viewed her.

Effie vowed to have a talk with her mother when she got home. She was going to remind her that she was twelve and more than old enough to have her fair share of chores and responsibilities. It was time for her to start standing on her own two feet. She should be able to do that—she had some really good braces on her legs, after all.

Chapter 19

I hereby proclaim today 'Do Nothing in Pinecraft Day,'" Mattie called out from her bed. "I'm exhausted."

Turning over onto her side, Leona gazed through the sheer curtains that covered the window. When she noticed that raindrops were steadily sprinkling the glass, she said, "Since it's raining, I think that's a *wonderful-gut* idea."

"We'll need to find lunch, though," Sara said, "since we slept through breakfast. I'm starving."

"You should've eaten last night," Mattie chided.

"You were eating pizza at almost midnight. That was a recipe for a stomach ache."

"Not for me," Mattie muttered. "I thought it tasted great, and I'm not hungry."

Leona flipped over on her back and closed her eyes, happy to let her girlfriends' bickering float over her.

They'd been in Pinecraft now for over a week. They only had five more days, then they were going to have to pack up, get on the bus, and leave sunny Florida.

The idea of leaving felt almost painful, and the truth was that she didn't want to go. She didn't want to leave this inn, or the happy times she'd shared with Sara and Mattie.

Most of all, she didn't want to leave Zachary Kaufmann. Opening her palm, she stared at his phone number before making a fist again. So far, neither Sara nor Mattie had spied Zack's writing on her hand. That was good, because it had been written in a permanent marker and was likely to be there for a while.

Kind of like Zack's impression on her heart, she realized, somewhat dreamily. Even if she tried to get rid of him, it was going to take a lot of work to erase him from her life.

"Leona, you're ignoring us," Mattie said. "Are you seriously trying to get back to sleep?"

"*Nee.*"

"I know what Leona's doing," Sara said to Mattie. "She's thinking about Zack."

Leona couldn't deny it, though she didn't particularly want to talk about just how often Zack occupied her mind, either. "I'm not thinking about anything," she lied.

"Come on, Le. We all know that you're thinking about a certain brown-haired, blue-eyed man with mighty appealing dimples. What are you going to do about him?" Sara asked.

Leona stretched before propping herself up on her elbows. "I don't know."

"Has he acted like he doesn't want you to leave?"

"He hasn't said as much, but I wouldn't expect him to. It's not like there's anything I could do about it even if he asked me to stay here every hour," she admitted. "No matter what happens in Pinecraft, we're going to be getting on that bus in just a couple of days."

"Well, I don't want to. And Danny doesn't want me to go,

either," Mattie said. Preening a bit, she added, "Unlike his friend Zack, he hasn't been shy about telling me his feelings."

"Oh, brother," Sara groaned.

Leona grinned. "I'm glad about that. You deserve to be happy, Mattie."

"You do, too."

"I am happy."

"You don't look all that happy. Actually, you look pretty tired," Sara quipped. "I've never seen you so eager to laze about, Leona."

"There's nothing wrong with being lazy," Leona protested. "And I'm happy enough. For sure. I just happen to be a lot more sleepy." She was also content to sit quietly and recall every moment she'd spent in Zack's company. The way he'd made her laugh. The way his attention made her feel like she was the only girl in the world.

Mattie merely smiled. "You look smitten, that's what you look like."

"Takes one to know one," Leona retorted.

Two raps at their door interrupted their laughter. "Girls, excuse me, but I think I need to talk to you."

"That's Miss Beverly's voice," Sara whispered. "Just a minute," she called out as all three of them grabbed their robes and threw them on over their T-shirts and pajama bottoms.

When they were all decent, Sara opened the door. "Is anything wrong?" she asked. "Were we too loud?"

"Loud? Oh, goodness, no," Miss Beverly said as she stepped just inside the door. "But, uh, I've just returned from meeting this morning's Pioneer Trails bus."

"Yes?" Mattie asked, her puzzled tone pretty much conveying the other girls' feelings.

Looking like she was preparing for battle, Beverly turned to Leona. "Dear, it seems you have a visitor."

"We aren't expecting anyone," Leona said.

"I don't know if you're expecting him or not, but this man, ah, sure seems intent on seeing you, Leona. It's put me in a little bit of a quandary. I have an extra room, but I'm not sure if you want him here. And it might be a bit awkward . . ." Her voice drifted off as she looked over her shoulder toward the stairwell, almost as if she were afraid the visitor was behind her.

A horrible, dark feeling of foreboding hit Leona hard. "Did he happen to tell you his name?"

Miss Beverly rocked back on her heels. "He did. His name is Edmund. Do you know him?"

"*Jah*. He is the man I told you about. My, uh, former fiancé."

Mattie groaned as she started scurrying around the room, gathering her clothes. "I canna even believe that my *bruder* is here. He has a lot of nerve showing up unannounced."

Beverly's look of bemusement turned to confusion. "I didn't know he was your fiancé."

"Edmund is my former fiancé," Leona bit out. "We recently broke up." Inwardly, she winced. She hated how flighty and uncaring she sounded, but another part of her felt more than justified in not sharing anything else. She already had her family, Edmund, her girlfriends, and the Lord to hold her accountable. At the moment, trying to appease Miss Beverly as well felt like too much.

The innkeeper shook her head in confusion. "Your former fiancé is also Mattie's brother. Boy, talk about an uncomfortable situation."

"You don't know the half of it," Sara muttered.

"All I do know is that he came off the bus looking for the inn and seemed mighty happy to follow me here once I told him that I managed it." She bit her lip. "Girls, I'm sorry if you didn't want to see him, but I really didn't feel like I had much choice."

Mattie replied to that one. "No, of course, you didn't. We'll take care of Edmund."

"I don't know how." Leona, who had been standing, walked to her twin bed and sat down. "I can't even believe he came here. Mattie, Edmund doesn't even like going to the Walmart in Millersburg because he thinks it's too far. He always goes to Graber's in Sugarcreek."

Mattie shrugged. "Graber's is a *gut* store. The best around. Everyone knows that. But you're right, Le. My brother, well, he ain't the best traveler. He's kind of a homebody."

Beverly's expression cleared. Obviously, she was beginning to understand a whole lot more about Leona and Edmund's relationship. "Well, since Edmund isn't the greatest of travelers, I think I had better get down there and make sure he's all right. I would hate for him to think that I forgot about him." After a pause, she added, "Girls, Edmund does need a place to stay. Do you want me to offer him the small room that just became available this morning?"

Edmund sleeping downstairs? Leona couldn't think of anything worse. "*Nee,*" she blurted, just as the other two girls practically shouted the same thing. Well, at least they were in agreement about that.

"Tell him I'll be down in ten minutes," Mattie said as she walked to their small closet. "He won't like waiting, but that's okay."

Eyes dancing, Miss Beverly nodded. "I'll do that. Girls, you all look pretty sleepy. Would you like me to make you a fresh pot of coffee?"

"Oh, yes, please," Sara said. "We're going to need gallons of coffee to get through this morning."

"That and a lot of prayer," Leona murmured after Beverly closed the door behind her. "I cannot even believe Edmund is here." She felt both irritated and betrayed.

"My brother just keeps getting more and more difficult," Mattie called from inside the closet. "Don't you worry, Leona. I'm going to take care of this."

Grabbing a pretty pink dress from a hook on the wall, Leona shook her head. "It's all right, Mattie. I need to talk to him. I don't know why he thought he needed to come to Pinecraft, but I intend to find out myself."

"We better hurry, then," Sara said. "I need *kaffi* and lots of it. And then I need some food. And if I know your brother, Mattie, Edmund is going to be in a bad mood if we three keep him waiting for much longer."

As Leona darted into the bathroom, she knew that Sara was exactly right. Edmund never had liked waiting.

But as she hurried to put on her fresh dress, she decided that she was only hurrying for Sara's sake.

As far as she was concerned, Edmund could wait all day for them. She was through putting his wants ahead of her own.

"NEVER THOUGHT OF calling a family meeting this early in the morning, Zack," Violet said as she walked out onto their parents' back patio with a carafe of hot coffee in her hands.

Looking at Karl, Effie, and their parents, Zack shrugged. "Not my fault that everyone's schedule is so busy. This was the only time everyone could meet."

Before Violet could dispute that, their mother started passing out cereal bowls. "We're on a time crunch, *kinner*. Pour some cereal and milk and start eating while Zack shares what's on his mind."

Immediately, Karl poured some cereal into his bowl and Effie's, added milk, then stared hard at Zack. "Anytime now, little brother."

"Well, it's like this. I think there's something special happening between Leona and me."

Effie clapped her hands. "I knew it! Every time I've seen you talk to her, you've looked really happy. And she has, too."

Violet put down her spoon. "I'm happy for you, too, Zack. I really am. But why did we all have to be together to hear this?"

"Because she's only going to be here for a few more days. And since that's the case, I want to be able to see her."

His father frowned. "I'm still not following you. You are far too old to be asking for permission to date."

"I know that." He took a deep breath and said a quick prayer to the Lord to help him find the right words to keep from hurting Effie's feelings. "What I'm trying to say is that I need more time to see her. Time to myself."

Effie looked down into her cereal bowl. "You mean time without me."

"I love being with you, Effie. But—"

"But you would like to have some time to yourself," his mother said quietly.

"And with Leona, *jah*?" Karl added with a small smile.

"*Jah*." That was exactly right. He wanted to spend time with Leona. She was becoming important to him.

She was *already* important to him.

Zack knew that even if she wasn't ready to start a new relationship now, he would be willing to wait. He'd waited this long to find someone that he was willing to risk everything for. He knew waiting another few months would be nothing to him.

As long as they both knew that they were going to eventually be together.

He didn't really care whether their relationship was in Ohio or Florida, either. If she didn't want to leave her family and only wanted to live near them, he now realized they could all work together to make that possible. He was starting to realize that he didn't always have to be the one to shoulder his sister's needs.

After waiting a few seconds, and not hearing anyone argue with him, he said, "I'm sorry."

But instead of accepting his apology, Violet, Karl, and even Effie started chuckling. Why, even his parents looked amused.

"What's so funny?"

"You are, Zack!" Violet exclaimed. "For months, we've all been trying to hint that you didn't have to do everything."

"Even I've been telling that to ya," Effie said.

"I brought this up to you just a few days ago, son," his mother chided. "Don't you remember?"

"I remember."

Grabbing the cereal box, his father poured a second helping into his bowl. "All we need to do is make some changes to our schedules. It's *gut* that you brought us all together, Zack. In a minute, I'll get out my calendar and see what I can do."

"And, Mamm and Daed, this means that you are going to have to remember that I'm still a part of the family," Violet said quietly.

Looking hurt, Mamm curved her hands around her mug. "I've never forgotten, daughter."

"Then let me help out. I know you're disappointed that I didn't want to be baptized Amish. I understand that you aren't pleased that Henry is Mennonite. But he's a *gut* man, and *wonderful-gut* boyfriend. Please stop acting like I don't want to be with all of you or do my part."

Mamm and Daed stared at her in shock before their mother jumped to her feet and gave Violet a hug. "I'm sorry, dear. I didn't realize you felt that we'd shut you out. You know we love you."

"I love you all, too." Smiling at her sister, Violet said, "So, that means I'm going to get to spend more time with Effie now, right? She's my baby sister, too, you know."

"And mine," Karl added. "Look, I know I'm busy, but that doesn't mean I'm too busy to pick up Effie once or twice a week. Or help her with her physical therapy. I can also help around the house. Even I can run a cloth over furniture or wash dishes or help in the garden. I can do that."

"*Danke,*" Daed said.

"I'm going to talk to the principal at school, too," Mamm said. "I'm going to ask to get off ninety minutes earlier every day. It shouldn't be a problem since I'm only supposed to help run copies and such."

Zack sighed. "Thanks, Mamm. *Danke,* everyone. I'm really glad we talked."

"Wait a minute," Effie blurted. "I haven't said my part yet."

"And what do you have to say, little sister?" Karl teased.

"Well, I just want to point out to everyone that I am twelve years old. I don't have to be watched over like I'm a small child."

"That is true, but it's your legs I worry about," Mamm reminded her. "Plus, sometimes you get too tired."

"If I get tired, I'll sit down. Or I'll trip," she said with a shrug. "It won't be the end of the world. I'm going to have this disease the rest of my life. I need to manage it, and the physical therapists say I'm doing pretty *gut* with it, too. You need to let me be more independent."

Their father pursed his lips. "Watch your mouth, Effie. You are sounding a bit too full of yourself."

To Zack's surprise, it was Violet who became the voice of reason. "Boy, I seem to remember being told the very same thing when I was twelve," she murmured before looking her parents in the eye. "And when I was that age, I looked after Effie."

Effie looked triumphant. "See? I am old enough."

"Give us a little bit of time to get used to that idea, Effie, but I do see your point," their father said. "We'll start giving you more freedom. But for the present, we need to think about Zachary. It's time we let him have a bit of freedom of his own."

"I don't know if freedom is what I'm looking for," Zack protested.

Violet chuckled. "I don't think you need more freedom at all."

Their mother turned to her in surprise. "But, Violet, we just agreed to step in for Zack."

"Oh, I'm not disputing that," Violet replied with a mischievous look. "I'm simply pointing out that Zachariah isn't really looking for 'freedom.' Instead, I think he's going to be looking for a certain brown-eyed, blond-haired girl."

When everyone started laughing, even Effie, Zack felt his cheeks heat. "I'm out of here," he said over his shoulder. "I've got some things to do."

"Oh, I bet you do," Karl quipped as Zack walked out the door.

Only when he was well and completely alone did Zack smile. His siblings were irritating, but they also had been right. He did have some things to do, and they all happened to revolve around Leona.

Chapter 20

It took a bit of convincing, but Leona persuaded Mattie and Sara to let her go downstairs to greet Edmund by herself.

"Just give me fifteen minutes, then you two can come down and join us," she'd said, trying her best to look far more optimistic about the upcoming meeting than she had felt. The truth was she'd felt a little sick.

Mattie hadn't been for it. At all. "Leona, he is my *bruder*. I know how he's going to be feeling, and it ain't going to be *gut*."

"It will be fine." Hopefully, she'd thought.

While Sara had looked extremely skeptical, Mattie simply shook her head. "I think it would be a good idea if we both talked to Edmund, at least at first. He's going to be on a mission to talk some sense into you. When he gets that way, it can be a bit overwhelming."

"Believe me, I know how he gets. Don't forget that I've known him for quite a while and have had many conversations with him, including breaking up over the phone. Right now I think I can handle just about anything he throws me," Leona replied, almost proud of herself for holding firm. Actually, she was mighty sure that every word Mattie had said was true; she wasn't looking forward to being lectured by Edmund.

But there were some things a person had to do herself, and this was one of them. "Mattie, I know you are his sister. But no matter how close you two are, I'm pretty sure he came all the way to Pinecraft in order to talk to me. I need to give him that chance."

"Leona has a point," Sara had said.

"All right, but I'll be watching the clock," Mattie grumbled.

"Watch all you want," Leona had replied.

Now, as she walked into the gathering room and saw his back to her, recognized the way he held himself, noticed that he was wearing his favorite blue shirt—the one she'd sewn for him as a birthday gift—Leona was scared to death.

"Edmund?" she whispered.

He turned around immediately. Examined her from top to bottom. She might have thought his close inspection would've made her feel a bit more attractive. Or maybe that he had been so anxious, he would have wanted to make sure that she was all right.

But instead, it felt vaguely like he was inspecting her for flaws.

"You are getting a tan."

She nodded. "*Jah*. I am."

"Must have been from your day at the beach."

Though she felt herself getting defensive, she tried to push through it. "Perhaps." Then, when he stayed where he was, merely looking at her intently but not offering any more hints about why he had come, she knew she was going to have to take the first step.

"Why are you here?"

"We needed to speak, Leona. Obviously."

"You could have simply called."

"I didn't have your phone number."

"You could have gotten the inn's number from your parents or my folks."

"I didn't want to talk to you on the phone." He sat down on the sofa, his long-sleeve blue shirt, dark pants, and heavy boots looking completely out of place in the bright and airy room. "May we speak now? Or would you rather we went somewhere more private?"

There was no way on earth she was going to go anywhere with him. Plus, he didn't realize it, but his sister and her cousin were just minutes away from joining them. "Here is fine." She sat down beside him.

After a generous exhalation, he blurted, "When we got off the phone the other night, I was pretty angry."

"I know you were."

"Leona, you played me for a fool. And no matter what you said about wanting to make friends in Florida and such, we both know that you should have never, ever considered accepting that man's invitation to go to the beach."

"I know how it must have made you feel."

"*Nee,* you have no idea. I felt betrayed. I was hurt, too." He ran a hand through his brown wavy hair. "But now that some time has passed, I've decided to forgive you. If you promise to never do such a thing again, if you vow to never act so impulsively, I will forgive you and we can be engaged again."

Leona felt a lump lodge in her throat, but she wasn't sure whether it was dismay that he could still think she'd want him back, or that she'd been mere months away from living with such a man for the rest of her life.

What she knew, without a doubt, was that if she still loved him, *nee,* if she had *always, truly* loved him, she would have agreed to his request right away. She would have promised to never accept another invitation because she wouldn't have ever wanted to be around another man besides him for the rest of her life.

But, in that moment, there was no way on earth she was going to put up with such a statement.

"Edmund, you were mad enough at me to break things off on the phone."

"You caught me off guard."

"I did? Is that why you didn't want to hear my explanations?"

"I told you, Leona. I have now changed my mind."

"Well, so have I. I've decided that I'm mighty glad this happened." When his head popped up, she felt a little bad, but she soldiered on. "I am grateful that we are no longer engaged. Obviously, God has been working overtime with us. He brought me here, He encouraged me to have new ideas. Marrying each other would have been a terrible mistake."

"What happened with that man at the beach?"

"Nothing." Then, remembering how she hadn't wanted to leave Zack's side, she amended her words. "I mean, nothing really. But I would be lying if I said that he doesn't mean anything to me."

"Leona, I came all the way down here on the bus to make things right."

To him "making things right" meant her giving in. Again. Yet again, he'd ignored everything she had told him and instead concentrated on only what he wanted to hear. That realization made her frustrated and sad and confused.

Why had she ever thought he was the man for her, anyway?

She was saved from coming up with a satisfactory comment when Sara and Mattie came barging into the room.

Leona turned to them, relieved. "Oh! Look who is here," she chirped.

"Edmund," Sara said graciously. "It's nice to see you here in Sarasota."

He got to his feet. "*Jah.*"

Mattie, on the other hand, was looking at Leona, asking her without words how it had been going.

Since it hadn't been going well at all, Leona tried to express just how frustrating the conversation had been through her eyes.

When Mattie's eyebrows rose and Sara visibly winced, Leona figured she'd done a pretty good job of that.

"Mattie, you are looking well," Edmund said.

"*Danke,*" Mattie said as she walked across the room and gave him a hug. "What a nice surprise to see my brother. We'll have to have a nice chat about why you are here. Unannounced and uninvited."

Edmund's eyes narrowed. "Mattie, now isn't a *gut* time."

"Sure it is." Looping her arm through his, she gave a little tug. "I'm starving, and we need to find you a place to stay. How long are you staying in Sarasota?"

"Only until the bus leaves tomorrow."

"That means we'll have to take you to Yoder's right now," Mattie said, just as if they were on the verge of an emergency.

"Goodness, yes," Sara said with a nod. "I'll join you. We'll give you a tour around Pinecraft, too. We're practically experts on the area now."

"I'm not here to see Pinecraft," Edmund said. "I came to talk to Leona."

"We've already talked," Leona blurted.

He turned to her. "Leona, you mustn't be so stubborn."

"I think I must."

Just as Mattie and Sara looked like they were tempted to yank Edmund out to the front porch, Miss Beverly entered the room. "I'm sorry to interrupt, but you have another visitor, Leona," she said, looking a bit apprehensive.

Leona gaped at the man behind the innkeeper. "Zack?"

"*Gut matin,* Leona. Sara. Mattie."

"Hi, Zack," Mattie replied. She stepped forward and not-very-subtly looked just beyond him. "Are you alone or is Danny here?"

Edmund's eyebrows rose. "Danny?"

"Zack's friend," Mattie supplied under her breath. "And mine."

"Yours?" Edmund blurted.

"I'm sorry, but I had to come alone," Zack said to Mattie. "Danny's working."

Mattie frowned. "That's too bad."

Zack's lips twitched. "*Jah.*"

Edmund crossed his arms over his chest. "What is going on?"

Zack looked from Leona to Edmund and back. "I hope I'm not intruding. It's just that, well, I remembered telling you how good the fruit was at Yoder's Market. So I picked you up a couple of pieces."

Leona couldn't have stayed on the other side of the room from him if she'd tried. "This is so nice of you."

"It was nothing." He smiled at her, then looked at Edmund again. "Zachary Kaufmann," he said, holding out his hand.

"Edmund Miller. I'm Leona's fiancé."

Zack's look of amusement faded. "Leona, I thought you two were through?"

"We are," Leona said.

"Have you already gotten back together?"

The expression on Zack's face mirrored the moment of panic she'd just felt in her stomach. "*Nee*, Zack," she said gently. "Although I feel mighty bad about how things happened, Edmund and I are no longer engaged."

"Then why did he say such a thing?"

"It's a mystery," Leona said, "because we definitely broke up."

"But he still came down here?" Zack asked. He was staring at her intently. As if they were the only two people in the room.

"It seems so." Her words were tart, but Leona knew what Zack meant. There was no way one could ever describe the twenty-hour bus ride to Pinecraft as something one did in the spur of the moment. The trip was long and it wasn't exactly inexpensive, either.

"You really had no idea—"

Edmund, however, didn't appreciate being ignored. "Leona," he interrupted loudly, "we still need to talk."

She glared at him. "We do not." Then she stepped closer to Zack and lowered her voice, almost to a whisper. "I promise, I didn't know Edmund was going to come here."

"I hope not." For once, there wasn't a bit of humor in Zack's expression. Instead, his gaze was serious, his posture protective, making her feel warm.

Making everything between them seem a little more sincere, a little more intent. Leona had the feeling if they'd been alone, Zack would have pulled her into his arms by now. She would have also stepped into those arms willingly.

"Leona," Edmund's voice was louder now. "You are being rude."

"*Nee. Nee*, I don't think so." Taking a deep breath, she said,

"Edmund, I think it would be best if you went with Mattie and Sara to Yoder's and looked for a place to stay tonight."

"Leona, I'm going to tell your parents about how much you've changed. They're not going to be happy."

Since she'd already talked to them, she knew they weren't thrilled about the change in plans. But she knew they were also not going to be happy with Edmund and his high-handed behavior. Moreover, they had made it clear that they loved her and wanted her to be happy. Therefore, she didn't say a word and let her silence speak for itself.

Sometimes there was simply nothing more to say.

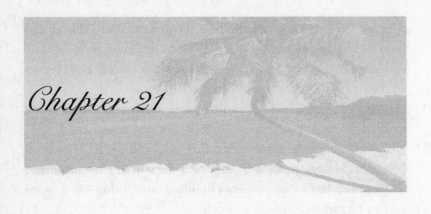

Chapter 21

Watching the sun set while sitting on the beach at Siesta Key was one of Beverly's favorite things to do, and she was delighted to have the opportunity to share it with Jean and Ida.

They'd taken beach chairs, a blanket, and a picnic supper with them for the trip. Beverly had even asked one of her friends from Palm Grove Church to drive them so they wouldn't have to lug everything on the SCAT. The bus was easy enough, but the older she got, the more she appreciated the ease of going to the beach in a car.

Now, as she sat on the sand next to Jean and Ida, the three of them quietly watching the sunset transform the blue sky into a dozen shades of red, orange, and pink, Beverly felt as if she had finally come full circle.

She'd gone from a life in Sugarcreek, where she'd had lots of friends and family surrounding her all the time, to a life in Pinecraft that centered around work. Little by little, the pain of her past had faded and she'd been able to reach out to the people in her life who cared about her.

Now, with Jean's and Ida's visit, Beverly was realizing that she was strong enough to start seeing these people face-to-face. She hadn't known she was ready. Only by the Lord bringing Jean and Ida to Pinecraft had He shown her that.

"I'm really glad you both came here to see me," she murmured as they continued to watch the sun slowly fade into the horizon. "It's been a wonderful couple of days."

"I couldn't agree more," Jean said. "Now I'm kind of sad that we made plans to go to Disney World, but it's probably for the best."

"Houseguests and fish, you know," Ida quipped.

"I don't think your company would ever be that tough to take."

Jean chuckled. "You never know. Plus, you've got a lot on your mind now that Mr. Wagler has shown up."

Beverly nodded. She'd told Ida and Jean a little bit about Eric the night before. "It's been on my mind, but I'm okay."

Wrapping her arms around her knees, Jean said, "That's good to know. Don't worry, dear, I'll fill everyone in about how you are doing."

"I've been writing lots of letters," Beverly pointed out.

"*Jah,* but this is different. Everyone is going to want to hear a full report."

Beverly bit back a smile. She was fairly sure Jean would tell everyone and anyone *all* about how she was doing. "*Danke.*"

Ida clucked her tongue. "Now that it's been brought up . . . what are you going to do about Mr. Wagler?"

These ladies were nothing if not tenacious! "I don't know what I'm going to do about him, or about the inn. I'm not even sure if he wants me to move out right away. I hate the idea of giving up everything to someone who doesn't even care about this place."

"If you do have to leave the inn, perhaps you should come

home," Jean ventured. "You might have left Sugarcreek, but I promise everyone there hasn't left you. I bet that once you see the rolling hills and all the familiar sights, you'll be glad you returned."

Home. Funny, after only three years, Pinecraft felt like home now. She liked going to the beach. She liked the warmth of the winter and the flowers that constantly bloomed. Most of all, she liked the idea of seeing the friends she'd made who didn't bring with them a whole host of dark memories that she'd rather forget.

She might be wrong, but Beverly couldn't imagine how Marvin's and Regina's betrayal would ever be far from everyone's minds.

But who knew what the Lord had planned for her? If she'd learned anything, it was that His will couldn't always be predicted.

"I don't know what I'll do," she replied at last. "But when I do, I promise to let you know."

Shifting, Ida curved her legs and brushed off the sand that had blown onto the fabric of her dark teal dress. "That's all we can ask, I suppose."

Just as the sun drifted lower, finally dipping into the waves on the horizon, Jean chuckled.

Startled, Beverly turned to her. "What made you laugh?"

"Oh, I was just thinking about those girls and those boys at your inn this morning."

Beverly grinned. "I didn't know you witnessed all that drama. It was quite the to-do."

"Who could miss it? Ida and I were in the kitchen, just about to take our cup of *kaffi* into the gathering room when we heard Leona greet that boy."

"And what words they had! She certainly gave him a mouthful."

"And then some," Ida added.

"It was certainly exciting. Like we were watching a play or some such!" Jean exclaimed.

Beverly chuckled because Jean wasn't exactly wrong. Every time she thought one of them was about to back down, things had only gotten worse. "I tell you what, I could not believe it when Zack Kaufmann sauntered in, bringing with him a quart of ripe, red strawberries."

Jean grinned. "Just like they were roses."

Ida waved a hand in front of her face. "I was worried that Edmund was going to toss those berries in the trash."

Beverly started laughing. "Then, when I found out that one of the other girls was the boy's sister! It made everything that happened to me almost pale in comparison."

"All we needed was popcorn," Jean said. Peeking over at Beverly, she murmured, "I guess you aren't the only lady with a bit of excitement in her personal life. Or who has had her share of disappointments."

"This is true," Beverly said. "This is very true. When does your van come to take you to Orlando?

"Early tomorrow morning." Ida grinned. "All the guide-books say to arrive at the park as early as possible."

Jean winked. "Ida doesn't know this, but I intend for us to hit every roller-coaster there. We've got a busy day planned."

LEONA SAT ON a stone bench on Bahia Vista Street and watched the bus leave. She'd elected to stay out of sight when Mattie and Sara met Edmund for lunch, choosing instead to sit with Zack on the Orange Blossom Inn's back patio. On their way outside, Leona had washed Zack's berries and deposited them in a thick earthenware bowl.

As they'd enjoyed the sweet fruit, warm from sitting in the morning sun, Leona had noticed that the tenuous bond that had formed between them had grown stronger. Conversation became easy and relaxed, then almost nonexistent as their awareness of one another became more apparent.

When Leona noticed Zack's gaze stray to her lips, she had shivered.

And that was when she had known that she'd made the right decision. No matter what happened with Zack, she'd felt more for him than she ever had with Edmund. Proving that her instincts had been right. No matter how hard she might have tried, she would never have been able to make herself feel that way toward Edmund.

Now, as she watched the rear taillights of the big bus fade into the distance with Edmund safely in one of the seats, she knew without a doubt that their relationship was officially over.

To her dismay, she felt a little bit sad. She hated that she'd caused so much trouble. Hated that the dreams she'd held so tightly a year ago had all unraveled. And she felt guilty about Edmund. Sure, he wasn't the right man for her, but he'd seemed to think that she was the right woman for him. She'd hurt him, and though she supposed there had been no choice, she still felt badly about it.

She was wondering how to deal with that guilt and when to try and smooth things over, when Effie approached.

"Hi, Effie."

"Hiya, Leona. I was watching the bus leave over at the post office with my sister Violet when I saw you sitting here."

"Where's your sister now?" Though Effie was twelve, Leona still felt mildly protective of the girl.

She waved toward a group of eight women standing in a circle in front of the post office bulletin board. "Oh, she's still over there, talking to some friends."

"So you're spending some time with her today?"

"*Jah*. Everyone in the family had a talk with Zack, you see. We all decided he was spending too much time looking after me."

Leona couldn't decide if Effie looked put out or was simply stating how things were. "He told me he likes to be with you," she said.

"He told me that, too. But I'm growing up, you see."

"I imagine you are. But at least you can now spend more time with your sister."

Effie grinned, obviously happy that Leona understood. "*Jah*. I am glad about that."

"Effie, I didn't see you cross the street," a dark-haired woman about Leona's age called out as she walked over to join them. "You should have told me you were going over here. I got worried."

"I did tell you, Vi."

"If you did, I didn't hear you."

"I did. And I thought you heard me."

"Uh-huh," the woman said as she reached them. After giving Leona a brief, commiserating look, she said, "I guess this means you're ready to be on your way?"

"Not exactly. I wanted you to meet Leona. Violet, this is Leona."

Leona got to her feet. "Hi. I'm Leona Weaver. I met Effie at Yoder's the other day."

"She's the woman I told you about. The woman Zack likes," Effie whispered, but it wasn't much of a whisper at all.

Violet gazed at her and smiled broadly. "Violet Kaufmann. Zack and Effie's sister."

"And Karl's, too," Effie said.

"*Jah*. And Karl's, too."

"It's nice to meet you." Then, feeling like she should add something more about herself, she added, "I'm here from Ohio."

"Oh, I know all about you, I'm afraid."

"Oh?" Leona had never been one to feel especially uncomfortable around new people, but she was beginning to think that there was a first time for everything. Violet's steady gaze was direct and assessing.

As if she knew how she was behaving, Violet's eyes lit up and she chuckled. "Don't worry. It's nothing bad. In fact, it's all good."

"I'm surprised anyone had much to say about me."

"Zack did," Effie chimed in. "Zack talks about you a lot. All the time, in fact."

While Leona processed that, Violet said, "Have your ears been burning? You've been quite the topic of conversation in our family this week."

Leona felt her neck turn red. "I hope not in a bad way."

"Not at all."

"We all think you're great," Effie said. "Well, I mean, me and Zack do. On account of we're the only ones who had met you until now." Looking pleased, she added, "Now Violet knows you, too."

Leona smiled.

"You've gotten Zack to finally start thinking about himself, which is a blessing," Violet added. "I've been after him for years to remember that he's *part* of a family, instead of thinking that he *is* the family."

"My *bruder* likes to be in charge. And to help. But he doesn't like to ask for help."

As Leona thought about how much of a change he'd spurred in her, just by being himself, she knew she had to be as honest as possible. "I'm not sure about how he is with his family, but he's been a great friend to me. Again and again, he's gone out of the way to spend time with me. I'm grateful."

"I think there's a mighty *gut* reason he's been doing that," Violet said.

Just as Leona felt her cheeks color, Mattie and Sara walked up. In the nick of time.

After introducing them to Violet and Effie, she knew it was time to move on. "It was nice to see you again, Effie, and to meet you, Violet, but we should probably be on our way now."

But Violet stopped her with a hand to her arm. "Hey, we're going to have some people over at the house this evening to play cards. Why don't you all come over and join us?"

"Do you think Zack would want that? I don't want to simply show up like an unwelcome surprise."

Effie waved off her worries. "Don't worry about that. Zack is gonna be real happy that you're there. I know he'll be."

"But still. We don't want to disrupt your plans."

"You won't. A bunch of his friends are coming over, too. So there will be a lot of people."

"His friends?" Mattie asked.

"*Jah.* Daniel and Jeremy for sure. And maybe Abel and Jay."

To Leona's amusement, Mattie brightened right up. "If you truly would like us there, I think it sounds like fun."

"We really would love for you to join us. Really. Right, Vi?"

"For sure. Plus, our parents will be around, so they'll be happy to meet you."

"Karl will, too," added Effie.

After glancing at her friends and seeing that they looked just as eager to go to the party as she was, Leona nodded. "*Danke*. It sounds like fun. Thank you."

Violet opened her purse and wrote down their address. "Come over around seven, after supper. We'll have some cookies and *kaffi*. Maybe some pop, too. It's nothing fancy."

"We'll see you then," Leona promised before they all said goodbye. Then, walking toward the inn, and once they were about a block away, Leona glanced at Sara and Mattie. "Are you sure that you both are all right with this?"

Sara nodded. "After spending so much time with Edmund, I think all of us are up for some fun. Besides, what could go wrong? We'll go over, eat a cookie, play some cards, and if it feels awkward, we'll leave."

"That's true." Leona nodded, but as they walked along the street, smiling at some of the Amish ladies and men who passed them, or were riding by on their bicycles, Leona had a feeling that this trip to Sarasota was becoming suspiciously like a lesson in Murphy's Law.

Whatever could happen, would happen.

And some of it might not be too good, either.

Chapter 22

Once word got around that the Kaufmanns were having some friends over, and that three girls from Walnut Creek—one of whom Zack had shown a particular interest in—were going to be there, everyone and their brother decided to join them. Zack had tried to take this news in stride. Having a lot of people over wasn't anything new. His family was social. Both of his parents had a wide circle of friends whom they liked to get together with often.

In addition, they'd made friends with other folks who visited Sarasota: snowbirds—the folks who regularly came south to spend the whole winter in the Florida sun—vacationers, relatives, neighbors, and chance acquaintances. Everyone and anyone eventually became known to one of the six Kaufmanns. Zach had always regarded that as a good thing; it meant their house was often filled with laughter and guests.

But this particular party? It was rapidly becoming more than a little out of hand. The number of people in their yard and house and patio had to be over fifty or sixty. It was truly something to behold, even for a family used to hosting events.

Zack hadn't known whether to hug his two sisters or give them a lecture when they'd come home four hours earlier, all smiles.

He'd been sitting on the back porch with his mother. She'd been writing letters and he'd been counting playing cards when Effie and Violet had burst in, full of news.

The first and most important piece had been that they'd seen Leona's former fiancé get on the Pioneer Trails bus and that Leona had most definitely not seen him off. The second piece of news was that Effie had introduced Violet to Leona and her girlfriends. Zack had been surprised about that, but not displeased.

But when he'd learned that Vi and Effie had extended invitations to their house—without asking him—and had coaxed Leona and her girlfriends into accepting . . . that had been more than a bit high-handed.

"Really, Violet?" he'd asked, giving his older sister a meaningful look.

"This is nothing to fuss about, Zachary."

"I think it is."

"Are you upset that Leona wants to come over and spend time with you and our family and friends? If you are, I would have to say that I am pretty surprised. I thought you liked her."

"I like her."

"Then you should stop acting so bothered, *bruder*," she replied with her trademark candor.

But the way she avoided his eyes told him everything he needed to know. She knew she'd been a bit overzealous, and that she would have had a fit if he had ever done such a thing.

Now that he knew they were both on the same page, at the very least, he kept his mouth shut. Effie was simply Effie.

She was guileless when it came to navigating how close or how far to push people. But Violet—and himself, for that matter—bordered on being experts.

"I must say that I'm surprised you aren't happier about this," his *mamm* said once she'd heard enough of their conversation.

"Do you not like Leona anymore?" Effie asked.

"Oh, I like her." He wasn't going to lie about that. When he'd shared those strawberries with Leona, he'd hardly been able to do much besides remind himself of the dozen reasons why kissing her was a bad idea, starting with the fact that she had just broken an engagement and ending with the fact that she was boarding a bus to Ohio in a couple of days.

"She seemed happy for the invitation," Effie added.

"That's *gut. Danke.*"

His mother stared at him. "So, if you do like Leona, what's the problem?"

"I don't have a problem with Leona." His irritation stemmed from having to discuss his feelings with not one but three women, one of whom was twelve and another of whom was his mother.

"But you are glaring at Violet."

"I don't mean to glare."

Violet took a seat next to him and gave him a little jab with her shoulder. "Sure you do. Something's bothering you. What is it?"

Of course she would say something like that. Violet loved being blunt, she always had. "I simply don't appreciate my sister setting up dates for me."

Violet waved off his concern. "Oh, stop. This isn't a date. It's just a bunch of people over playing cards. Plus, her girl-friends looked happy about the idea, too."

"They did?" Maybe things were going smoother for Leona with Mattie and Sara.

"Oh, *jah*. There's only so much you can do on your own here in Pinecraft, you know. The best part is socializing with everyone."

"I suppose you're right."

"I know I am."

His mother's lips twitched as she shared a smile with Zack. Obviously, Violet's headstrong, bossy nature was still alive and well.

Effie turned to Zack. "Are you mad at us?"

"Never," he said quickly. "I'm glad to have the opportunity to see the girls again. And having everyone over is sure to be fun."

And though he'd said all that in order to diffuse the situation, Zack had realized that everything he'd told Effie had been true. He *was* looking forward to seeing Leona again, and he did think his family threw some of the best parties in Pinecraft.

Effie relaxed and they all started chatting some more. But within an hour, their mother started getting that look about her. The one that signaled she was about to clean the house, prepare more food, organize guests, and start weeding her garden. And since she'd never been one to work while her *kinner* lazed about, Zack knew that they were about to be run ragged with her feverish plans.

And sure enough, within the half hour, all of them had been given rooms to clean. She'd even gotten on the phone with their father and asked him to bring home plastic cups, napkins, and some apple cider after work. Then she commandeered Violet and started baking up a storm.

After Zack had straightened up the living room, he'd walked down to Danny's house to tell his family about the impromptu party and to borrow some card tables and chairs.

That, of course, set more people in motion. Danny's siblings told other people and his parents decided they'd stop by, too, which meant that Danny's mother also decided to bake a pie. And Danny thought they should go tell a couple of their friends he'd just seen at the park.

An hour after that, it felt like half of Pinecraft was planning to come to the Kaufmann house around seven that night.

By a quarter after six, Zack was hopping into the shower, and by a quarter to seven, he was setting up tables. Then Karl showed up, saying he'd told the manager he had a family function to attend that he couldn't get out of.

Zack was so pleased at the opportunity to hang out with his brother, he almost didn't care about the reason. "It's been forever since you've been home for a neighborhood get-together."

"*Nee,* it's been *never* that I've been home to see a girl that you are courting." He smirked.

"I'm definitely not courting Leona."

"Are you sure about that? Because that's not what everyone's saying."

"People like to gossip too much."

Karl waved a hand in dismissal. "People are interested. That's all."

"I don't want everyone staring at her or asking her too many questions."

"Oh, they will. You can be sure of that." Seeing their *daed* approach, Karl gave Zack a light slap on the back before walking over to join him. Almost immediately, they started talking shop.

And then the front door opened. Danny and his family came inside, bringing with them two of their neighbors, two pies, and a basket of plastic forks.

On their heels were more family friends, and on *their* heels were the two girls Effie had introduced him to at Yoder's.

As Zack watched Effie shyly greet them, then walk them over to the kitchen to have sodas, he relaxed. Seeing Effie with friends made everything they were going through worth it.

Then, when he saw Leona, Mattie, and Sara enter the house and Leona waved to him from across the room, he knew for sure that he'd been absolutely wrong about doubting the get-together.

This party was, indeed, a fantastic idea. Maybe the best idea his sisters had ever had in their lives. Because of them, he was going to get to spend the next couple of hours with Leona.

He didn't even try to hold back a wide smile when he walked over to greet them.

Chapter 23

Leona's pulse started beating double time the moment Zack turned around, spied her, and smiled broadly. Though she was a little aware that his attention on her had caught the attention of several other people, she didn't care in the slightest.

No one, not even Edmund when he'd proposed to her, had ever looked at her the way Zack was looking.

As if no one in the world mattered to him as much as she did.

Beside her, Mattie sighed rather dreamily. "Leona, he really likes you," she whispered.

Leona felt that way, too, but she hated to jinx herself. "Maybe. I mean, I hope he does."

Mattie shook her head. "I'm not just making conversation. I think this Zachary Kaufmann *really* likes you. I realized that at the beach. Whenever he wasn't by your side, he eyed you as if you were on the other end of his fishing pole."

"Fishing pole?"

"*Jah*. Like he couldn't wait to reel you closer to him."

Leona giggled at the image. "*Danke.* I think."

Then Sara clutched her arm. "I have to admit that I didn't understand any of what you've been doing, Le. But now that I've observed how both Edmund and Zack treat you, and was able to compare them on the same day, I've got to admit that you've made the right choice."

Sara's words meant the world. Thinking that she'd disappointed her friends had really bothered her. But Sara's words also reminded Leona of how the Lord had actually been the one to orchestrate what had been happening between herself and Zack.

"I don't know if I actually made a choice," she pointed out. All she'd done was come to the conclusion that Edmund was not right for her. And she'd done that far too late. Then she hadn't been able to resist Zack's smiles. And that, without a doubt, had been rather foolish. "All I did was follow my heart, and I'm not even sure if my heart knows what it is doing."

"I think it might," Sara said.

"Really?"

But before Sara could explain herself—though she really didn't need to—Zack was right there.

"You came," he said, his gaze warm.

She smiled right back, not even caring that she probably looked decidedly dreamy. "I did. I mean, we did."

"I'm glad." He smiled at her and then nodded his greetings to both Mattie and Sara. "Girls, come on in and I'll introduce you to everyone."

Everyone? There had to be at least a hundred people milling around. "There's no need for that," Leona said quickly. "We'll just hang out with you and your friends."

Looking a little sheepish, he said, "I don't think that's possible. Everyone is really looking forward to meeting all three of you."

Leona liked how Zack automatically included her girl-friends in his statement. So far, she'd noticed him doing things like that a lot. It seemed he never wanted anyone to ever feel left out.

As they walked farther inside, and she realized that there had to be almost thirty people in the living room alone, she looked at him curiously. "When Violet said that your family was having a couple of people over for cards, I thought maybe you'd have six or eight. At the most."

He looked a little pained. "It started out that way."

"Started?"

"Things got a little out of hand fairly quickly."

"Only a little?" Leona teased.

He shrugged. "When word spread that you, Sara, and Mattie might be here, a lot of people decided that they would like to stop by." He smiled over at Mattie and Sara. "I hope you girls are hungry. There are more pies, cakes, cookies, and other snacks here than you can imagine. It seems every lady who walked through the door decided to bring dessert."

"Except the three of us." Leona frowned. "I didn't even think to bring anything."

"You shouldn't have brought anything but yourselves. You're the guests."

"But so is everyone else who is here."

"I meant, you're the only ones who are living in a B and B."

"Ah." Because she couldn't argue with that point, she let the subject drop. Just then, Danny and Jeremy joined them along with some of the people Mattie and Leona had met on Siesta Key. Mattie and Sara began chatting with everyone.

Leona was relieved that both of her girlfriends looked happy to be talking to Danny's and Jeremy's friends. Almost right away, Mattie was laughing at something and Sara was smiling at one of the girls.

Next thing she knew, Leona found herself smiling, too.

Zack noticed. "What brought on that smile?"

Meeting his gaze, she realized that he was staring at her. Like her sudden smile meant something to him. "I was a little worried that they might feel left out if you and I spent much time together. But now I think they're going to be all right. I'm relieved."

Looking in their direction, Zack nodded. "I promise, Sara and Mattie will have fun. We've got a real nice group of friends and neighbors."

"Thank you again for inviting us."

His gaze warmed before he shrugged off her thanks. "No reason to thank me. Like I said, I'm glad you could come over." After a moment's pause, he rested his palm on the small of her back.

That gentle touch both calmed her nerves and heightened her awareness of him—as if she needed any reminding! Realizing he was waiting for a response, she said, "I'm glad, too."

He smiled. "Let me introduce you to some people."

Before she could answer, he guided her into the kitchen, where Violet and a couple of other ladies were setting out fruit kabobs. "Everyone, this here is Leona."

Most of the women smiled gamely in her direction or said hello, but one of them stopped what she was doing as they approached. One look into her eyes told Leona that she had to be Mrs. Kaufmann. She had the family's blue eyes and likeable, easygoing manner.

Zack winked at Leona as the lady walked around the kitchen counter to greet her. "Get ready," he warned in a tender tone. "My family is a bit enthusiastic."

Leona flashed a grin his way before holding out her hand to the lady who approached.

"Hello, dear. I've been looking forward to meeting you."

Leona smiled as they clasped hands. "By the looks of your eyes, I'd guess you are Mrs. Kaufmann. I've never met another group of people who have such striking eyes."

"Thank you for the compliment. It's nice to meet you, Leona. Now, please, call me Ginny."

"*Danke*, Ginny."

Ginny looked around the crowded area. "Did your girl-friends make it here, okay?"

"Oh, yes. They're with some of Zack's friends." She smiled at the other women who were listening shamelessly. "I can't believe you're hosting such a big party."

Looking vaguely like she was hiding a secret, Ginny shrugged. "It doesn't usually work out like this, but word of our get-together spread like wildfire tonight. I hope you and your friends will enjoy yourselves. We're happy you came."

"*Danke*. I'm sure we will."

Ginny's eyes lit up. "Now, dear, how about I introduce you to some of our—"

"I'm going to take her to the backyard first, Mamm," Zack interrupted.

"Oh, all right."

After giving his mother a meaningful look, Zack took Leona's elbow and guided her through the people and out the back door.

Once they were outside, Leona exhaled. There were far fewer people on the deck and patio than there were out front or in the house. Someone had lit little torches and a fire pit, too, so there was a soothing glow against the twilight sky.

It was pretty and also fairly quiet. She looked at Zack in surprise. "Why did you bring me out here?"

"For a couple of reasons."

"Oh?"

"Well, I wanted to make sure you were all right."

She smiled a little self-consciously. "I've been to parties before, Zack. I think I can handle myself just fine."

"I wasn't concerned about that."

"What were you concerned about?"

"I was thinking that a lot has happened to you lately."

"You could say that," she hedged, hoping he wasn't going to make her relive Edmund's surprise visit all over again.

But instead of turning judgmental, his expression softened. "Don't look at me like that. I'm not being critical."

"Oh?" She knew she sounded tongue-tied, but she felt that way. There was that same pull between them again. That pull she'd never felt before and wasn't sure she wanted to fight.

While she simply stared, he stepped closer, then reached out and took her hand. Ran his thumb lightly along her knuckles. "I'm sure it had to be difficult. Are you all right?"

"I'm all right." And she was. Especially since Zack was holding her hand and looking at her like everything she thought mattered to him a great deal.

His expression, his touch, the way he honestly cared about her, it all combined and made her shiver. He was being wonderful, and it was so different from how Edmund had treated her, it was almost overwhelming.

Seeing her response, his blue eyes narrowed. "You don't have to tell me a thing, but I want you to know that I care."

Feeling even more emotional, she dropped his hand and leaned against the back wall of the house. She needed a bit of space between them. Otherwise, she was going to be completely drawn into everything he was saying.

If she did that, she would be even more heartbroken when she left Pinecraft.

"Leona? I didn't mean to make you upset." After a beat, his voice hardened. "Or does thinking about Edmund make you upset?"

"*Nee*. He was . . . he was fine."

"Then what is wrong?" Reaching out, he took her hand again. This time folding it between both of his own. "You look like you are about to cry."

It was his concern, ironically, that was making her feel choked up. He was treating her the way she'd always hoped Edmund would treat her but never had.

"I'm sorry," she murmured. "It's just that for the last few days, everything has been really stressful."

"I can only imagine. I've never been engaged, but—"

She cut him off. "It isn't because of what happened with Edmund. It's because of you."

"Me?"

"I don't mean to embarrass you, but I guess you can tell that I really am glad we met. I've liked spending time with you."

"You know I've felt the same way." He looked at his feet. "Gosh, I've been half worried that you thought I was being too forward, being at the same restaurant you were, inviting you to the beach"—he winced—"showing up at your B and B with a bag of fruit. I'm not usually so pushy or awkward."

"I haven't thought you were awkward at all. I've liked everything you've done."

"So what is wrong?"

"Edmund and I are officially through. He's on the bus back to Ohio now, and I have a feeling he's probably already told all thirty people on that bus how horrible his former fiancée is."

"Surely not."

"No, I'm afraid so." Closing her eyes, she added, "Then, unfortunately, he'll tell more stories when he gets home. I'm going to have a hard time showing my face anywhere in Walnut Creek when we get back."

"No one would ever believe bad stories about you."

She opened her eyes and gazed up into his again. "You sound so certain."

"That's because I am." He exhaled. "Leona, I don't want to scare you, but I'm really enjoying your company. A lot. I wish you didn't have to leave Sarasota in just a couple of days."

The right thing to do was nod and say something appropriate. Or say nothing! Saying nothing would be a very good idea.

But instead, Leona blurted out what was spinning in her head. It was completely inappropriate. And completely too bold.

"I've been wishing for that, too, Zack," she admitted. "Actually, I've started to wish for a whole lot of things where you are concerned."

When his body tensed, Leona feared she'd just said the absolute *wrong* thing.

Chapter 24

I didn't know your family was so popular," Melanie told Effie as they stood in her home's front lawn. "Everyone is here." She giggled. "Even Josiah."

Effie's stomach churned, but she tried her best to act like Melanie's statement wasn't a big deal. It kind of was, though, because this was the first time that so many people her age had come to one of her family's get-togethers. It did seem as if half their school was standing on the lawn and driveway.

It was also the first time that Josiah Grimm had paid her much attention. The idea that he'd come to her house was thrilling.

So were the smiles he'd been sending her way.

Not that she was about to let Melanie know about that, though. "Josiah is here?" she asked, trying to keep her voice particularly calm and unaffected. "I haven't seen him yet."

But of course she had. She'd noticed the cutest boy in their class the minute he'd arrived.

"You haven't talked to him yet?" Looking a bit like she was

harboring a secret, Melanie circled her hand around Effie's elbow. "Let's go say hi, then. He's over there with Jennifer, and half the kids from our class."

Effie didn't want to do that. Actually, she would have liked to do just about anything other than walk toward half the class, with another thirty people observing her. But it wasn't like everyone didn't already know she had Perthes disease and had to wear braces.

"All right."

"Do you need help walking?" Melanie asked.

"I'll be fine."

"Oh? *Gut.*"

Effie was relieved that Melanie hadn't stayed by her side while she plodded over to the other kids—honestly, nothing was more embarrassing than that—but now she felt just as conspicuous as she made her way over to the kids. Her gait wasn't smooth, it was choppy. And she even had her crutches—her mother's orders, since she was bound to be on her feet for hours tonight.

As she got closer, she saw more and more kids watching her walk. Some looked sorry for her. Others embarrassed. Others, like Melanie, looked a little unsure. Almost as if they weren't sure whether they should offer her a hand or not.

The only good thing about the short journey was that Josiah was simply staring at her face, watching *her.*

When she finally got near them, she called out a greeting. "Hi, everyone."

"Hey, Effie," Beth said. "Thanks for having a party."

She grinned. "You're welcome." She didn't bother to explain that the party was actually just an excuse for Zack to introduce Leona to everyone. "If you all get thirsty or hungry, you should come inside. There's tons of lemonade, pop, and food."

Josiah smiled again, just like he had that one day in class. "*Danke*, Effie."

Feeling a little braver, she smiled right back.

Melanie noticed. And, just as everyone was starting to talk and Beth was asking Effie about the rumor she'd heard about Zack having a girlfriend, Melanie's voice rose. "I hope you won't think I'm being rude or anything, but I've been wanting to ask you something."

"What?" Effie was completely taken off guard.

Melanie smiled at Jennifer C. before turning back to Effie. "Are your legs ever going to be normal?"

Immediately, a new, ugly tension filled the air. Jennifer C. looked horrified, Beth's eyes turned to saucers, and a couple of other kids looked embarrassed.

Effie had no idea what to say. Helplessly, she looked around for one of her brothers or Violet. They'd always been her rescuers during situations like this. But now, of course, she was completely alone.

"I don't know," she finally said. Because, well, she didn't. Her legs were stronger now, a lot stronger, but she didn't know if she would ever be completely free of braces and crutches. A lot depended on how her hips handled her growing body.

"Really, Melanie?" Josiah said.

Melanie turned to him. "What?"

"You know what." He sounded almost mad.

"Oh! Did I embarrass you, Effie?" Melanie asked. "Sorry."

But it was obvious—at least to Effie—that Melanie wasn't sorry for hurting her feelings. Instead, she was sorry that the most popular boy in their class had heard her be so mean.

Exchanging pained glances with Beth, Effie felt more alone than she ever had in her life. Even Beth wasn't saying anything.

No one wanted to become the new target of the popular girls' attention.

What she needed to do was get away. Feeling her neck turning bright red, she mumbled, "I'm just going to go inside for a minute."

Josiah hurried to her side. "Great. I'll come with you."

"That's okay. I mean, you don't have to."

He lowered his voice. "Don't let Melanie get you down. She's being pretty ugly."

She stared at him in surprise. "*Nee,* she's really pretty, Josiah."

He leaned toward her ear. "You know what I mean. She can be ugly inside."

His comment was a little shocking, but it was also honest. Melanie was the type of person who could do the sort of things that made her seem rather ugly.

Effie looked up at him and smiled. And when he looked at her, his gaze steady and sure, but now with a bit of warmth settled in it, she felt like maybe she actually already was "normal." Maybe she needed to finally trust her brother, listen to his words, and remember that everyone had something about themselves that they wished they could change. She would be extremely selfish if she started imagining that her problems were greater than everyone else's.

Still looking at her, Josiah said, "Were you serious about there being a ton of food inside?"

"I was. Are you hungry?"

"Yeah." At last, he grinned.

"Oh, look out!"

Effie dragged her attention away from Josiah with a start.

She looked behind her and saw someone had brought their dog. And that dog looked like a cross between a Labrador and a Mastiff. It was huge, really friendly, and bounding right toward her.

It barked happily, then lunged . . .

Right as Effie inadvertently stepped backward on a sprinkler head.

The puppy barked again. Josiah darted from her side and reached for it as it barked happily, obviously thinking Josiah was joining in a game.

Unfortunately, Josiah's rescue came too late.

The dog's jump and her subsequent shift in weight was too much for her hip joints and muscles. In seconds, her left leg gave out.

She fell hard, the metal sprinkler head hitting the fleshy part of her arm with a sharp pinch. And since she'd refused to wear her braces, opting for her crutches, there was nothing to brace her legs—or her bones—for her fall.

"Effie? Effie, are you okay?" Josiah said after calling out for help with the dog.

Effie knew she wasn't. She was on the ground, her leg was in terrible pain, her arm was stinging, and her muscles felt pulled and out of sorts. But the worst of it had been hearing the snap of the bone as her leg hit the ground.

She couldn't help it; she cried out in hurt and frustration and disappointment.

Josiah knelt on the ground next to her. "Don't worry, help's on the way," he said.

His promise was sweet, but Effie also knew it hardly mattered. She was going to have to go to the hospital again. Tears blurred her vision, so she closed her eyes. She knew what had happened.

She'd broken her leg again.

THE CRY WAS shrill and piercing. And the commotion that followed was even louder as a kid about Effie's age ran up to Zack and Leona in the backyard.

"Zack, Effie fell."

"Where is she?"

"On the ground in the front yard."

He bit back a sigh. Effie was really going to need to be more careful. They'd all told her not to wear herself out. When her muscles started tiring, accidents happened. "She'll be all right," he said. "I bet she's already on her feet." And no doubt completely embarrassed.

But the girl shook her head. "*Nee,* Zack, you don't understand. She's hurt bad!"

"How bad?"

"I think she broke her leg. Josiah heard a pop. She's crying something awful. And bleeding, too."

Every muscle in his body tensed. "Go make sure someone has told my parents," he called out. "And Violet." He stared at the kid. "Do you know my sister Violet? She's Mennonite now. Her boyfriend has a car." The moment the kid ran off to do what he asked, Zack turned to Leona. "I've got to go."

Only compassion shone in her eyes. "I know."

"I hate to leave you like this—"

Cutting him off, she said, "I'll be fine, Zack. I promise." With a tender smile, she squeezed his arm for a second before lightly pushing him away. "Go on, now. I'll see you at the hospital. And I'll pray for your sister, too."

THREE HOURS LATER, Zack was sitting in an uncomfortable chair in the middle of Sarasota Memorial Hospital's crowded waiting room. Effie had, indeed, sustained a broken leg. She'd also needed seven stitches on her arm.

Because of the nature of her disease, everything had taken a lot longer than it might have with another child her age with the same injuries. Her specialists had wanted to view the X rays before any decision had been made about whether or not she needed surgery.

Thank goodness everyone had agreed that surgery wasn't necessary. Now his parents were sitting with her and conferring with the doctors about whether or not to keep Effie overnight.

He was thankful also for Leona. When she'd first arrived at the hospital, she'd taken a seat next to him in the waiting room and whispered, "I wanted to be here with you, Zack, but you needn't feel obligated to sit with me the whole time. I'll be fine."

He had sat beside her most of the time. It was only after his parents had left the room that he'd decided to sit with Violet and Karl. Still, just seeing her nearby had helped.

And a few minutes ago, she'd taken everyone's coffee orders and was now passing out cups with Violet's boyfriend, Henry.

Now that it was only the three of them, he said something to Violet and Karl that had been on his mind from the moment they walked through the hospital's electric doors.

"This feels pretty familiar, doesn't it?"

Looking drained, Karl nodded. "This time we know what we're dealing with, though. We know what to do with broken legs and cut arms."

Violet pushed a chunk of hair that had gotten loose from her pins around her ear. "I hate thinking about two years ago, when Effie was first diagnosed. I was so mean to her."

They'd had this discussion many times. Effie's first complaints had sounded like normal growing pains. And because she was so much younger and had been quite coddled by their parents, Zack, Violet, and Karl hadn't given Effie even the smallest amount of sympathy.

"I was worse than that," Zack said. "I kept questioning Mamm and Daed when they took her to the doctors. I thought she was creating a lot of expense for a few sore limbs."

Karl rested his elbows on his knees. "Even now, my behavior isn't much better. I'm off working while you've been helping her get to her physical therapy sessions."

Zack wasn't going to go down this path again. Their guilt hadn't caused the Perthes disease. It was simply a condition that the Lord had seen fit for Effie to bear. "We ought to stop double-guessing ourselves. She was fine. We've all been doing the best we can, too. It was just an accident."

After a moment, Violet nodded. "You're right. Just an accident."

"Thank goodness you brought Henry, Vi," Karl said. "Because of him, we were able to get her here right away."

Violet looked over at Henry and Leona talking to some of Effie's friends who were at the party. "He's a good man," she said softly. "I love him."

"Is he ever going to propose?"

After making sure Henry wasn't looking their way, she smiled. "He already has."

"So you are engaged?"

"*Nee*. I haven't said yes yet."

"Why on earth not?" Karl asked.

She shrugged. "I wanted things to be better between me and Mamm and Daed. I know I'm disappointing them, but I still want them to want me in their lives."

"They love you," Karl said. Then he looked at Leona, who was still chatting with Effie's friends. "And what about you, Zack?"

Zack felt an immediate blush all the way to the tips of his ears. "There's no way I'm talking about that now."

Violet's eyes sparkled. "But?"

"But you and Effie were right on the mark," he said as he glanced Leona's way.

They all sat up when the door opened and their father came out. He looked far more relaxed. "She's going to be just fine, but because of the late hour, they've decided to keep her overnight."

"Where's Mamm?" Violet asked.

"Sitting with Effie. She's going to spend the night by her side."

Violet shook her head. "Mamm's exhausted. I'm going to go see if I can stay instead."

Their father looked at her in surprise. "Are you sure you want to do that?"

"She's my little sister, Daed. Of course I'm sure."

"All right, then," Daed said, giving her a hug. "*Danke.*" After he released her, he gazed at Zack and Karl. "We are a blessed family," he murmured, "for sure and for certain. It is surely a blessing to have you *kinner* to lean on in times like these."

Quickly, Zack shared a smile with Violet. If she had any doubts about their parents' acceptance of her, he had a feeling those doubts had now faded away.

Chapter 25

Beverly was in the kitchen making oatmeal cookies when she heard a knock at the front door. She wiped her hands with the dishrag tied around her waist and turned on an additional porch light.

But when she peeked out and saw who had arrived, she was tempted to turn right back around and go back to spooning cookie dough onto baking sheets while waiting for the first batch in the oven to finish. Why in the world had Eric Wagler decided to stop by at this time of the evening?

Bracing herself, she opened the door. "Eric. Hello."

"Beverly."

"What brings you out at this hour?"

He looked at his watch. "It's only a little after ten."

"Eric, it's almost ten thirty!"

He still looked confused. "Is that a problem?"

What he didn't realize was that ten at night was considered late in Pinecraft. Far too late for social visits. "It's a little late, but never mind. I'm up, anyway."

"I thought you would be. See, earlier tonight, I was in Yoder's when a group of people came in, talking about how you saved the day at some party with your next-door neighbor's van."

"Oh, that."

His gaze warmed, looking more than a little amused. "Yeah. That."

"It was nothing. Three of my guests were at someone's home and a little girl had an accident and broke her leg. She'd already gone to the hospital with her parents, but her siblings and some family friends wanted to be there with them. My neighbor George is on retainer. He didn't mind picking them up and driving them over. He's the one who saved the day."

"You act like your helping wasn't any big deal."

"That's because it wasn't," she replied, shrugging off his impressed look. "As I said, I didn't do anything besides ask George if he would drive some folks to the hospital."

"Do things like this happen a lot?"

"Girls getting their legs broken in the middle of a family party?" she asked. "I certainly hope not."

"You know what I mean," he pressed. "I'm talking about you offering a helping hand to a bunch of strangers."

These people weren't strangers. They were her friends and neighbors. If Eric was going to take over the inn, they would be his friends and neighbors, too.

But a sixth sense told her that he wasn't ready to hear that. He still seemed to view what she did as merely a job when it was really so much more.

Therefore, she measured her words carefully. "Well, Pinecraft is a small place. We help each other out when we can. It's our way, you know."

Eric nodded. But, actually, he looked as if he didn't understand.

And that made her wonder a little bit more about him. What type of man was he? She looked at him curiously. "Are you familiar with the Amish or the Mennonites?"

"Some. As you know, my neighbor, John, was Amish. However, I grew up in a fundamentalist household. I can't tell you the number of times my mother talked to people she met about Jesus Christ." He met her gaze then, and looked more than a little bit embarrassed. "Sorry, it's late and here I am, telling you my whole life story."

"Actually, I like hearing that. I feel like we share so much but are virtual strangers."

"I suppose we are." He waited a beat, then murmured, "Maybe one day we won't be."

His words were as unexpected as they were sweet. They gave her comfort, too, which was a blessing since his appearance in Sarasota and her life was a real source of worry. "I hope that is true," she said. "I hope one day we won't be strangers, virtual or otherwise."

"I also came over to ask if I could come back tomorrow or the next day. I want to take another look around. When I stopped by the other day, it was only for a few moments."

He'd stopped by soon after Jean and Ida had left for Orlando. She'd had tears in her eyes, and Eric saw them. After just a few minutes, he'd told her he'd stop by another time.

Eric sniffed the air. "Do you have a candle burning or something?"

"Oh my goodness, it's the cookies. Come on!"

Fearing that she'd just burned a whole sheet, she tore down the hall, only vaguely paying attention to the door slamming and the footsteps following her.

As soon as she got into the kitchen, she grabbed a dish-towel and pulled out the sheet of cookies. Thankfully, she'd gotten to them and found they were only slightly well-done.

"What do you think?" Eric asked.

Setting the tray on the counter, she heaved a sigh of relief. "A little crisp, but definitely salvageable."

"I'm not too sure about that."

"Really?" They weren't the prettiest cookies she'd ever made, but she didn't think they deserved to go directly into the trash.

With a new gleam in his eye, Eric said, "I think they need to be tested. You know, just to be sure they are edible."

Now understanding that he was teasing, she played along. "*Jah,* I suppose that would be the right thing to do. Any chance you would be willing to do the honors?"

He sighed. "I guess I could. I mean, someone has to."

When he looked ready to reach down and grab one, she slapped away his hand. "Be careful. You're going to burn your-self. I'll give you a couple to take home in a minute or two."

His lips quirked. "If I'm a good boy?"

"And *only if.*"

"That would give anyone all the incentive they need to be on good behavior."

"Let's hope you fall into that category."

He laughed, then walked around the large kitchen. "This is amazing. It's huge. Was it like this when you moved in?"

Looking at the stainless steel appliances, the two dishwash-ers, the granite countertops, and the butler's pantry, she shook her head. "Not at all. I've put all my time and extra money right back into this place." Pointing to the industrial-sized oven, which in her mind really was a work of art, she said, "It all started with the oven. I'm afraid the projects grew from there."

"Do you have a contractor?"

"There's a local man here, Frank Kaufmann, who does good work. He does a lot of remodeling and refurbishing of homes in the area." She gasped as she put two and two together. "Oh my gosh, Eric. I think it was his youngest daughter who broke her leg." Without thinking, she added, "I've been so stressed out, thinking about—"

"About me coming to take over your place?" He pursed his lips.

She supposed there was no turning back now. "Yeah. But I had some other things happen, too." Such as Marvin's sisters' surprise visit.

Turning back to the tray of cookies, she frowned. "I'll have to make them a cake or something tomorrow."

His expression looking more solemn, he nodded. "When would be a better time for me to look around, Beverly?"

She met his gaze. Realizing that he suddenly looked fairly uncomfortable. Was it the reminder about how much his visit had rattled her, or something else?

"How about you come over the day after tomorrow? Tomorrow, I've got quite a few new guests arriving. One of the couples is very nice but a little high-maintenance, if you know what I mean."

If anything, that made him frustrated. "You know what? I don't."

"Eric—"

"Beverly, please don't apologize. I'm the one who is disrupting your life, not the other way around."

She'd like to think that she'd learned a few things over the years. "You're not disrupting anything," she said, realizing for the first time that she'd let go of her anger. "What happened with your friend John and my aunt and this inn . . . it's just life. The Lord gives us only one life, but He seems to enjoy packing it in."

"You do have a point there." His eyes lit with a new warmth and understanding.

"Let me get a bag and I'll give you some cookies."

"Don't trouble yourself. I'll come back in a day or two."

"That sounds good, but I'll send you home with some cookies in the meantime." She found a zip lock bag in a drawer and popped a half dozen inside for him. "Here you go."

"Thanks."

"Anytime," she replied, then found herself blushing at the phrase. It seemed she really would look forward to seeing him at any time.

Slowly, he smiled. "I'll see you soon, Beverly."

She smiled weakly as he turned and left. And because things were feeling so awkward and she really had no idea where they were going to go next, she stayed in the kitchen instead of walking him out.

She was pretty certain that they both needed that. Space and time.

"You DIDN'T HAVE to walk me back to the inn, Zack," Leona said as they walked side by side late that evening. "I know I have a pretty poor sense of direction, but I would have been okay."

They'd elected to take the SCAT from the hospital to the stop in the heart of Pinecraft. The stop was almost directly between the Orange Blossom Inn and his house. Since a couple of people were still walking or riding bikes on the street, she'd felt pretty safe walking home by herself. But Zack had looked horrified about that idea.

"It's too late for you to be walking by yourself. It must be after eleven."

"I'm sure I'll be fine. Plus, I bet you're tired. I don't want you to feel obligated."

"You didn't have to come to the hospital and sit with me in that waiting room, but you did."

"I'm glad I did," she said, realizing that she meant every word. Though they hadn't actually spent a lot of time together, she'd seen him glance her way often. She could tell that he was worried about his sister, and feeling a little guilty that he hadn't been by her side when she'd fallen.

Though she hadn't been able to solve any of Zack's problems, she'd known enough to caution him not make things worse than they were. The last thing in the world Effie needed was to have her favorite brother blame himself for a dog leaping on her.

"I'm glad you did, too," he said.

As they walked along the sidewalk, the streetlights glowed, as did a couple of the lights from different peoples' front porches. And though it wasn't exactly warm—the temperature was lurking in the mid-fifties—it was a far cry from the cold, wet winter they'd been experiencing back in Ohio.

"It feels so good out here. I'm going to miss the warmth of Florida. Even thinking about putting my winter coat back on makes me grumpy."

"And here I was just going to ask you if you would like to have my jacket over your shoulders. If feels a little brisk out to me."

"You Floridians," she teased. "So spoiled when it comes to the weather."

He chuckled under his breath. "That's a fact."

They passed another couple, forcing Leona to move in front of Zack for a couple of paces. When it was just the two of them again, Zack moved to her side, steadying her by placing his palm in the small of her back.

From there, when he reached for her hand, Leona took his without hesitation. She liked his touch. Liked having a connection with him even though they walked together without talking.

Zack seemed just as pleased to clasp her fingers in his own.

He smiled at her as he gently squeezed her hand. "You're going to laugh at me for admitting this, but I have to say it's been a mighty long time since I've walked in the moonlight, holding a girl's hand."

Leona tried to remember the last time she'd held Edmund's hand. Try as she might, she couldn't.

Which, of course, made her both sad and irritated with herself for never realizing that she should've been doing those things with "the love of her life."

"Actually," she admitted, "I'm not laughing at all."

"Why is that?"

"Edmund never held my hand," she murmured, "but what's worse was I never expected him to. Which, now that I think about it, seems pretty sad."

Instead of replying, he gently squeezed her hand again.

And he was right. Nothing else needed to be said.

Chapter 26

In the three days since the accident, Zack's house had turned into a big mess. Effie's doctors had suggested she stay home from school a few days. Since she was wearing a bulky cast, everyone in the family had agreed that was a good idea. They'd also been taking turns to be with her.

Even though Zack had said it was his job.

But what was funny was that everyone in the family—Effie included—had decided that he should definitely *not* be the person to stay by her side. It seemed everyone in the Kaufmann family was smitten with Leona and believed that he needed to spend every spare moment he could with her before she returned to Ohio.

And because he also wanted to be with Leona as much as he could, he'd given in gracefully.

There were consequences to this decision, however. Many hands got involved, as well as many Kaufmanns, each with particular ways of doing things.

Which meant schedules were changed.

And only *some* of the shopping got done.

Effie now had three different people offering to help her with her math, giving her three different ways to solve her division problems. She was getting hopelessly confused but was unsure of whom to ask for help.

Everyone had also decided to take turns in the kitchen, which would have been helpful if either Violet or Karl could actually cook a decent meal.

In addition, friends and neighbors stopped by at all hours of the day. They visited with Effie, dropped off casseroles, flowers, books, and cookies. In short, the house was overflowing with good efforts.

This was a blessing. It truly was.

But the chaos brought on by good intentions was not.

"Am I ever going to find my magazines again?" Zack heard his mother mutter as he walked through the living room. His mother had an inordinate fondness for *Better Homes and Gardens* Magazine. She stacked them neatly all year long then spent much of New Year's Day cutting out the previous year's favorite articles. No one in the family could quite understand her love for this, but to each his own, they guessed.

"Last time I saw them, they were on the bottom bookshelf."

Eagerly, she looked in that direction. When she saw nothing but a blue spiral notebook, she gave an exasperated sigh. "Those magazines aren't here now." Placing a hand on her hip, she muttered, "They're probably making friends with my missing sewing basket and favorite serving platter. I tell you, Zack, while I love having people over, I am beginning to wish they wouldn't try to help out quite so much."

It was a struggle to keep a straight face. His mother was as guilty as anyone about making herself at home in other people's kitchens. "Try not to let it bother you too much, Mamm. You know what they say about many hands and all that."

"Too many hands in this house. Every time I get home from work, someone has helpfully rearranged my things."

"At least Effie has been enjoying herself," he pointed out.

"That she has." Her eyes softened. "Have you noticed how many of her classmates have come over?"

"I have. Both boys and girls." He was tempted to add that this was something new. Effie rarely talked about her friends at school. He couldn't remember her ever having more than one or two classmates stop by over the years. "She's seemed happy to see them."

"I noticed that as well." She paused. "Zack, I think something happened with one of the girls in her classroom."

"Like what?"

She lowered her voice. "A couple of my friends heard one or two girls being a little uppity with her."

"Kids tease, Mamm."

"I know. But, I'm starting to wonder if one of them had something to do with her falling. Have you heard anything about that?"

"Some." He shrugged. "But I don't think her problem with a girl had anything to do with her falling. She promises that the dog was just an overactive puppy and he merely got a bit rambunctious."

"What if someone did hurt her feelings during the party? Should we try to get to the bottom of it?"

He shrugged. "Mamm, you know how private Effie is. She's not going to come out and tell us if something is wrong. Plus, there's always a chance we could make things worse if we get involved."

"I know. I just want her to be happy."

Thinking about some of the rumors he'd heard of a certain boy being especially kind to Effie, Zack smiled. "I think she's doing okay, Mamm. Let's worry about her leg and not her social life for now."

"I suppose you're right."

"I know I am."

Focusing on him, she blinked, as if she'd suddenly realized that he had on fresh clothes. "Where are you off to?"

"I'm going to see Leona and her girlfriends. Maybe take them out for pizza."

Her expression fell. "She's leaving today, isn't she?"

He nodded, not really trusting his voice, though he didn't know why. There wasn't anything to say.

"What are you two going to do?"

He knew she was talking about the future. "I don't know."

"You haven't made plans?"

"Not really. Though, what could we say? It's not like we've made any promises to each other."

His mother looked a little taken aback. "You two seemed like you meant more to each other than you're letting on. I've noticed the way she's looked at you . . . and the way you've looked at her."

"Mamm, like I told ya, Leona was engaged to be married when she arrived here." He held up a hand before she got the idea that he actually wanted to talk about that with his mother. "Granted, she had already begun to have doubts about the relationship before we met. But even if she had some misgivings, I don't imagine that she'll be ready to enter a new relationship with me so soon."

"Or, maybe, you two already have started a relationship," his mother softly suggested.

"I don't know how to respond to that."

"You know what I mean, Zack. The Lord has already been working through you both. He might have already decided that the two of you need to enter a relationship, whether you think that's a wise thing to do or not."

His mother had a point, but that didn't mean he was ready to embrace a romance with Leona that she wasn't ready to have. "How about I'll let you know what happens *if* something happens between us?"

She nodded. "I think that sounds like a fine idea. Now, in the meantime, I think I'll start looking for those magazines again."

Zack chuckled to himself as he left the house and set off for the Orange Blossom Inn. When his grandmother was alive, she used to tease his *mamm,* saying that she always had been a bit absentminded.

Her heart was in the right place, though. He knew that she also made some good points. There had to be a reason the Lord had put him and Leona in each other's paths. Perhaps he should stop putting up obstacles and simply be open to letting things happen instead.

When he got closer to the bed-and-breakfast, Zack couldn't help but compare his lonely walk to the one that had taken place three nights before, when he'd offered to slip his jacket over her shoulders and her smile had made a difficult night so much better.

He'd felt such hope that night, but for once, he had also felt selfish and possessive. He'd wanted to claim the rest of Leona's time as his own. Had wanted to tell his family that no matter how much they needed him to pick up the slack, he was going to be unavailable until Leona left.

Of course, the ironic thing had been that he hadn't needed

to make such statements. His family had been more than eager to steer him toward Leona.

And, as a matter of fact, he had spent a lot of time with her. But it had never been alone, and they'd never discussed anything serious. That had been by her design, he realized. She'd needed to retain some space between them.

When the front porch came into view, he slowed, seeing that there was a woman sitting on the front steps. Then his heart started beating a little bit faster as he realized that it was Leona.

She smiled as he approached.

"Leona," he said. "It's *gut* to see you."

Her brown eyes warmed. Then she gave a somewhat wistful sounding sigh. "I feel the same way."

He almost stumbled. From the time they first met, he'd felt as if he and Leona had been destined to meet. Then, from their visit at the restaurant to Pinecraft Park to Siesta Key to that party at his house . . . he'd seen a dozen reasons why his instincts had been correct.

There was something special about this woman. But more than that, there was something special about the way he felt about her. She'd been kind to his sister, firm with her ex, and adorable with her friends.

But only now was he able to put what had been happening between them to words. Right now, with Leona gazing at him with trust and tenderness, he knew.

In her eyes was the promise of everything he'd ever wished for and the fulfillment of everything he'd always wanted.

He'd found it, the very day she was leaving him.

Chapter 27

To Leona's pleasure, Zack took a seat beside her on the steps. Immediately, she smelled the clean cotton scent of his clothes, noticed again the hard lines of his jaw, felt how solid and strong—and, well, how much bigger—he was compared to her.

He resonated with confidence and assurance. Yet, there was more to him than that. Kindness tinged his actions, whether it was caring for his sister, his behavior toward her girlfriends, or the way he held her hand.

She was drawn to that kindness as much as his looks or his confidence. To her, being around a man who so easily thought of others was mesmerizing.

"How is Effie?" she asked.

"She's recovering well. Anxious to return to school."

"I bet. Staying home in bed always sounds more fun than it is. I'm sorry I didn't have time to see her yesterday."

They'd planned to go by the Kaufmann's house but time had gotten away from them. She, Mattie, and Sara have been so busy buying souvenirs and going to all of their favorite places one last time.

He grinned. "If you had stopped by, it was likely that you wouldn't have been able to see her. It seems everyone we know has been visiting the house. My *mamm* has even had to limit my sister's visiting hours."

"It's nice she has so many friends."

"*Jah.*" Still gazing at her, he said, "So, are you ready to leave?"

"Well, my things are packed. But I'm not ready to leave Pinecraft." She also wasn't ready to leave him, but she was too shy to tell him that. "It's going to be hard to go back to Ohio."

His expression turned strained. "I'm sure you'll miss the warm weather."

"I will, for sure. But . . . ah, I'm going to be missing the friends I've made, too." Throwing caution to the wind, she added, "And there's the fact that I'm going to have to deal with everything in Walnut Creek."

"Have you talked to your mother again?"

She nodded. "I talked to her again yesterday, but we didn't talk about anything of importance." Remembering the wary tone in her mother's voice, Leona knew she was going to be having many conversations with her mother about what she'd done. Though she never doubted her parents' love, she knew they would have something to say about how she'd handled things with Edmund. "I have a feeling she's waiting to see me face-to-face to discuss things."

"That's for the best, I bet."

"I suppose." She looked down at the rubber flip-flops on her feet and felt that they were a fine symbol of everything that was about to change. Gone would be the sun and the dazzling blue skies and the warmth and the freedom. In their place would be stockings and boots and snow and gray skies. Also her parents' watchful eyes and Edmund's resentment.

Zack rested his elbows on his knees. "Leona, I want to tell you something before everyone joins us."

"Yes?"

"I . . . I hope that you will consider staying in contact with me."

Though she was pleased about that, his somewhat stilted statement was a bit of a disappointment. "Oh. *Jah*. Yes, of course."

He tilted his head, staring at her intently. "Of course?"

"*Jah*." *What to say? What to say?* "I mean, I'd like to stay in contact with you."

"I am going to miss you. A lot." As if embarrassed, he looked down at his feet. "Even though we haven't known each other long, I want you to know that I've developed feelings for you."

"You have?"

"*Jah*."

"Ah."

He nodded again, this time almost looking as if he was embarrassed by his admission. "Strong feelings." He exhaled. "I wasn't going to do this, but I can't help myself." With a sudden, forceful movement, he reached for her hand and clasped it between his. The way he held her hand, as if he was staking a claim, made her pulse beat a little faster. And right then and there, she knew. Zack was serious about her, serious about their relationship. So much so, he didn't want to let her go.

His next words proved her suspicions to be correct. "I want to see you again. Actually, I am dreading the thought of going weeks without seeing you."

"I've been feeling the same way," she admitted. "But, Zack, I can't make you any promises about the future until I get my life settled."

"I understand. But may I write and call you?"

Her gaze warmed. "You better. I would be sad if you didn't."

"We can't have you sad."

"Please don't make me sad, Zack." She smiled then, because their conversation made her so happy.

And because, if she didn't share a smile with him, she was going to be tempted to do something really stupid and lean closer to him . . . just as if he was going to share a kiss with her on the front stoop in broad daylight.

The worst part about that, of course, was what she knew her reaction to that would be. She knew if he made the first move, she wouldn't turn her head away. She wouldn't get mad at him, either.

Unfortunately, she had the terrible idea that she would no doubt be glad he kissed her.

She'd probably kiss him back, too.

She wouldn't care that they were sitting on the stoop of the inn in broad daylight.

She wouldn't care what her girlfriends would say—or her mother, when she found out.

"Leona," Zack said as he brushed his fingers down her cheek. Along the edges of her mouth. Then, as she gave a little gasp, he leaned closer.

She tilted her chin up. He was going to do it. He was going to kiss her, right there on the front porch.

She had as much control over her ability to stop what was happening between them as she had over the weather.

Just then the door opened. "Zack, you're here!" Mattie called out. "You're just in time, too! I was telling Sara that I'm starving."

Leona jerked away as Zack practically jumped to his feet, releasing her hand like her touch burned him.

Mattie stopped, looked from Leona to Zack and back

again. Then a rosy blush stained her cheeks. "Oh my gosh! I'm so sorry. I didn't mean to interrupt."

"It was nothing," Leona said quickly.

"Do you want me to step back inside for a few minutes?"

Leona could only imagine how embarrassed she'd feel then! "Of course not," she said as she got to her feet. "Let's eat." She smiled at Mattie, then motioned for Sara to come out and join them. "I'm starving, too."

But when they started down the sidewalk, she wondered if she was ever going to be able to eat a thing again.

THAT FEELING ONLY intensified as they watched their bus pull into the parking lot a few hours later.

"It's here," Mattie said in a particularly un-Mattie-like way.

"We should probably take our things over there," Sara added. But for once, not even their most organized member was in a hurry to move.

Sitting beside Zack, Leona felt tears prick her eyes. For the last two hours, she'd been doing her best to hold them at bay, but now that they were only minutes from boarding the bus, crying was inevitable.

"Hey, Mattie!" Danny called out from the parking lot. He was walking with several of the men and women they'd met at the beach and at Zack's house. "We came to see you off."

Mattie immediately got to her feet. "I'm glad you did," she said as she grabbed Sara's hand and pulled her, along with their suitcases, toward the crowd. "You two coming?"

"We'll be there in a minute," Zack said.

"Take your time, Leona," Sara said as she took hold of Leona's suitcase too. "I'll give this to the driver for ya."

"*Danke.*"

As soon as they were sitting alone, Zack leaned closer. "If you start crying, I won't be able to let you go," he teased.

"Then you'd be stuck with a crying woman."

"I think she would be more than that," he said softly.

His sweet words were her undoing. With a sigh, she let the tears fall. "I'm going to miss you so much, Zack. I'm going to miss you and your friends and your sisters and the sun and . . . and everything."

He chuckled. "I know you will. And I'm going to miss you just as much." His expression turned concerned as he watched her swipe away a tear, then he pulled a worn bandanna from his back pocket and dabbed at her cheeks. "Don't cry anymore, Leona. This separation won't be forever."

"You sound so certain."

"That's because I am," he said, wiping her face. "Too much changed for us to drift apart. That's not going to happen."

Everything he said made sense. Too overcome with emotion, she simply nodded.

Leaning closer, he brushed a strand of hair away from her face. "Don't forget, we're going to write and call and make plans."

"I won't forget," she replied.

"*Gut.*" With a frown, he glanced toward the parking lot. "It's time, Leona," he said as he got to his feet. "Come now. People are boarding."

She let him pull her to her feet, then slowly walked by his side toward the crowd surrounding the bus. "We'll talk soon, I promise. Safe travels," he murmured before they were surrounded by their friends.

"We thought we were going to have to drag you onto that bus," Danny teased.

"You almost did," Leona said, summoning up a smile for

Danny and the rest of Zack's friends. "This is a hard place to leave."

"That just means you've got to come back again soon."

"Everyone needs to board," the driver announced.

"Bye, Zack," Mattie said with a smile, leading the quick, chaotic process of everyone saying goodbye to everyone else.

Then, next thing she knew, Leona was boarding the bus and trying not to cry again. This time, Mattie and Sara were sitting together, and for now, Leona sat by herself.

As the bus started up, she peered through the glass at Zack, who was standing in the outskirts of the group.

Leona noticed that he had at last let his guard down. Now that he wasn't trying to look brave, he looked just as devastated as she felt.

With effort, Leona pushed away the fresh tears that were threatening to fall. She'd promised herself that she wouldn't cry until the bus was dark and everyone was asleep.

"Leona, do you see Miss Beverly?" Sara asked.

She scanned the crowd and saw Miss Beverly standing with a couple of ladies who the girls now knew were some of her best friends.

But Beverly's gaze was settled directly on Leona, and her expression seemed almost wistful. It made Leona realize that she and her friends had been as special to Beverly as she'd become to them.

"Don't you hope you end up as great as she is?" Mattie whispered. "She's so warm and friendly, but there's an elegance about her, too."

Leona nodded. "She is elegant. But sometimes, when she doesn't think anyone is looking, I think she looks a little melancholy, too. I wonder if she's truly happy."

"She seems like it. Do you think maybe she's not?"

"I don't know. I simply got the impression that there was lot more to her than most people cared to see."

"Everyone is like that, though, don't you think?" Sara asked as the bus turned down Bahia Vista. "We all try to be the person the world wants us to be. But sometimes it's too exhausting."

Leona glanced at Sara quickly, realizing that her friend had become a champion of doing just that. Keeping everything inside while hiding so much confusion.

"It can be very tiring," she admitted. Then, much to her dismay, she felt tears fill her eyes yet again. And because it was so, so hard to hide her sadness any longer, she turned straight ahead, closed her eyes, and let the tears slide down her face.

Leona was so grateful that Mattie and Sara pretended not to notice.

Chapter 28

"Another day, another bus gone," Sadie announced as the crowd started to break up. "I have to tell you that I'm going to miss those girls from Walnut Creek. Having them around certainly livened up the place."

Beverly smiled in agreement. "I'm going to miss them, too. There's something about a trio of girls laughing and staying up all hours of the night that makes me happy. They were noisy and full of spirit, and they practically cleaned me out every teatime! Did we ever eat so much?"

Sadie winked. "I think I still do."

Beverly grinned as they started down the sidewalk toward their homes. "Yesterday, I even made an extra chocolate-cherry pound cake. Those girls sure loved their chocolate."

"You do make a *gut* chocolate pound cake, Beverly." After they walked another block, Sadie added, "Maybe when we see those girls, we remember how we used to be."

Beverly thought about that. "Maybe so. Gosh, I wonder if we were ever that lighthearted?"

"Speak for yourself, Beverly," Sadie said. "I know I was. Why, I'm still lighthearted. And I've been known to eat you out of house and home at teatime."

Sadie did, indeed, have an appetite, though Beverly would never tell her such a thing. "I'd be lost without friends like you, Sadie."

"I feel the same way."

They were almost back at the inn when Beverly noticed Zachary Kaufmann standing alone against a fence. She knew people often congregated there to watch the buses parade down the street.

But noticing he was staring down the street with a lost expression, she felt compelled to speak to him. "Sadie, I'll see you later. I'm going to go talk to Zack."

Sadie's gaze warmed on the boy. "That's a *gut* idea. Poor guy."

Beverly smiled at her friend, liking that they were of the same mind. Then she walked to Zack. When she got just a few feet away, her approach seemed to push him out of his reverie.

"Hi, Beverly," he said politely.

"Hello, Zack."

He pushed back from the fence. "Is there something I can help you with?"

"Not at all. I just happened to notice that you, too, came to see off the bus. I bet this is a hard day for you."

He nodded. "I guess it's no secret that I've become pretty close to Leona."

"Not a secret at all." If all their togetherness hadn't been enough of a hint, the rumor of them almost kissing on her front porch would have been a sure sign.

"Do you two have plans to see each other soon?"

He shook his head.

"I'm surprised about that."

"I thought I had better give her a little bit of time. She wants some, too, I think," he said after a thoughtful pause. "She just broke up with another man, you know."

"Yes, I heard about that." She tilted her head to the side. "Are you afraid she's going to go back to him?"

His eyes widened. "Actually, I never even thought about that. Do you think that's a possibility?"

Oh, but she could have bitten her tongue. "I have no idea, but based on the glow of happiness she wore whenever the two you were together, I'd be shocked if she did. She really seemed to like you, Zack."

"I've been more worried that when she gets back to her normal life up in Ohio, she's going to imagine that what she had with me was just a vacation romance."

"There's only one way to keep that from happening. You'll have to make sure Leona knows she means more to you than that."

"Matter of fact, when you walked up, I was just standing here, thinking about when I should visit her." He shook his head. "I'm embarrassed to tell you that I was even thinking about going to Walnut Creek at the end of the week."

"Nothing embarrassing about wanting someone to know they mean a lot to you," Beverly said gently, realizing that she meant every word she said.

It was what Ida and Jean had done, after all. They'd made all kinds of attempts to see her despite the fact that Beverly had been sure that they didn't want to know her anymore.

"As someone who has been the recipient of other peoples' efforts to stay in touch with me, I can tell you that reaching out to others is well worth it."

"You think so?"

"I promise you that, Zack."

His shoulders relaxed as his lips curved up. "You're right. I'll call her when she gets home and go from there."

"That sounds like a perfect plan." Worried that she was about to step over the line between being a concerned friend and a nosy neighbor, she said, "Well, I should get back to the inn. I have guest rooms to prepare, you know. I really came over here to tell you that if you ever need someone to talk to, or even if your family needs help with Effie while you are away, please don't forget about me."

"I won't. *Danke*."

She waved a hand. "Have a *gut* afternoon."

"Wait. Hey, Beverly?"

"Yes?"

"How hard was it for you to move away from Ohio to Florida?"

She swallowed, thinking about how lost—and betrayed— she'd felt and how terribly kind Aunt Patty had been. Then she remembered her fascination with the foliage and her love of the citrus trees. The constant sun. And the way people arrived all the time from Holmes County, so it wasn't like she'd ever completely left behind the things she remembered.

And that was why she smiled softly and was able to say with complete honesty, "It wasn't hard at all, Zack."

"Really?" He looked stunned.

"Really. See, for me? Well, it was the right decision."

LEONA'S PALMS WERE damp with worry when they stepped off the Pioneer Trails bus in front of the Alpine Village shops in Berlin. During the last hour, as the bus had traveled closer and closer to home and the landmarks became more and more familiar, she'd become more and more agitated.

What if her parents yelled at her? What if her sisters lectured her, reminding her that she was very far from perfect and a true disappointment to them all?

Worse, what if Edmund had had a change of heart and met the bus, too?

Imagining the scene, Leona had an idea of how he would handle it, too. He would claim that he'd met the bus to greet Mattie, but she would know that he'd come to take a good, long look at her. Almost as if he'd come to see a fallen woman.

Both Sara and Mattie had shaken off her concerns.

"You're getting yourself worked up for nothing," Sara had said. "First of all, your parents would never embarrass you by creating a scene in the parking lot. Secondly, I know your *mamm*. She's a nice lady, and a very honest one, too. If she was still mad at you, you would know about it."

"Maybe."

"And you shouldn't worry about Edmund, either," Mattie said. "I can't imagine him meeting the bus. Plus, if he is mad and hurt, he's not going to want everyone to see him like that."

Feeling a little bit better, Leona had nodded. "You're right. I'm overthinking things."

Sara had clasped her hand. "It's going to be a hard couple of days, but you'll get through it."

"You sound so sure."

"I am. The Lord wouldn't have put you in this situation if He didn't think you could handle it."

That reminder had meant the world to Leona, because it was so true. She did have His blessings on her side. And with His help, she knew she was going to be able to handle anything.

Lord, I could sure use your strength right now, she silently prayed as they scooted up the aisle, then finally walked down the steps and planted their feet in the parking lot.

Immediately, a burst of February wind stung her cheeks.

"Hello, winter," Mattie muttered behind her. "I haven't missed you one bit."

Looking around, Leona noticed that large mounds of snow had been plowed into different sections of the parking lot. As was the norm, the sky was a dismal pale gray, diligently reminding them that even on clear days, the sunny days of summer were still months away. Funny, she'd been so wrapped up in her worries, she hadn't given much thought to the weather.

All she'd thought about was that she was going back home. Almost a thousand miles from Zack Kaufmann.

"Leona!" her mother called out, rushing toward her with a tender expression in her eyes. "It's so good to see you."

"Mamm, it's *gut* to see you, too," she said as her mother enfolded her in a long hug.

That hug was everything she'd ever wanted. And exactly what she needed right that very minute. Her mother might be disappointed in her, but this hug told her that she was still loved and cherished.

And that meant everything to her. So much so, that tears filled her eyes. Yet again.

When they separated, her mother noticed her tears right away. "No reason to cry, dear. Everything will be okay."

"Are you sure?"

"I am," Naomi said as she pushed her way through the crowd to join them, Rosanna just steps behind.

"Naomi? I can't believe you came to meet the bus."

"Why wouldn't I be here?"

"I thought you might be upset with me," she admitted softly.

"I'm never too upset to welcome you back home," she teased as she wrapped an arm around Leona's shoulders and squeezed tight. "Leona, you always did bring a lot of drama into our lives. And now, here you are, doing it again with this broken engagement of yours."

"Some things never change," Rosanna said, enfolding Leona into a hug of her own. As Leona wrapped her arms around her eldest sister, Rosanna pressed her lips to Leona's cheek. "It will be okay. I promise."

She was so relieved, the tears started falling harder.

Suddenly, a tissue was planted in her hand. "*Danke.*"

"Blow your nose. We're going to get your things together, then take you out for sandwiches."

Leona wiped her tears. "Is Daed here, too?"

"*Nee,*" Mamm said. "He thought you might need your sisters right now."

"We all thought that," Naomi said. "David and Michael are home with Daed."

"So come on, dear. Let's get your bags, load up the buggy, and get some lunch."

"Okay. Let me just say goodbye to Mattie and Sara." She found them in the crowd. Both pulled away from their parents and hugged her tightly.

"I miss you already," Mattie said. "I'll come see you in a day or two."

"Me too," Sara said. "I promise."

Leona promised to make an effort to see them soon, too. She knew she was going to need their support while she at last dealt with the consequences of her broken engagement. Then it was time to hurry back to her sisters and mother. They had found her bags and were wheeling them to their waiting buggy.

As she rushed to catch up, she whispered, *"Danke,"* to the Almighty. Once again, He'd shown that she was always on His mind. She was ever so grateful to Him.

Chapter 29

Zack waited two days before calling Leona. He had actually considered waiting another day before picking up the phone. He didn't want to rush things, scare her off, or overwhelm her, especially when she was probably busy reuniting with her family and getting back to work.

But as his every thought seemed to be centered around her, and because, since she'd left, he'd felt as if he were missing a limb, he knew he couldn't wait another day. Waiting even another hour to hear her voice was going to be an impossibility.

After assuring himself that he had privacy in the kitchen, Zack unfolded the note card he'd been carrying around. The one on which she'd carefully written both her address and phone number. He didn't want to think about how many times he'd opened the card and looked at Leona's neat handwriting. If he dared to guess, it would be embarrassing.

Yes, his eagerness, where she was concerned, seemed to know no bounds.

Which was why he knew he should probably wait another day to call. The way he was feeling now might give too much away. He wanted her to know that he liked her, not that he was verging on becoming obsessed.

But, as if his fingers had a mind of their own, he punched in Leona's telephone number, then drummed his fingers on the kitchen counter as he waited for the call to go through.

After hearing three lonely rings but no answer, his high spirits deflated. It served him right, too. All he'd done for pretty much the last forty-eight hours was debate with himself about when he should actually call.

It honestly hadn't occurred to him that once he finally made this momentous decision, she might not answer.

He let it ring one more time. Then two. Then at last gave up.

"Hello?"

He blinked. He'd been such an arrogant idiot, it also hadn't occurred to him that there was a very good chance she wouldn't be the person to pick up the phone.

"Hello," he replied quickly. "This is Zachary Kaufmann. I'm calling for Leona."

"Hi, Zachary. We were wondering if you were gonna call. I'm Edie, Leona's mother."

"Hello. It's nice to meet you."

"I'll look forward to meeting you in person."

He couldn't resist smiling in his empty kitchen. Her wanting to meet him in person was a *gut* sign. As was her comment about them wondering when he was going to call. "I, as well."

"Leona said she enjoyed meeting your family," she continued, just as if it wasn't a long distance call.

"I'm glad. They like her verra much."

"And how is Effie? Leona mentioned that she fell and broke her leg."

"Oh. Yes, she did. Effie, she's doing better, *danke*." He paused, unsure whether he was supposed to let her continue to ask him questions or remind her that he'd called for Leona.

"Is Leona around, by chance? I was hopin' to say hello to her."

Edie chuckled. "I know. I'm sorry I didn't tell you right away. I just wanted to get to know you a bit. Leona is at work."

"Oh."

"She works five days a week at the notion shop in Berlin."

"She mentioned that," he murmured, now feeling embarrassed. "I guess I wasn't thinking about that when I picked up the phone."

"Doesn't sound like it." Again, she sounded amused, not irritated. "Does Leona have your phone number? I imagine she'll want to give you a call when she gets home."

He remembered her saying she wasn't comfortable calling men. "She doesn't. But I can call back. What time do you think would be best?"

"She'll be home after six o'clock. But let me have your phone number, too. I know she'll be disappointed that she missed you."

Zack figured if she was even half as disappointed as he was, he would consider himself lucky. "I'll give you my number, but please let Leona know I'll call her this evening."

"You sound determined to do the calling."

"I think she'd prefer if I did the calling," he blurted out before he realized that Leona probably had no desire for him to be chatting with her mother about things like this. "I mean, well, never mind," he said. "I don't think I'm making much sense right now."

"As a matter of fact, I think you are making a lot of sense, Zachary. Thank you for calling."

After giving her his phone number, Zack hung up the phone with a sigh of relief. He had to get his act together. The sooner the better, too.

"Class, I need a volunteer to walk Effie down to the assembly," Mrs. Bishop asked from her desk.

"I'll be fine, Mrs. Bishop," Effie said. "I'm pretty good on crutches." Actually having a broken leg and crutches wasn't such an unfamiliar situation. For most of the last two years, one or the other of her legs had needed special support.

"I know you can hop around on crutches like no other, Eff, but we're going straight to the buses after the assembly. That means someone needs to help you with your books."

"I'll help Effie," Josiah called out, already on his feet.

"That is very nice of you, Josiah. Thank you," Mrs. Bishop said. "Uh, Josiah and Effie, you two may leave as soon as you're ready."

Effie had learned to always keep her things in order, since needing help wasn't anything new, and now she plopped her backpack onto the top of her desk. Just as she was reaching for her crutches, Josiah bent down and retrieved them for her.

"Here," he said without a lot of fanfare.

Which was a really good thing, because the rest of the class—Effie and Mrs. Bishop included—were staring at him like he'd just solved every problem in their math book.

"*Danke,*" she forced herself to say in a rather cool way.

In no time, he was holding their backpacks and she was crutching down the hallway.

The gymnasium was practically empty. The assembly bell wasn't supposed to ring for another eight minutes.

"It's nice getting out of class early," she said, just so Josiah wouldn't think she thought he'd offered to help her because he liked her, or anything.

"Getting out of class is great. But that's not why I volunteered to walk with you."

"Why did you?"

His lips twitched. "Maybe because you've been avoiding me since you've gotten back to school."

"I have not."

"I think differently. You talked to me a lot when I visited you at your house. But now that we're at school, you'll hardly look at me."

"I didn't want to put you in an awkward position."

Josiah frowned. "What are you talking about?"

Now she felt even more embarrassed. Did they really have to be talking about this? "I thought maybe you were only being nice to me because you felt sorry for me."

He stared at her, his expression serious. Then, to her surprise, he suddenly smiled. "That wasn't the reason, Effie," he said at last.

And when that smile finally penetrated, Effie realized he was telling the truth. She returned his smile. Because it was pretty obvious that nothing else needed to be said.

AS THE CLOCK's hands moved again, proclaiming it to now be a quarter after six, everyone who was seated at the kitchen table stared at the phone expectantly.

But nothing happened.

Naomi leaned back in her chair. "This waiting is killing me. Leona, you need to get up and call him."

"*Nee.*"

"Why not?"

"He wanted to do the calling," Leona said.

"Actually, he made it sound like he was going to do the calling because you wanted him to call you," her mother murmured. "Did you tell Zachary that you didn't call boys?"

"Maybe." When the other four people at the table grinned at each other, she said, "What?"

"Nothing, dear," her father said. His expression was the most composed of all of them, but that wasn't saying too much. Everyone at the table looked like they were on the verge of laughter. Even Naomi's husband, David, looked like he was having a grand time witnessing her embarrassment.

"Daed," Leona said, "if I did say something like that, it was because we were in Pinecraft."

"Though it ain't my business whether you want to call young men or not, I don't see how who calls who matters," her father replied.

"It does to me."

Naomi neatly stacked her bread plate onto her empty dinner plate. "I think you need to call him now. We're going to have to start the dishes soon."

"Don't push, Ni," David murmured.

"But—"

"I mean it," Naomi's husband said. "Leona needs to do what she wants." With a scowl, he added, "That Edmund hardly ever let her voice an opinion. He was *always* sure he was right. Now that he's out of the picture, I have to admit I'm not sorry that I won't be sharing a bunch of meals with him in the future."

"I couldn't agree more," her father grumbled.

Noticing how the four of them didn't even attempt to shy away from bad-mouthing Edmund, Leona looked from one to another with a sense of frustration. "I sure wish all of you would have told me how you really felt about Edmund before now."

Mamm shifted uncomfortably in her seat. "We didn't want to hurt your feelings. I mean, we weren't the ones who wanted to marry him."

"Mamm!"

"I'm sorry, but that is the truth," she said around a blush. "We all thought you loved him, dear."

"We thought you thought his quirks were cute," Naomi added. "Just because Rosanna and I didn't like him, it didn't mean that you couldn't."

"Rosanna didn't like Edmund, either?"

David covered his bark of laughter with a napkin. "Sorry, Leona," he murmured. "All I know is that Michael wasn't real eager to be sitting across from him too often, either."

Leona inhaled, feeling like she should defend herself or her judgment . . . or something. After all, it wasn't like she'd gone into that relationship blind. She'd really thought she would come to love Edmund.

The ringing of the phone stopped all conversation.

Talk about divine intervention!

Her father glanced at the clock. "Might want to give that young man a lesson in telling time, daughter. It's now almost twenty after the hour. Best go get the phone before he hangs up."

She scampered to the side of the kitchen and picked up the receiver. "Hello?"

"Leona. You're home," Zack said. His voice sounding smooth and perfect. Like butter.

And though it was foolish and a bit on the dramatic side, she felt like *she* melted right then and there. "*Jah*," she replied, not even caring that she sounded breathless.

"Did you hear I called?"

"*Jah*."

When she didn't say anything more, he added, "Your mother said you might call, but I'm glad I got to you first."

"Me too," she said around a sigh. "It's so good to hear your voice."

"I was just thinking the same thing."

She knew she was probably grinning like a fool, but she couldn't help herself.

Across the room, her family stared at her in silence, each person looking more intrigued and surprised than the next.

Then her mother abruptly stood. "Off we go. Into the hearth room."

"Oh, hold on, Zack," Leona whispered, then loudly she said, "You all don't have to leave."

"Oh, yes, we do," her mother replied. "Leona Weaver, you are my daughter, and I've seen you through all sorts of things: chicken pox, disagreements with friends, stitches on your hand. A broken engagement. But in all of your twenty-two years I've never, ever seen you look like this."

"Like what?"

"Like you're the happiest girl in the world," David said with a wink. Then, to Leona's amazement, her brother-in-law started leading the way to the hearth room, and everyone else followed on his heels.

And then she was alone in the kitchen with stacks of dirty

dishes and Zack on the other end of the line. "I'm sorry. My family said something . . ."

"I heard," he said, his voice warm and kind. "Now, talk to me Leona, tell me how you are doing. I've missed you."

She pulled the cord out, sat down on the wooden floor, and did just that.

Chapter 30

A little more than a month later, after delaying the inevitable for a good ten minutes, Zack wrapped the telephone cord around his fingers and made himself do what had to be done. "*Gut naught,* Leona," he murmured. "Sleep well."

"Good night, Zack. Will you call again tomorrow night?"

He smiled, because the anxiousness he heard in her voice sounded a lot like how he was feeling inside. A little desperate. "*Jah.* I will call," he promised. Just like he'd done for the last eight nights in a row, and several weeks before that.

"*Gut.* Good night, then."

"Bye, Le," he murmured, then hung up before he found a way to extend their conversation yet another ten minutes.

When he finally put the receiver in the cradle, Zack sighed. Something was going to have to be done, the sooner the better. It had now been more than a month since she'd left Florida. If he didn't see Leona in person, he was going to start climbing the walls.

After that one day when he'd called and spoken to her

mother, then talked to Leona later that night, their conversations had gradually become longer and more frequent. He'd gone from having short, ten-minute conversations every other night to talks twice that long every evening.

Tonight, they'd been on the phone over an hour. It was getting a bit ridiculous. Expensive, too.

"Zack, you need to buy a bus ticket," Violet said from the doorway.

He could tell by the tone of her voice that she wasn't teasing him. Turning to look at her, he nodded. "I know. I keep offering, but she doesn't want me to come see her yet."

"Why on earth not?"

He shrugged. "She said she wanted me to wait a bit." Actually, he was trying hard to not take her request wrong. If she hadn't kept refusing his offer, he knew he would already be in Walnut Creek.

"Is she still recovering from her breakup?"

"*Nee.* I mean, I don't think so. But maybe she is. She's just disrupted her whole life, you know."

Violet tapped her foot. "Do you think her family is upset with her?"

"*Nee.* I know they aren't. She's put different family members on the phone to say hello." He chuckled in an attempt to hide his embarrassment. "I think she simply wants more time. There's nothing wrong with that."

"I know. But it still seems a little strange." Her eyes brightened. "I know! Maybe she's afraid to be too forward. Maybe you should go on up there and surprise her?"

He actually had been thinking about that, but then he remembered how Edmund had never listened to her. He didn't want to be that way, too.

"I don't think that a surprise visit is the way to go."

"Sure? She might find it romantic."

When a dreamy look appeared in her eyes, he laughed. "Believe me, I've thought about it. But I'm not going to pay her any surprise visits. See, I've been praying about this," he confided. "I think the Lord is reminding me to have some patience. I've waited this long to find Leona, I can wait a little longer until she's ready."

"You love her, don't you?"

"*Jah.* I really do love her," he said, not even embarrassed to admit it. "And because I want her love, too, I'm willing to wait until she's ready to love me back."

He just hoped she would come to her decision sooner than later.

"KNOCK, KNOCK."

Glancing up from the letter she was attempting to write Zack, Leona frowned at the unwanted interruption. "*Jah,* Mamm?"

Without another word, her door opened. But, to her surprise, it wasn't her mother who had come to see her.

"Daed?"

"Don't act so surprised," he said gruffly. "I, um, had a little bit of time this afternoon, so I thought maybe we could visit for a bit."

"Is everything all right?" After flipping her letter over, she scrambled to the side of her neatly made bed just as he pulled over the chair from her desk.

"Everything is fine, I think," he said.

She wasn't sure about that. Actually, she couldn't remember her father ever stepping into her room simply to chat. And, judging by the way he was sitting—his hands practically holding his knees in a death grip—she was pretty sure he didn't have a simple chat on his mind.

When a full minute passed, Leona searched for something, anything, to say. "I was, uh, just writing Zack a letter."

His shoulders eased. "I'm glad you brought that up. See, that's just what I wanted to talk to you about."

"My letters to Zack?"

Looking at her intently, he said, "Leona, I'm thinking those need to stop."

"What!?" Before he had a chance to answer, she shot off another question. "Why?" Foolishly, she felt tears fill her eyes. And wasn't that just the worst? It seemed all she'd been doing since she'd said goodbye to Zack in Pinecraft was attempt to hold her tears at bay.

"Calm down, Leona." Looking at her with a tender expression, he added, "My word, you always did wear your heart on your sleeve."

"Daed, I like writing Zack. I know we talk a lot on the phone, too, but I feel like I need to write him every day, too."

"Leona, what I'm trying mighty hard to say—in between all of your interruptions—is that it's time to stop fussing around and start making plans to see him."

He might as well have been speaking Greek. "Daed, you're saying you want me to go back to Pinecraft to see Zack?"

"Last time I checked, that's where he was. And, I might add, we all think he sounds just as miserable as you do on the phone." While she gaped at him, his brown eyes—eyes which matched her own—filled with humor. "Leona, it's time you were happy, don't you think?"

"You . . . you don't think it's too soon?"

"Too soon for what?"

"You know, Daed. Too soon to fall in love again?"

She inhaled, waiting for some special words of wisdom that only her father could share. But instead of spouting out anything of worth, he tilted his head back and laughed.

She hopped off the bed. "Daed, I'm being serious."

"Oh, daughter. Of course you are," he murmured as he got to his feet as well, then promptly enfolded her into the warmest hug ever. After pressing his lips to her brow, he pulled back and looked her in the eyes. "But what you don't seem to understand is that you already have fallen in love again. It's done."

She blinked. Then realized he was exactly right. All she'd been doing since she'd returned from Pinecraft was biding her time until she thought everyone else would be able to accept her new relationship. Her mind—and her heart—had already decided that Zack was the man for her. The right man for her.

"You're right," she said.

Stepping away, he grinned. "I know I am. You can't stop love, child."

Watching him walk out of her room, then close her door softly behind him, Leona repeated his words in her head.

Her father was now officially the smartest man she'd ever known. He was exactly right. No matter how hard she'd tried, she hadn't been able to stop love.

She hadn't even been able to slow it down.

Marching to the bed, she picked up her letter and tore it in half. She now had a far different letter to write. And after that, she had a bus ticket to buy.

Chapter 31

Leona held a bus ticket in one hand, a backpack on her shoulder, and a matching quilted duffel bag in her other hand. She was ready to return to Pinecraft.

Standing on either side of her were her two best friends in the world. And they were currently looking forlorn.

"I can't believe you're going back to Pinecraft without us," Mattie exclaimed. "I'm so jealous."

After sharing a smile with Mattie, Leona chuckled. "I bet you are. After all, one Daniel Brenneman is pining for you."

"I wouldn't say he's *pining*. But in his last letter, he did say he wanted to come see me soon," Mattie admitted.

"I hope you told him to get on the bus," Sara said.

Mattie lifted her chin. "Of course I did. I'm not as stubborn as some people we know."

"I haven't been stubborn. I just wanted to be sure I was making the right decision this time."

Sara shook her head in exasperation. "Leona, you were sure from the moment you saw Zack in that tree."

"This is true."

"So, you're going to stay with Miss Beverly again?"

"*Jah,* though it's going to feel strange, staying in a regular guest room instead of our attic space."

"You'll have to tell us all about it. Write fast!"

"I will."

At her sisters' urging and her parents' blessing, she'd decided to spend two whole weeks in Pinecraft. She wanted to be able to spend as much time with Zack as possible, as well as have a real idea about what her life might be like living there.

She and Zack had talked about a lot of things during their many, many lengthy phone calls. They'd discussed their love for their families and their goals for the future. No matter where their conversations took them, though, they always ended up at the same place.

Both wanted to be with people who made them happy, who lifted them up. And, it seemed, they'd found these things in each other.

Neither of them had wanted to be coy about where their relationship was headed, especially not after she'd relayed her father's words of wisdom. Leona knew while she was in Pinecraft, she was going to be making plans with Zack about their future.

It felt so different than everything she'd done with Edmund, it was hardly worth comparing.

Suddenly, aware of everyone boarding the bus behind her, she hugged her girlfriends goodbye. "I love you both," she whispered. "I would never have survived all of this without you two. I don't know how I'll ever be able to repay you."

Mattie winked. "Don't worry, Le. I'm sure I'll be enough trouble soon enough. Sara, too."

After hugging them again, Leona boarded the bus. She had brought some knitting, two books, and a pillow. She wasn't worried about how to pass the time.

She just wished she knew how to convince the driver to drive as fast as possible. Now that she was about to see Zack again, she could hardly wait.

SIXTEEN HOURS LATER, Zack was standing next to Beverly in the parking lot. Next to her was another man, Eric Wagler, who she'd introduced as the new owner of the inn. Zack had a feeling they weren't the best of friends, though they seemed to be getting along all right.

Beverly and Eric had kindly offered to take Leona's things back to the inn so Zack could be alone with her as soon as possible.

Practically everyone in the parking lot knew his and Leona's story. After sharing with his family much of what Leona had told him, his family had done what they did best—they'd told everyone they knew that love had bloomed and Leona was on her way.

Now, as he looked around, Zack was certain that only about half the people in the crowd were there to greet the newcomers on the bus. The other half were hoping to get an unobstructed view of his much anticipated reunion with Leona.

With the exception of Effie, who was still at school, his whole family was there, though they were standing off to the side. His mother had even taken the day off work, saying she had a welcome-home party to prepare for.

Yep, his family was hosting another party this evening, and chances were good half the town was going to be there again, all to welcome Leona back.

He was just considering going to chat with his brother and sister when the atmosphere in the parking lot changed. A couple of cheers rang out, and his heart started beating a little faster.

The bus had arrived.

He stood still as it pulled forward and parked, even as the doors opened. The occupants started descending the stairs, and around him, familiar scenes unfolded. Relatives hugged. Old friends greeted each other with handshakes and wide smiles.

And then he saw her.

Blond hair. Brown eyes. Pretty cheeks. Sweet smile.

His girl.

Without a thought for anyone else, he walked through the crowd and reached her just as her feet touched the pavement.

But that lasted only a second. Because he picked her up in his arms and twirled her around, much to the amusement of everyone.

Leona rested her hands on his shoulders as he held her, her eyes bright with happiness. "You were here waiting for me," she said.

He knew she was talking about much more than just waiting for the bus, and she was exactly right. He had been.

After Zack set Leona down, he pulled her into his arms and kissed her temple. "I promised I would, Leona. Remember?"

"I remember," she murmured. "I remember all of your promises, Zack."

"Every one?" he teased.

"Every one. See, there are some promises that are just so special, just so right . . ."

"Just so right?" he prodded.

"That they become the promises a girl never forgets," she finished at last.

Right before he smiled.

And then he twirled her around again . . . until her joyous laughter filled the air.

About the author

About the book

Insights,
Interviews
& More . . .

Read on

Meet Shelley Shepard Gray

The New Studio

PEOPLE OFTEN ASK how I started writing. Some believe I've been a writer all my life; others ask if I've always felt I had a story I needed to tell. I'm afraid my reasons couldn't be more different. See, I started writing one day because I didn't have anything to read.

I've always loved to read. I was the girl in the back of the classroom with her nose in a book, the mom who kept a couple of novels in her car to read during soccer practice, the person who made weekly visits to the bookstore and the library.

Back when I taught elementary school, I used to read during my lunch breaks. One day, when I realized I'd forgotten to bring something to read, I turned on my computer and took a leap of faith. Feeling a little like I was doing something wrong, I typed those first words: *Chapter One.*

I didn't start writing with the intention of publishing a book. Actually, I just wrote for myself.

For the most part, I still write for myself, which is why, I think, I'm able to write so much. I write books that I'd like to read. Books that I would have liked to have in my old teacher tote bag. I'm always relieved and surprised and so happy when other people want to read my books, too!

Another question I'm often asked is why I choose to write inspirational fiction. Maybe at first glance, it does seem surprising. I'm not the type of person who usually talks about my faith in the line at the grocery store or when I'm out to lunch with friends. For me, my faith has always felt like more of a private thing. I feel that I'm still on my faith journey—still learning and studying God's word.

And that, I think, is why writing inspirational fiction is such a good fit for me. I enjoy writing about characters who happen to be in the middle of their faith journeys, too. They're not perfect, and they don't always make the right decisions. Sometimes they make mistakes, and sometimes they do something they're proud of. They're characters who are a lot like me.

Only God knows what else He has in store for me. He's given me the will and the ability to write stories to glorify Him. He's put many people in my life who are supportive and caring. I feel blessed and thankful . . . and excited to see what will happen next! ᥩ

Letter from the Author

Dear Reader,

Thank you for traveling with me to Pinecraft, Florida! I hope you will enjoy reading the Amish Brides of Pinecraft series. I know I am truly enjoying writing the books.

I've been wanting to set a series of novels in Pinecraft for some time. Several years ago, when I visited some of my Amish friends, I noticed one of the ladies seemed especially tan. It was March and we'd had quite a winter! And that's when she told me that she and her family had recently returned from a vacation to Pinecraft.

I have to admit to being very surprised. I'd had no idea that the Amish liked to go to the beach. Then, as she told me about the Pioneer Trails bus that traveled from Sugarcreek to Sarasota, Yoder's Restaurant, the beach at Siesta Key, the bicycles that everyone rode . . . I started wishing I had vacationed there, too!

This was why I was so excited when my editor was just as happy about setting a series of novels in sunny Florida as I was. The moment I got off the phone with Chelsey, I told my husband that we were going to have to visit Florida for some research. The sooner the better!

I was so happy when I discovered that my Amish friend was going to be in Pinecraft a few of the same days that my husband and I were. She very graciously spent the afternoon with us. Together, we peeked in shops, ate lunch and pie at Yoder's, and even walked down to Pinecraft Park, where a number of people were playing shuffleboard.

And with every hour that passed by,

I became more and more charmed by, well, everything that is Pinecraft.

I hope you will enjoy the series, and most especially this first book, *The Promise of Palm Grove*. In this novel, you'll meet Leona, who must decide whether to hold close everything she's ever known . . . or to take a chance on the promise of what could be.

I love this story. I hope you will enjoy it, too.

With blessings,
Shelley

P.S. I love to hear from readers, either on Facebook, through my website, or through the postal system! If you'd care to write and tell me what you think of the book, please do!

Shelley Shepard Gray
10663 Loveland Madeira Rd. #167
Loveland, OH 45140

Questions for Discussion

1. The following scripture verse guided me through the writing of this novel. I thought it was a perfect verse to describe Leona's journey. Can you think of a situation when the Lord changed some of your plans?
   We can make our plans, but the Lord determines our steps. Proverbs 16:9

2. I found the following Amish proverb to be especially helpful when creating my own "community" in Pinecraft, with the Kaufmann family and Beverly in the center of much of it! Describe your community of people, those who see you through. *We are not put on this earth to see through one another, but to see one another through.* Amish Proverb

3. What are your first impressions of Leona?

4. I loved the idea of Beverly "dreaming in color." I liked the idea of having her life so much brighter than the life she left behind. Can you relate to Beverly's color-filled life? What in your life brings you happiness and bright days?

5. How do you feel about Leona's friends? Were they supportive enough? How do you see the girls' relationships evolving after the book ends?

6. Some of my favorite scenes in the novel revolved around the interaction between the different members of the Kaufmann family. I especially liked Violet's character, and how she struggled to still be included even though she wasn't doing exactly what her parents

wanted her to do. Were there any relationships that you could relate to?

7. Beverly's story begins in this novel and continues through the entire series. What do you think are some areas in her life that she needs to work on before she's able to handle her own romance?

8. I truly loved setting my book in Pinecraft, Florida. It was fun to mention some Pinecraft landmarks—and adding some fictional places in order to make the story my own! What place would you like to see more of in the rest of the series?

9. Do you or disagree with Leona's father's pronouncement that "You can't stop love"? What experiences have you had that support this? ∿

Orange Pie

2 cups sugar, divided
1 tablespoon cornstarch or Clear Jel
1½ cups water
1 tablespoon orange Jell-O (or Kool-Aid)
Juice of 2–3 oranges
1 (3 ounce) package cream cheese, softened
4 cups (12 ounces) nondairy whipped
    topping, divided
1 baked pie shell

Cook 1 cup sugar, cornstarch, and water
until clear and thickened. Add Jell-O
and cool. Juice oranges and add to sugar
mixture. Beat cream cheese, remaining
sugar, and 2 cups nondairy whipped topping
until fluffy. Spread into bottom of baked pie
shell and pour orange mixture on top. Top
with additional whipped topping and enjoy.

(from Arlene Mast, Pinecraft, Florida)

Taken from *Simply Delicious Amish Cooking*
by Sherry Gore. Copyright © 2012 by Sherry
Gore. Used by permission of Zondervan.
www.Zondervan.com

Shelley's Top Five Must-See Spots in Pinecraft

HONESTLY, I FELL in love with everything about the tiny village of Pinecraft, nestled in the heart of Sarasota and nearby Siesta Key! Here are five places to start your journey:

1. *Yoder's Restaurant.* I've been to a lot of Amish restaurants. I've eaten a lot of coconut cream pie at each one. But nothing has compared to this well-known restaurant. The lines to get in are always long, usually at least a thirty-minute wait. But the long lines allow everyone to chat and make friends.

2. *The Produce Market at Yoder's.* The market next to Yoder's is full of beautiful Florida-fresh produce. We couldn't resist picking up two pints of strawberries and five oranges. Just to snack on—in between servings of pie, of course!

3. *Pinecraft Park.* It's the social center of the community! The night we were there, kids were playing basketball, men and women were playing shuffleboard (women have their own lane), and there were at least another forty or fifty people standing around and visiting.

4. *The Bus Parking lot.* This is where everyone meets to either board one of the Pioneer Trails buses or to watch who is arriving and leaving.

5. *Village Pizza.* It's located right behind Olaf's Creamery. You can order a pie and take it right over to one of the picnic tables outside. The pizza is delicious. Eating pizza outside in the sunshine in January or February in the Florida sun? Priceless. ᴄ∾

Scenes from Pinecraft

Photographs courtesy of by Katie Troyer,
Sarasota, Florida

The Pioneer Trails bus arrives in Pinecraft.

Siblings and friends at Big Olaf in Pinecraft.

Enjoying a Song Fest at Pinecraft Park.

Playing bocce in Pinecraft Park.

A Sneak Peek of Shelley Shepard Gray's Next Book, *The Proposal at Siesta Key*

THE MINUTE PENNY Troyer placed one foot outside her front door, she knew it had been a big mistake.

No matter what her mother was doing, no matter what part of the house she happened to be in, she always, *always* heard the distinctive snap of the deadbolt on the front door disengaging.

Penny froze, feeling vaguely like a burglar caught red-handed. Mentally began to count to five.

She barely made it to three.

With all the fanfare of a trio of trumpeter swans, her mother's high-pitched call flew down the hall. "Penny? Penny, what are you doing?"

And, as often happened lately, Penny bit back an irritable retort. "Nothing."

"It must have been something. I am fairly positive I heard you at the door."

God had really blessed her mother with too good hearing. "I'm simply going to sit on the front porch."

In the twinkling of an eye, her mother appeared in the entryway. Her hands clutched the sides of her apron and a blurred concern shone in her truly beautiful periwinkle-colored eyes. "Why?"

The question was so unnecessary, Penny almost smiled. But that would be wrong to do. Instead, she kept her voice even and respectful. "No real reason. I simply wanted to sit outside."

"But you'll go no farther?"

The correct answer was the one she'd given for the last twelve years of her twenty-four years of life. No, she would not. She would stay close. Free from harm.

But she simply wasn't sure if she could do that anymore. "I don't plan to go anywhere. But I might."

Her mother froze in mid-nod. "What in the world does that mean?"

"It means that I'm far too old to be forced to promise to stay on my parents' front porch," she said. Almost patiently.

Immediately hurt filled her mother's expression. "You know I like you close because I care about you, dear."

Penny knew that. She really did.

But of course, she knew that her mother asked for other reasons, too. They both knew those reasons. And they both knew that her mother would do just about anything to refrain from speaking of them.

But today was the day Penny finally had had enough.

Steeling herself for the drama that was about to ensue, she gestured toward the open doorway. "Mamm, why don't you come out on the porch, too? I think we need to talk."

"Penny, you know I don't have time to lollygag. Your grandparents are coming over for supper."

"I know that everything is ready. I helped you set the table, make the casseroles, and marinate the chicken."

For a moment, Penny was sure her mother was about to argue, then at last she followed Penny out to the porch swing that was situated exactly in the middle of the wide front porch that spanned the entire width of their tidy, one-story home.

Surrounding them were her mother's carefully tended pink roses and a quartet of blooming azalea bushes. Daisies and snapdragons and begonias lined the walkway.

After they were seated side by side, Penny tried to think of the best way to say what was on her mind. But as she mentally tried out different approaches, she knew there wasn't a single explanation that would be accepted.

Sometimes there really was no way to deliver bad news, even if that news was only going to be regarded as bad by one of them.

Steeling her spine, she decided to go for the direct approach. "Mother, it has now been twelve years since Lissy died. She's been gone for half my life."

Her mother flinched. "We don't need to talk about your sister."

"*Jah*, we do," Penny said gently, but took care to thread resolve into her tone. "Mamm, everything we do is a consequence from what happened to Lissy." Before her mother could get up, Penny wrapped ▶

her fingers around her mother's wrist and held on tight. "Mamm, what happened to Lissy was a terrible thing. I know that."

Before her eyes, her mother aged another ten years. As she always did when she thought about what happened to Lissy. "It was worse than terrible."

Yes. Yes, it was. One winter's day twelve years ago, back when they'd lived in Ohio, Penny's older sister, Elizabeth—Lissy to all who knew her—had been lured away from the girls she'd been walking home with by a very bad man. He raped her. He beat her. And then he left her in a field. She died alone and in pain.

The event had sent shock waves throughout the community, both English and Amish. Everyone in the area held memorial services, set up funds in Lissy's name; some even began neighborhood watch groups.

Within a week, the police had caught the man. A week after that, the man had mysteriously died in his jail cell.

Many had been secretly pleased about that.

But for the three remaining people in the Troyer family, the man's death hardly mattered. Nothing mattered except their loss. As each grueling hour turned to days and then weeks, it became obvious nothing was never going to ease their pain, and nothing was ever going to bring Lissy back.

Two years later, her parents decided to move to Sarasota, claiming they needed a change of scenery. Someplace fresh to start new. Someplace that would never be cold and snowy. Where there were no reminders of that horrible day.

Penny had been eager for the move, too.

But though they now lived in a place where the sun always shone and nobody knew about their hardships until they were told, the grief and worry in her family didn't change.

If anything, it began to imprint on everything in their lives.

Over the years, instead of venturing out into the world more, her parents had become more reclusive. Their fears began to center on Penny. Her restrictions became more and more pronounced. At first, Penny had been glad for all the rules. She'd been afraid of strangers and most of her nights had been haunted by memories of her sister and visions of what must have happened at the kidnapper's hands.

Eventually, however, the memories faded. And Penny had begun to feel the pinch of her circumstances. She'd kept her silence out of respect for her parents.

But their rules and fears had begun to chafe. Their refusal to see her as a grown woman instead of a susceptible child was aggravating.

It had festered. Now it pained her. And when she woke up this morning, she knew she couldn't take it another day.

Not for one more hour.

"Mamm, you and Daed are going to have to give me more freedom." Truly, she was proud of her firm tone of voice.

But even that didn't make an impression. "Don't be silly. You have freedom, Penny."

"Not really. You haven't let me take a job, you don't like me walking anywhere alone."

"That's because it's not safe."

"Mamm, if I was still a child, I would agree with you. But I am a grown woman. Of course it's safe."

The skin around her mother's lips tightened. "Things can happen."

"That is true, but I will be careful."

"Bad things can happen even when one is careful."

"I know that. But I can't live like this any longer. I have a feeling if you let yourself actually see me as I am, you would see that, too. Why, many women my age are married and have their own children."

"Is that what this is about? You are wanting a husband?"

"*Nee!*" How could her mother have jumped from her needing to be able to walk down the street by herself to her wanting a husband?

Her mother's expression gentled. "Don't worry, dear. We'll all go to more gatherings. You'll meet a man."

"You don't understand. I am not simply looking for a husband. I am looking for friends, activities." Around a sigh, Penny added, "I am looking for a life."

"You have a life. And a good, safe one, too. Daughter, everything we've done has been to protect you."

"*Jah.* But it's also been to protect you and Daed. Mamm, you and Daed must loosen your hold on me."

"I'll speak to your father. Perhaps we can come up with a plan . . ."

"Mamm, tonight there is a gathering at Pinecraft Park. A missionary group, the Worldwide Address, is speaking. I am going to go with Violet Kaufmann."

"Violet? But she's not Amish anymore."

"I know. But she is a nice girl from a nice family." She was also one of Penny's few friends. "I'm going to go with her."

"Your father is going to be upset when he hears about this." ▶

A Sneak Peek of Shelley Shepard Gray's Next Book, *The Proposal at Siesta Key* (continued)

"I know and I'm sorry about that. But I can't live my life trying to make him happy with me." Especially since she knew that nothing was going to truly ever make her father happy again. "Please try to understand my point of view, Mamm. I feel like I'm trapped. No one wants to live like they are confined and restricted."

"I'm sorry, child. But you know I cannot support this . . . this whim of yours." She paused, looking as if she was trying to add something more, but then merely stood up and walked back inside.

Penny slumped against the back of the wooden bench. In that moment, she knew she had two choices. She could either back down so she wouldn't hurt her parents . . . or she could finally please herself.

And suddenly, her decision was so very easy. Everyone at some point in their life had to stop being someone's daughter and start being their own person.

It seemed that it was finally time to do that.

With a new resolve in her heart, Penny stood up and started walking. It was time.